Evolved

ARCHER MILLER

Evolved

Epitome Press Publishing, Seaside, CA.

An Epitome Press Book

Cover Image and Design by CL Fors

ISBN: 1943212058
ISBN-13: 978-1943212057

Printed in the United States of America

DEDICATION

SKIP: For my wife Sue, who stood by me and had faith that one day I would write something worth reading. Who believed in me through three computer crashes. Who suffered, having to read my story every time I needed someone to say, "that's good, honey." A writer can't survive without one great fan. That's my Sue.

KC: For my Mother, who introduced me to reading in general and to reading sci-fi in particular. She loved the great writers in the genre and held them up as my role models. Most of all, she gave me permission to dream. Thanks, Mom..

ACKNOWLEDGMENTS

To Robert Heinlein, who pointed the way; to Anne
McCaffrey, who showed us that a story goes on from
generation to generation; and to Isaac Asimov, who taught
us that the best science-fiction begins with real science.
And, finally, to our friends at Epitome Press, for believing
in us.

CHAPTER ONE

On the hillside overlooking Novgorod, Pieter lay on his back, watching the lights dance in the sky. Flashing ribbons of green and gold gyrated against the starry backdrop. On the horizon, the small nearer moon raced to catch up with its larger, more distant cousin.

The cool night breeze carried the sounds of small nocturnal creatures out foraging for their supper. The sounds gave him no pause. The smaller creatures of The Steppes were no danger to the humans who now called this world home.

His eyes drifted shut and he breathed deeply of the night air. Even in the chill, he teetered on the brink of sleep, so at ease was he here. This was his special place to clear his mind and feel his connection with his world.

He turned to look back toward the center of town, where the gold-leaf onion dome of Saint Basil's dominated the skyline. He had dedicated two weeks of his precious summer break to the great work.

His fingers rubbed an itch on his ear, careful not to brush his hair away, lest he uncover his deformity. He felt the rough callouses from last summer and many weekends since. They gave him pride and satisfaction. *Pavel will be there*, he thought. Will his other friends still want to work with him?

Turning his head, he could see lights from the spaceport, the exclusive property of Golden Door Corporation. He had taken the guided tour with his school to receive the official message that they should be grateful to the corporate entity that sold this planet to his ancestors. The facility was overgrown from disuse. Only the occasional supply ship arrived to bring replacement parts and personnel to be rotated to new posts.

Pieter had once played inside the vast warehouses with his best friend, Pavel. He would tag along when Pavel's father had been called upon to check on the inventory or move a piece of heavy equipment from one place to another. His chest tightened, his brows pinched, and his mouth drew in to a tight line remembering the incident that ended his excursions into the warehouse district.

The chill deepened, from his bones out. He would be late getting home. He stood, snatched up his blanket, and followed his heavy feet down the hill. The slope shallowed as he entered the civilized areas, where a copse of short bristly trees had reclaimed this part of the terrain, once scraped clean by bulldozers. Their dark orange and gray bark resolved out of deep shadows in the light of the street lamps.

His road carried him past rows of identical cement houses. Over time, the residents had lent them some degree of personality, but beneath the veneer they were the same efficient, sturdy homes produced in sections at a local factory and assembled on site.

Ceramic pots by his front door held several *Camellia sinensis* plants. They clung to life, thanks to his mother's constant attention, on a world that was too heavy and too cold for them. Still, they were his mother's treasures, to be shared on special occasions. Pieter brushed the fragile stems, gathering the aroma of green chai on his palms.

The door was set deep in the thick, load bearing wall, and as he opened it, a savory aroma seized his nose and led him toward the kitchen. The chiller held a plate of berry filled blinis as well as thinly sliced corned beef and dark bread left over from supper. His stomach pleaded for attention. Hunger had been his constant companion since turning thirteen. His father often laughed and called it a common affliction of boys his age.

In the dining room, his father was bent over the chessboard, trying to avoid defeat at the hands of his younger son. They took little notice of him as he sat with his plate and a cup of milk.

Anton waited, silently, for his father's futile exercise in staving off checkmate. His eyes danced in anticipation of a rare victory.

"I think you have him," Pieter whispered.

"I think I have him too," Anton replied.

Their father stroked his solid jaw, catching his short cropped beard between his thumb and forefinger, tugging briefly before repeating. His dark eyes darted from piece to piece, searching for a way. His brows arched and a grin formed where a scowl had been.

"Someday you will have me, Anton," he rumbled in a rich baritone. His fingers grasped his king and deftly slid it past his rook and flipped their positions. "But that day is not today."

A single word burst from Anton's lips, "Damn."

Pieter laughed. "You left him open to castle. Now the leesha has slipped away to live another day."

"I'll have him yet."

"No, he has you in four moves."

There was a tinkle of china cups and spoons from the kitchen. Pieter's mother entered with a tray of koren kofe. Coffee was carefully rationed on a world where it could not be grown. A native root could be ground into a powder that carried a warm, spicy aroma and could be mixed with coffee to stretch the supply. Many locals had acquired a taste for the substitute brewed on its own.

"Did you enjoy your walk, Pieter?" she asked as she set the tray on the table. "Were the lights out tonight?"

The sharp acid taste melded with the smoky aroma of the root. He sipped and drew breath to lift the flavor to the nose. A splash of milk and a drizzle of honey rounded out the notes. He felt the warmth as it slipped past his tongue.

"Yes, Matushka, beautiful as always."

Her hand rested on his to bring his eyes to hers. "Don't be late, sinochick; you have a big day tomorrow."

"Yes, mama."

He downed his cup, kissed his mother's cheek, and headed for bed.

****

S dniom rozhdenya tebia,

S dniom rozhdenya tebia,

S dniom rozhdenya mily, Pieter,

S dniom rozhdenya tebia!

A chorus of adolescent voices rang through the room and out into the hallway. Pieter sat in the chair of honor and listened to his classmates. Like many boys in Pieter's class, Pavel's voice broke as he wavered between the voice that was and the voice that would be.

What a cruel joke God plays on us, he thought. To make us sound like clowns when girls are just beginning to take notice.

The girl he hoped would take notice was Sophia. She was proof that even this harsh world could produce a rose among the hard scrabble.

He was grateful he did not have to sing. When they reached the last line and the last high note, he had to bite his lip and hold his breath or he would have laughed out loud.

His prepodavatelnitsa, Miss Lada, stood over him and smiled. She was the new teacher this year, filled with energy and ideals. Lada's small stature barely contained her bright spirit. He would miss her kindness and patience when he started school next fall. Most of all, he would miss how she treated him despite his difference. She laid a bouquet of spring flowers in his hands and clapped along with the others.

His mother had sent a huge Medovik for his class to share. He ate his slice of the honey cake in silence. Indeed, the whole room was quiet, save for the private expressions of pleasure and delight. His mother had taken the trouble to pile on fifteen thin layers, one for each year. It was sweet and smooth on his tongue.

There were many small, mostly homemade gifts. Pavel's was a handmade Jacob's ladder that marveled him: a dozen or so brightly painted wooden squares, strung together on ribbons. Images of Baba Yaga, Father Frost, the White Duck, and the Firebird performed an impossible aerial dance on command. He thanked Pavel and kissed his cheek.

His friend was given the task of writing the names of their classmates on slips of paper and putting them in a cup. The cup was held above Pieter's head for him to draw a name for the honor of ritually pulling on his ears.

His fingers sifted through the papers while he whispered a secret prayer. He closed his eyes and pulled a slip from the bottom of the cup. His teacher plucked the paper from his fingers and read it aloud.

"Sophia, will you step behind our birthday boy and do the honors for us?"

He sat while she stood behind him. She leaned close and whispered, "You will let me know if I do it too hard, won't you, Pieter?"

He felt his heart pound in his chest and his face burned where her breath caressed it. Her fingers rubbed his ears from tip to lobe, and then playfully pulled while the rest of the class counted.

He loved her, of course. Not just because she was the most beautiful girl he had ever seen, but also because she knew of his deformity and did not seem to care. If anything, she seemed as drawn to his exotic variance as he was to her golden hair and deep blue eyes, so rare among his people. Still, she was careful to keep the tops of his ears tucked behind his cascade of dark hair.

He blushed as he felt her perfect fingers pulling on his fleshy lobes. She pulled him toward her until the back of his head brushed against her budding breasts. At first, he thought it was by chance but then she did it again and again.

"I'm not hurting you, am I?" She pulled until he was looking up into her face. She had a crooked grin and caught her lower lip between her teeth. She teased him until he thought he would go to heaven.

He would ask Brother Maykl for absolution and do penance later, but this was the greatest day of his brief life. They sang and danced and laughed until it was time to go home.

Pavel helped him carry his treasure. "I think she loves you, Pieter."

"Don't play the fool; Sophia is a Goddess I am not worthy to worship."

"So you say. But she smiled while she caressed your ears. And she was not put off by them."

Pieter paused to let the thought settle in. They walked in silence for a few minutes. There were no sidewalks on their road, unlike the streets closer to the center of town or the spaceport. What did it matter, when there were no cars to disturb the peace here on the outskirts of the city? A few squat fruit trees, struggling against the gravity, insisted on flowering. Chickens roamed freely, electing to walk exclusively rather than try their wings against the heavy pull of The Steppes.

"You'll come in for sbiten and cake, Pavel?"

"Of course."

Music streamed from the open windows into the warm afternoon air. The white star flowers that covered the sun-washed southern wall of his home were blossoming, attracting a chorus of hungry bees. In mass bloom, their scent was so sweet as to be intoxicating. His mother liked to pick them fresh to mix with her chai.

Pieter's mother greeted them with hugs and kisses. Her smile radiated love and pride in her family. Her black hair and eyes, like dark glass, had passed down to both of her sons. "Pavel, come in," she smiled, then plucked the bouquet from Pieter's hands and took the flowers to her kitchen for a vase and water.

No sooner had Pavel and Pieter unburdened their arms than Anton crept around the corner and rummaged through his brother's gifts. He poked and probed and examined each package until his curiosity was satisfied. Pieter watched Anton, making sure nothing was damaged, then cut him a stern look from the corner of his eyes.

Boris hugged his eldest son and led Brother Maykl into the room, his black robes and kalimavkion hat in stark contrast to his bright smile and boisterous laugh. Brother Maykl was Pieter's confessor, and had been both his spiritual guide and friend since his first communion.

"I bring you a birthday gift from our holy mother church, Pieter." The monk produced a long narrow box, tied with a purple ribbon, and gave it over to Pieter.

Inside was a Chotki, a long strand of polished prayer beads with the traditional three-bar cross and a Madonna medallion. Pieter kissed the silver crucifix and draped the long strand of beads across his palm. The round stones felt cool and smooth against his skin.

"It's beautiful, Maykl." Pieter blinked and

sniffed back a welling of tears. Thank you."

"May it bring you peace in times of trouble, Pieter."

The young man threw his arms around his friend and hugged him tight. The dignified monk smiled and replied with a hug of his own. "Perhaps, in a year or two, when you have finished with your schooling, you will consider my invitation to take a retreat with the brotherhood."

Pieter released his hold and stepped back. "Perhaps I shall. I must confess to dealing with great temptation."

"You would not be a fifteen-year-old boy if you did not. But you are a good boy with great faith, Pieter. You will know the right thing to do when the time comes." He grinned and nudged Pieter's ribs. "You must tell me of this girl. She must be a beauty to distract you so much."

Pieter smiled as his cheeks flushed. "It's no secret, Maykl. You have seen her at church. Her name is Sophia."

"Ah, yes. She turns many young men's heads when she takes her seat. She is a sweet child whom God has blessed with beauty and grace."

Maykl took the strand of beads and draped them around Pieter's neck. They were cold at first, but then warmed to the touch of his skin.

"Come, everyone," Risia called from the dining

room. "Let us drink to my son's birthday."

Her precious formal cups with their silver holders were on the table with steaming, golden liquid in each. Small tea cakes, dusted with fine powdered sugar, were set on brightly-colored plates. Cookies filled several more on the side board.

The sbiten was hot, and sweet, and tasted of spices and blackberries and honey. He savored it on his tongue before feeling it warm his belly. The cookies were warm and chewy, the way he loved them. Occasions like this were a special indulgence that dipped into the family's sugar and flour ration, but his mother would not have it any other way.

His father sat in a chair and picked up his balalaika by its long, narrow neck. The triangular body, crafted from a local wood, almost glowed from its hand rubbed finish. He plucked a few strings and waited for the raven-clad monk to get his instrument and join him on gudok. Maykl held his three-stringed instrument on his knee and stroked the strings with a deeply-curved bow. Their deep voices blended in a traditional folk song and floated through the open windows.

It was long after sunset when Brother Maykl offered to see Pavel home on his way to the monastery, and even later when Pieter went to bed. The cotton sheets were soft and smelled of sunshine under his nose. The goose down in his pillow caressed his face and lured him to sleep.

****

Blinding lights screamed past his eyelids; even his hands glowed pink where he covered his eyes with them. Coarse shouts of men filled the air. A BOOM shook his home, and he could hear his mother scream in her room. His father shouted at the top of his lungs.

Then his door exploded.

The lights bore down on him. He tried to see who it was, but he was blinded. His mother screamed his brother's name, and he lashed out. A bright flash of light filled his mind and a surge of heat welled up in his gut. The lights crashed to the floor; one smashed to pieces on impact and the other folded like a cheap can and continued to draw in upon itself until it winked out of existence.

Now he could see men in simple uniforms reaching for him. Their fingers were a few inches away when they crumpled to his bedroom floor. He had never used his strange ability to harm another person. It felt oddly satisfying.

"Ebat!" one of the men pinned to his floor managed to scream. He stepped over them and into the hall. More men in the same uniforms confronted him. In the door to his brother's room, a man held Anton up against his wall. His chest was pressed against the plaster and his arms were pinned behind his back. Pieter's eyes narrowed, and Anton's captor collapsed like a marionette with its strings cut.

"Svloch!" he managed to shout as the air left his lungs.

Someone else cried out, "Kill the son-of-a-bitch! He's dangerous."

The normal houselights came on and a chill froze his blood. A man stood behind his mother with a pistol held to her head. Behind him was another with a gun on his father.

"On your knees," the man barked. "We have orders to take you alive, but they don't say shit about your family."

Pieter stood, still holding the man in Anton's room against the floor. In the moment that he hesitated, a thick, black piece of cloth slipped over his face. Something tightened around his neck and a searing pain ripped across his back. He lost contact with his legs as hot agony ran down his spine and he fell to his knees on the hard wooden floor. Robbed of sight, all the men he held were released to exact their revenge. A booted foot rammed into his stomach. What could only be a gun butt struck his face. The world spun, and a second blow found the back of his head. He could hear his mother scream his name as blackness closed in on him.

****

Pieter's eyes opened, but it was an exercise in futility. There was nothing but darkness for him to see. He knew he was awake because of the lancing pain running down his back and across his chest; the cover on his head was stifling and smelled of sweat and blood. He was upright in some sort of chair, but he was unable to move. The back of the chair was straight and hard, and he was bound to it with his arms pinned behind his back. He struggled to breathe. His chest was stretched as his shoulders pressed into the chair behind him. A cry of pain rose in his throat, but he clamped his mouth tight to hold it prisoner.

As he gasped for air and strained to ease the pain in his chest and back, a voice from beyond the pain alerted him to another presence.

"Suka is awake."

"Good. I want this suka blyad to remember this."

With no way of knowing or seeing its approach, a hand struck his face, slamming the back of his head against the hard chair. He could stop the scream, but not the tears that rained from his eyes.

"Little boy wants to play," the voice taunted him.

Something hard crashed into his stomach, forcing the air from his lungs. He tried to breathe, but was unable.

What do they want from me?

A second fist slammed into the side of his face, whipping his head to the right.

"Don't kill him," the first voice warned.

"I won't. But he'll wish I had."

Why are they doing this?

The voice of his assailant whispered into his ear, "I want to hear you scream, mu'dak."

Again, a fist slammed into his stomach, hard enough to move the chair. He tried to cry out, but nothing would come from his open mouth except blood and bile.

Then…nothing. As suddenly as the beating began, it stopped. Pieter could not know if they had left him or had simply grown tired of inflicting pain. The voices were unfamiliar to him. He did not know these men. He thought he knew everyone in this human outpost, but these men were strangers.

"What have you done to my family?" he called out.

"Family?" a voice replied softly. "You have no family, suka. No one is coming to save you."

"What did you do to them?"

"They are no longer a concern."

He wept, silently. Hot, salty tears ran down his face, across his swollen lips and into the cloth bag covering his head. He thought of his father and what he would want him to do. Boris, he was sure, would want him to be strong and not give in to his tormentors. So he bit into his lower lip and staunched the need to cry out. He hoped he would make his mother proud and ached to hear her voice again.

They left him. Time was meaningless in the stifling confines of the bag. A throbbing pain wrapped itself around his ribs and squeezed. His jaw ached and his mouth was filled with the astringent iron taste of his own blood.

The strap that held his arms cut into his skin just above his elbows and pulled his arms behind his back. As the hours slipped past, the pain's dull ache became a numbing agony.

He wondered if Jesus suffered this way.

No, you cannot compare your little pains to our savior. He prayed for forgiveness. He prayed for his mother and father. He prayed for his brother. He prayed for strength. He prayed for forgiveness for the men who hurt him.

He felt the polished, black stones against his skin and the silver crucifix below them. It gave him peace to feel the Brother's gift against his skin. He could not roll the beads between his fingers, so he said a prayer to his Guardian Angel.

"O angel of Christ, holy guardian and protector of my soul and body, forgive me everything wherein I have offended you every day of my life, and protect me from all influence and temptation of the Evil One. May I never again anger God by my sins. Pray for me to the Lord, that He may make me worthy of the grace of the All-Holy Trinity, and of the blessed Mother of God, and of all the saints. Amen."

If he was going to die here he would first make peace with his God. Again and again he prayed, until he passed into the numbing grace of sleep.

****

He was shaken by the sound of a chair being dragged across the floor. The legs screeched where they rubbed against the concrete until they stopped in front of him. Someone was sitting face to face where he was bound.

A prodding finger tapped his head. "Boy. Boy, can you hear me?"

He tried to answer, but his mouth was dry and crusted with blood and his tongue was swollen from lack of water. He nodded.

"Good. I'll make this plain. I want to remove the bag, but you made things difficult for us before. We have your family. Do you understand?"

He nodded.

"Here is what I want to happen. I will take this bag off and you will behave, or we will kill everyone you love. Do you understand?"

He nodded.

A hand clawed at the top of his head. The lights would have probably hurt his eyes if they were not already swollen shut. Cool, fresh air filled his lungs for the first time since he was taken. The strap holding his elbows was removed, and his arms and shoulders protested at their new freedom.

One of his jailers passed a wet rag across his face and pressed a cup of water into his shaking hands. He blinked and swallowed a mouthful of water, swirling it around his leathery tongue to loosen the paste that filled his mouth. He spat on the floor, drank the remains of the cup, and held it out for more.

The man across from him wore a uniform like the men who raided his home that night, only clean, and with some braid on the collar to indicate he was a man of importance. On his shoulder the Golden Door logo, an outline of The Mother of Exiles, identified the man's employer. Pieter drank, slowly, letting the cool water satiate his throat. It was almost sweet on his tongue.

"We need to make some accommodation for you, boy. We need to hold you safely until we hand you over."

Why? Why do you need to hold me? Who are you handing me over to?

I'll make you a simple bargain, boy."

"Pieter."

"What?"

"My name is Pieter, Pieter Varushkin."

"Of course it is."

"I want to see them."

"I know you do, but you are in no position to make demands."

"How can I know they are alive?"

"You're going to have to trust me, Pieter."

Pieter shook his head and scowled, "Why should I trust you?"

"Because you have no other choice." His voice was chill like the late autumn wind.

His gut roiled and something dark and cold escaped from inside him. Words that frightened him to say. "I could kill you," he hissed. What he considered doing was against everything he believed. To kill was to violate the fifth commandment and would damn him for all eternity.

"I don't doubt you could. But if you do, you will never leave this room alive and your entire family will be killed. Is that what you want?"

Pieter paused while their eyes locked. Something feral had been awakened in him. "Nyet."

"Good. That's settled. We've decided to hold you in a secure place, and in a way that will protect our people. You understand the necessity for this,

Pieter?"

"Da."

"Good. I'm glad we had this chance to talk. Someone will be along soon to move you to your new room."

CHAPTER TWO

The helmet on Pieter's head made his neck ache. Chains on his wrists and ankles shackled him to a ring set in the cement floor. He could not move from the spot or stretch out farther than the place where he slept. Awake, his gift kept his home world's strong grip from making his suffering worse. Asleep, he pressed into the rock-hard floor. The taint of iron from his own blood still colored his mouth, a souvenir of his most recent encounter with his keepers.

He stirred against his chains, drawing a sharp toe to his ribs from the nameless man set to watch him.

"Urod," his keeper hissed under his breath. A word he knew well, *freak* in his native Russian. Something hard rapped the opaque visor that covered his eyes. "Make no trouble for me, urod."

Pieter retreated in on himself, as much from the hateful word as the abusive man, but he fought back the urge to cry again.

Time was meaningless. All he had was the darkness and his hate. He hated these men, he hated the men who sent them; but most of all he hated himself for not being strong enough.

They had buckled the helmet onto his head and kept him in darkness. It covered his face down to his nose and smelled of sweat and paint, but it also masked his warm tears. He would not wish to appear weak to his father.

The concrete floor sucked at his life energy and he shivered against the chill that crept into his marrow. Bitter bile filled his mouth, mixed with the salt of his own tears. His mind echoed with his mother's pleas and his father's torrent of angry curses, and his soul burned with every outcry. In his mind he vowed, *I swear to the Blessed Holy Mother, I will make someone pay for this.*

A thin, metallic sound raced across the floor to where he lay. The plate of food was close enough for him to sniff the stale bread and porridge. His first urge was to reject the tasteless mush and send the plate sailing back the way it came, but his empty stomach forced him to accept the ration. No spoon. He used the bread to shovel the sticky mass into his mouth. He gagged. The flavor reminded him of the simple paste he and his mother made from flour and water for a school project.

The door closed behind his jailers. He could hear them talking. Someone was coming from Golden Door to take him back to Prime. His grandfather had told him stories about the home world, tales that were handed down from his father and his father's father before him. He had seen pictures in his history reader. They showed scenes of green trees and swaying grassland, and strange animals roaming free.

But according to his father, the pictures were a cruel joke. The paradise they portrayed had disappeared ages ago. The world they left behind was now a desert of concrete and ash.

Footsteps echoed into his cell. A key rattled in the lock. He wanted to curl up and hide, but hands took hold of his shoulders and sat him upright. A jerk on his chains pulled him to his feet. Pain from his cold joints and a multitude of bruises set him on fire.

Even in his native tongue, the voices were harsh. "On your feet, brat," his keeper hissed.

Shuffling his feet kept him from tripping on his chains as they clanked and scraped against the floor. A cold draft of air swirled around him, sending a shiver running along his arms and legs, working inward through his chest. It was warm on the hill on his last full night of freedom. The spring flowers were blooming with a promise of a fine summer. He had missed it all; now, the chill winds of fall had come to The Steppes.

A prod to his back sent a tingle down his spine. It reminded him of when he was a child, walking barefoot through a construction area. He had stepped on a damaged electrical line that left him trembling out of control and unable to stand or walk for several days.

The door closed behind him, blocking the wind. Electric motors whirred to life, and the transport bounced and swayed across a rough, pitted road. He felt the large bodies pressing in against him from either side. The motors whined for several minutes before he heard them spool down to a smooth stop. A door slid open and one of his guards urged him to stand. Another poke to his ribs, and every nerve in his body was on fire. His scream of agony was blown away on the wind. His mind blazed. He wanted to strike back. He knew he could hurt them, but with the helmet on he was blind.

Wind whipped around his bare arms, raising goose bumps. A few steps farther, and a rush of warmth enveloped him. *Where am I?* he wondered. *What is this place?* Distant echoes sounded like voices, but with his ears covered he couldn't make out what they said. He was led down a long corridor until his keeper pulled on his chain and brought him up short, tripping him. His knees buckled, sending him sprawling on the floor.

"Son-of-a-bitch," a new voice spoke unaccented English. "What the hell does the boy do, eat people?" The male voice carried not a trace of honest concern.

"Very funny, Blue. You and lady sign here and this gryaz is yours." A voice thick with the local accent replied.

A cloying, sweet scent like the tiny, white star flowers his mother grew flowed to his nose. A woman's voice touched his ears. "What have you done to this boy? Take this off at once." She spoke with a sharp staccato, like an angry teacher taking a student to task.

"We were instructed to treat freak as dangerous. Take no unnecessary risks. That is what directive say."

"I don't care what the directive said," Her voice was piping, like a flute, but tempered with indignation. "This is inhumane."

"Hey, could you be a pal and hang on to 'em long enough for us to grab something to eat?" the one they called Blue asked. "I mean, really, the kid is rank. I'm hungry, and I don't think I could keep anything down if I gotta sit next to that."

The helmet was unlatched from his chin and neck, and finally pulled from his head. The sudden flood of light forced him to shut his eyes and look away. He blinked away fresh tears while his shackles were removed. The Guard chuckled, "No chance, Blue. Rebnok give me creeps. Po'shyol 'na hui."

Blue called back, "Hey, Ivan, you kiss your mother with that mouth?"

The woman leaned in to consider his face. Her fingers gently brushed the tangle of hair from his face. She inhaled sharply and her quick brown eyes darted from one mark on his face to another. "My name is Clair Jones." She put her right palm on her chest and repeated, "Clair Jones." She moved her hand to his chest. "And you are?"

Pieter looked up at the woman. On her face was the first smile he had seen since he had been taken. He wanted to smile back but his rage wouldn't permit it. She was a colorless woman. Her clothes were plain, no makeup, and thin lips against pale skin and high cheeks, but it was her eyes that caught him. They were kind, but held a deep loneliness. He tapped his own chest and answered, "Pieter."

"That's a nice name, Pieter. Do you speak English?"

"I speak English little."

"Are you hungry, Pieter?"

Pieter nodded and replied, "Da."

Captain Jack Blue waved a hand in front of his face, as if to brush away something unpleasant. "Whew, kid could use a bath. Make sure he gets cleaned up, okay, Jones?" He ran his fingers through his long, shaggy hair and turned back toward the main terminal. "I hope we can get a decent knish and maybe a pirog before we have to lift off."

Blue walked with the swagger of someone who pretended to have power.

Don't be afraid, a voice whispered to him. Pieter glanced from side to side but there was no one near him except for the woman, Captain Blue, and the retreating backs of his former tormentors. His head spun, looking for the author of the spectral voice. He looked at the people around him, but no one appeared to have heard anything.

You can stop looking, I'm not there. The voice was decidedly female, like that of a young girl. It set off a tingling inside his head. It was a voice he had never heard before, with no hint of an accent. He stared into nothing while his attention grasped at the voice. His steps slowed and his shoulder glanced off a wall.

"If you are not here, where are you?" he whispered.

I'm on board their ship. You'll be

joining us soon.

"How are you doing this?"

I'm like you, Pieter.

"You know my name?"

Stop whispering. You don't need to talk out loud. Just think what you want to say. And of course I know your name, silly. I can read your mind.

Pieter's eyes glazed over. *How are you like me?*

I mean we're different. You'll find out soon. There are already six of us and we're all different.

Six?

Yes. You make seven. Be nice to Miss Jones. If it weren't for her, we would all be locked up and probably chained to a wall.

Why are they doing this to us?

Don't you know?

Nyet.

Tell me about your ears.

My ears? Pieter clinched his hands at his side, resisting the urge to cover his deformity.

Your ears aren't like other people's, right?

How do you know?

You'll see.

****

"Three years and no incidents. Are you so sure these...oddities are worth the trouble?" First Secretary James Paul leaned heavily in the chair across the desk from his Defense Secretary. He loosened his tie and tugged the closure at his collar free.

"This could have gone quicker if you had let me use a new ship. We might have cut the transit time in half." Doctor Stephen Mills sat in his ergo-chair and spilled some whiskey into a pair of cut crystal shot glasses. The ice made musical sounds as he swirled the amber liquid. Mills stood and paced past the clear wall that overlooked the city far below. Through the toxic haze, he could see the flashing lights that dominated the skyline. Cold drops slipped past his fingers where he gripped the glass and splattered on the floor. "As it is, I had to contract with Charlie to send a retread that was half way through being stripped. Minimal crew so we don't attract attention, right? Isn't that what you wanted?"

Paul sipped his whiskey. "Yes, it is. You've stirred up enough fear over these... anomalies. We don't need to spook the colonists. It's bad for business."

"Well, if they stuck to the schedule they should have left The Steppes by now. So, it's seven down and one to go, then the return trip."

"How much do you trust this Jack Blue?"

"I don't. But he's just smart enough to feed the monkey and dumb enough to keep his nose out of places where it doesn't belong."

"And this Jones woman?"

"She's good enough to be the caretaker and she follows orders. That's all we need. Old ship, skeleton crew, no frills to draw attention."

Paul leaned closer, "I still don't see why this is so important to you, Stephen; they're just kids."

Mills looked into Paul's eyes and glared at him. "They're not just kids, James. They're un-Godly abominations. They're a threat to humanity, and I, for one, will not stand idly by while they and their progeny spread like a cancer through the population. This may be our only chance to cut the tumor from the body before it kills us."

"I hear what you're saying, Stephen, but isn't it a bit extreme?"

"No," Mills stood and slammed a fist into the desk, "it's not. We must be God's good shepherd and cull these abominations from the flock."

****

Miss Jones opened a menu and held it up to Pieter's face, "I really don't know anything about the food here, Pieter. What do you recommend?"

Pieter's mouth watered as he gazed at the list of fare offered in the port restaurant. He pointed at an item and pronounced the name, "Kasha."

"Kasha," Jones repeated.

He pointed at another. "Kalduny. Stuffed dumplings." Hunger made his stomach churn.

"That sounds good. What's this?" she pointed at another item.

Pieter scanned the few patrons in the ports dining room for a young girl, the source of the voice in his head. Distracted, he hesitated to answer the woman. "Shashlik? Umm, lamb on stick," he replied.

The Captain simply jabbed a finger at the menu to indicate his order.

Pieter devoured the first hot food he had enjoyed in months while Miss Jones ate slowly and with delicate manners. Blue ate quickly and in silence, his uniform overalls catching what his mouth did not. He wiped his fingers on the stained front of his jump suit, using the napkin only for his mouth.

Pieter forced himself to eat slowly, to cherish each bite. The dumplings were not as good as his mother's, but it made little difference to him now. They were swimming in a hot broth that warmed his insides for the first time in months. The borsch was delicious and the tea was sweet. Slowly, he felt his life returning.

Blue flashed a voucher chit for their meal and lead them out of the café toward the loading ramp. The ship was long, sleek, and still intimidating enough to inspire awe in his young mind. As Pieter got closer, he could see the fading insignia, oil and grease stains, and the occasional sloppy weld. Gun ports still bristled with the business ends of rail guns, but the muzzles were plugged. The vessel was an old tiger with its teeth pulled. He walked between the Captain and Miss Jones as they climbed the gangway into the ship.

"How many on ship?" he asked.

Blue laughed, "We're it, kiddo. Don't worry. It's mostly automated. I just punch in a destination and the ship's computer takes it from there. I hardly have to touch anything."

"Thank God for small favors," Clair whispered.

Blue appeared oblivious to the remark. He rubbed the dark stubble on his jaw and tugged the closure on his jump suit down far enough to expose a flannel chest.

Pieter's nose twitched at the musty smell of recycled air. The floor was scuffed and worn to the metal sub deck in spots. At an intersecting corridor Blue turned left while Clair Jones placed a hand on Pieter's shoulder and led him in the opposite direction. They stopped at a door marked "Rec Room" about 50 meters into the passageway. The automatic door rattled and squeaked, then opened on an area set aside for the detainees.

Pieter watched a reflection of himself and Miss Jones walking into the center third of the room. As he watched, the dark plastic panels became clear, revealing four separate tanks on each side. Faces appeared as each room was revealed. They reminded Pieter of stuffed animals on display.

They continued to the end of the isle where Clair led him into the fourth cubicle. Inside was a bunk bed folded against the wall, a few drawers, a computer terminal above a small desk that disappeared into the wall. "This is your room, Pieter. And here is the food dispenser." She touched the screen above the desk which flickered to life. "You can also use this to call up books and movies, or anything in our data bank. If there is anything else you need, just push this button."

He touched a display above the sink, and the screen flickered to life. The face looking back at him from the screen was his own; or at least it looked familiar. Long, black hair hung across his face and down his neck. His dark eyes were puffy and crusted with dried salts from his tears. His lower lip stuck out, swollen and split. Dark blotches on his cheeks and forehead testified to his rough treatment. More surprising were the first long strands of facial hair on his cheeks and chin.

Clair Jones passed her fingers over a few buttons to the right of the sink, "If you want to take a shower, just press these two buttons. This one gives you privacy, and this one opens the shower."

His fingers ran through his hair, sweeping stray locks out of his eyes. He took a moment to run water into his cupped hands and splash his face. He cupped a second handful of water and swirled the cool liquid in his mouth. He spat into his sink and watched the pinkish flow disappear down the drain. The water was as flat and tasteless as the recycled air, but it was cool and wet. He took a small towel from the drawer below the sink and wiped his face dry.

As he looked up again, his brow pinched and his eyes smoldered with rage. Every bump, bruise, and cut reminded him of the men who beat him and, if he could believe them, held his family hostage. He wanted to give sway to his anger, to find an outlet and release his rage. Then he remembered what the voice told him about the woman in his room, and did his best to force a smile.

He looked into the face of Miss Jones and saw

fear in her eyes. She couldn't meet his gaze and turned for the door.

"Goodnight, Pieter. Sleep well."

She slipped out the door and pushed it closed with an electronic click. She paused to look across the room and caught the eyes of their other prisoners staring back. Clair Jones disappeared into the outer corridor.

Pieter laid out one of the suits and some clean underwear then went to the switch and pressed the button marked privacy. The transparent wall became opaque and he was alone. A second push caused the sink to drop back into the wall, revealing a tiny shower space. For the first time in months he had a chance to clean himself, wash his hair, and get the smell of prison from his skin.

The water was hot and eased the pain in his joints. He lathered himself, twice, and scrubbed hard enough to draw blood from some of his shallow wounds. He poured a palm-full of shampoo into his hair and worked it deep with his fingers. Finally, he just stood under the water and let himself cry as the soap drained away.

Wrapping a towel around his waist, he stepped out. The sink and mirror reappeared. He looked at himself and winced at the deep purple blotches that dotted his pale skin. He turned to look at his back and found the marks left by boots and fist and prods. His rage bubbled up again and he slammed a fist into the wall.

He stood at the opaque wall as it turned clear and the voice appeared in his head again. *Feel better? Good. Welcome to our home away from home, Pieter. My name is Mary.*

Is that you I see across from me?

No, the girl flirting with you from across the hall is Joan.

Pieter stared into a pair of dark, shimmering eyes, like marquis cut basalt, and long, straight black hair. Her fingers brushed her hair back and he noticed she had the same deformity as him. The top of her ear was peaked instead of rounded. A word came into his mind, Elf.

Don't gawk, Pieter. We all have them.

"I thought…"

We all did. Until we met, we all thought we were the only ones with these ears. Put on some pants; then we can get out.

"What…"

He slipped into the jumpsuit he had laid out earlier. A moment later, the lock clicked and the door moved slightly. Pieter pushed it open and was surrounded by the rest of the group. "How did you do that?" he asked.

A short, sandy haired boy held his hands in front of his chest. Sparks flew from fingertip to fingertip. "No big, hey. Electric locks are my thing." A sharp, acrid aroma of ozone lingered in the air.

"You make electricity?"

"Make, control, it's all the same." The other boy thrust his hand into Pieter's. "Hi, I'm Billy."

"Preevyet," Pieter replied with a firm squeeze. Billy winced but his grin returned in an instant. Billy's face was round with baby fat and pre-adolescent down that wouldn't see a razor for another year or two. His warm brown eyes danced with mischief.

"Be careful where you point that thing, big guy," Billy released his grip.

Pieter stood half a head taller than anyone else in the room. He used his advantage to scan the crowd. "Who is Mary?" he asked.

The frail looking girl from the first cubicle raised her hand. As Pieter watched, she floated toward him, her feet several inches above the floor. His eyes widened and he whispered, "You can fly?"

Laughter rippled through the crowd. Mary drifted closer, her dark curls bobbed with each burst of laughter. "No, I can't fly or float or levitate or anything like that. Your planet's gravity was making it hard for me to breathe and stand, so Billy is giving me a lift. He's telekinetic."

Mary's hand motioned toward the pale, black haired girl. "Sue is a healer. She's good for what ails you."

The girl called Sue stepped closer and cupped Pieter's chin. Her touch was gentle, but still caused him to hiss and wince. She placed her soft hands on either side of his face. Slowly her hands glided down across his chest and stomach. His skin warmed under her touch like a flow of warm honey. In a few seconds, the pain from his abuse at the hands of his guards began to fade.

Mary giggled as his cheeks glowed. "Relax, stud. She's not getting fresh, just fixing what they did to you."

As Sue backed away she smiled. He touched his face and found the swelling and bruising gone along with the lingering pain.

"Spasobi," he thanked her.

Mary pointed to the girl from the cubicle directly across from his. "And Joan is a shapeshifter."

Pieter turned to face Mary for a second, then returned his attention to Joan, only to find Mary's identical twin looking back.

"Bozhe moy!" he shouted and stepped back.

Billy laughed. "Yeah, I bet she's a scream at

masquerade parties."

As Pieter stared her face elongated and her hair returned to its raven sheen.

"She can change what you look like too."

Pieter reached for her hand and raised it to his lips. "You are amazing."

Joan blushed and turned away.

"And her?" He pointed to the blond girl with light blue eyes.

"That's Leeann," Billy replied. "She blows bubbles."

Leeann's eyes narrowed and she frowned, baring her teeth. Billy disappeared for a split second then reappeared as the shimmering sphere of energy surrounding him transitioned from black to clear.

"I swear to God, Billy, if Mary didn't need you I would leave you in there for the rest of the trip," Leeann shouted.

The sphere disappeared leaving Billy hanging in mid-air. His fall was interrupted when Pieter held out his hand.

"Hey, big fella, that's pretty cool," Billy grinned, "So you and I are the same."

"Nyet." Pieter smiled. "I am not holding you up. I am stopping you from falling."

Joan gasped, "You're what?"

"Stopping gravity, so Beely is not getting hurt."

"You stop gravity…" Joan breathed, "Do you

know what that means?"

Mike interrupted. "Joan is our resident science expert. She's also a computer genius. That's why Bob's on our side."

"Bob? Who is Bob?"

Joan chuckled. "Bob is the name I gave the ship's mainframe computer. I hacked it not long after they picked me up. Since then I've been tweaking it and setting it up to work for us."

"You are smart one, yes?"

"She is smart one, yes," Mary answered. "I think Miss Jones suspects that we get out when there's no one watching. But the Captain, if you can really call him that, is oblivious. When he checks the monitors, the camera shows him a loop of us in our rooms."

Mike looked up from where he sat, making tiny lightning bolts dance between his fingers. "There's one more passenger to pick up, then a three-year trip back to Prime."

"Then what?"

"Then we find a way to get off this boat trip before we reach our final destination."

A vibration thrummed through the hull and up through the deck plate into the soles of Pieter's feet. "Cheto eto?"

"English, please, Pieter," Joan called as she returned to her own room.

"Sorry, what is that?"

"That's the engines warming up. We're going to head back into space in a few minutes. You better get strapped into your G-chair."

Pieter followed the others' lead and retreated to his room. The form fitting chair turned to face the nose of the ship. His arms slipped under the straps and the buckle latched across his chest. In a few minutes, the vibration spooled up to a high-pitched whine and powerful gee forces pressed him into the chairs thick padding. Tears began to run down his face. He wondered what had become of his parents and his younger brother.

We'll be breaking orbit for Asgard in a few minutes and then we can get out again.

"Are you all right?" He called out to Mary.

I'm fine. Billy takes good care of me.

A final burst of acceleration, and the ship's auto-pilot plotted a course for the mission's final pick up.

CHAPTER THREE

Pieter sat captive in his chair. Joan's fingers combed through section after section of his long black hair and snipped at them with a pair of scissors. Discarded ebony strands floated to the deck and clung to his arms and shoulders. He could feel the warmth of her hands as they worked their magic. He remembered the feeling of Sophia's fingers as she tugged on his ears on his birthday. It felt like another lifetime ago, but the memory still made him blush.

"If you don't stop squirming I'm going to nick you with these scissors, and then we'll have to get Sue in here."

Pieter craned his neck to look up at her. "Serri."

"English only, please. You need more practice."

"Oh, sorry. I am doing my best but this makes me a little…"

"Calm down, cowboy, I'm not going to bite you."

"Cowboy? What is cowboy?"

"A word nobody uses anymore. It's a name for someone who works on a cattle ranch."

"I have never worked on a cattle ranch. Why would you call me this name?"

Joan stopped snipping his hair and put both of her hands on his shoulders. She looked up into the screen in front of them and stared into their reflection. He was looking back with his deep brown eyes. "Legend has it that cowboys are supposed to be strong, handsome, and very independent. They can be very tough but very kind at the same time. I guess you make me think of them."

Pieter blushed again and looked away. He stared into his lap to avoid her gaze. He felt Joan's fingers brush across the back of his neck. Then he felt the smooth beads of his Chotki slide across his skin. "These are beautiful, Pieter. What are they?" she asked.

"We call them Chotki. They are for making prayers. It was a gift from a good friend."

Joan reached into her pocket and pulled out a string of small black beads with a tiny silver cross dangling from a strand attached in the middle. "Like this?" She held them out where he could see. "I may be Japanese by birth, but my great grandparents converted to the Catholic faith. In fact, they were Catholic missionaries and helped found the school I attended back home."

Pieter reached up and cupped her rosary in his palm. "So, we are same but different. You are Catholic, but I am Russian Orthodox."

"Am I wrong to think you are a person of great faith?" She let his beads settle back into place, then put her own rosary back into her pocket.

"I am having good friend at Monastery. He is frequently speaking to me about joining the brotherhood, even becoming priest. But I am young man with young man's temptations. Brother Mykel says this is normal and that I have time. But I don't have time."

"The way you looked when they brought you in… I can't imagine how bad that was."

"When they took me and locked me in cell and beat me, I prayed. I prayed for my family, I prayed for deliverance; I even prayed for men who hurt me." He raised the three-bar cross to his lips then tucked it back inside his shirt.

Joan set about trimming his long locks again, humming happily as she did.

****

Billy sat with his arms folded across his chest while he watched random objects move through the air at the whim of an invisible juggler. "Are we there yet?" he asked, for the untold time.

Mike leaned back in his seat at the table and raked his fingers through his sandy blond hair, singeing away any that disobeyed his rule for perfect length. The acrid scent of burning hair drifted through the common room.

Sue covered her mouth and nose with her hand then stomped her foot in frustration. "Damn it, Mike, I asked you not to do that out here. If you want to give yourself a buzz cut, do it in your own room."

Pieter sat in his cubicle and watched the drama in the common room, while Mary's voice whispered in his mind.

Classic case of cabin fever. The trip to Asgard is taking too long for their liking. What they need is a strong leader to calm them down.

Pieter chuckled under his breath and stared into empty space. *I am thinking you would make good leader, Mary. You always know who is doing what.*

Sorry. Not my style, if you know what I mean. They get uncomfortable thinking

I'm in their heads all the time. Mary's voice in his head made him recall the buzzing of the bees in his mother's garden. *You, on the other hand, would make a very good leader for this rabble.*

Nyet, he protested with a shake of his head. *I am just like the rest of you.*

No, you're not. You're older, bigger, stronger, and very smart. Believe it or not, they already look up to you. We need you, Pieter.

Nyet, nyet. He held up his hands as if warding off a bothersome insect. *Not me.*

Think about it.

Why do we need a leader? We're prisoners.

Because we cannot, under any circumstances, reach our destination. If they all knew they would panic.

What would make them panic, Mary? Pieter sat and pinched the bridge of his nose between his thumb and finger.

I picked up a thought from Miss Jones. She tries not to think about it because it upsets her.

You are upsetting me. What is so bad for us to reach Prime?

They're going to dissect us, Pieter.

What is dissect?

They're going to kill us, cut us open and take us apart-- especially our brains, see what makes us different. But first they'll run a lot of tests. Then they'll treat us like bugs in a collection.

"Why? Who would do this thing?" he asked aloud, his voice rising in pitch and volume.

Mary's mental voice was sharp and scolding. *Be quiet. You can't tell anyone. Not yet.*

Who would do this? His teeth ground together with the effort to control his anger and keep his mouth closed.

A man named Mills. From what I can gather he's high up in the government on Prime.

Why?

He's afraid of us. At least, he's afraid of what we could become.

Then we must not make it to Prime.

Good idea. Now all we need is a leader and a plan.

****

Dr. Mills paced the length of his opulent office, nearly colliding with a dark grained end table before the window glazing brought him up short. His face was florid with rage and impatience. A solitary officer stood carefully out of the way near the ornate desk. Mills' voice rose in pitch and volume, "Son-of-a-bitch is an idiot. He's an incompetent fool." He flung the glass in his hand. It shattered against the teak paneling and settled as a hundred tiny shards in the Turkish rug. "And to send an obsolete ship, run by a washout and a spinster with no family, to handle the most important mission in a thousand years."

He continued to pace, ignoring the other ears in the room. "Paul is nothing but a temporary roadblock in my way. But why am I worried? If the mission somehow succeeds, I get my gaggle of freaks to show what's left of mankind the threat to their existence. If it fails, we can lay the blame on Paul and push him out the door. Either way, I win."

The officer standing near the desk looked down at his feet to avoid any possibility of making eye contact. Mills continued his rant, "Jackson had the Cherokee, Forrest had the freed slaves, Hitler had the Jews, Mussolini had the communists, and I've got these freaks. I can ride them all the way to the top of the political food chain. Then I will be free to do God's will." His voice became a whisper. He looked up into his own face reflected in the window and grinned like a shark contemplating a juicy meal.

Mills turned and looked at the officer. "Are we

prepared to transport the last prisoner?"

The officer stood at attention and answered, "Yes, Secretary Mills. We had to take special precautions to keep him confined, but everything is ready and waiting for the Corsica."

"I want to know the moment they arrive and the moment they leave."

"Yes, Secretary Mills."

CHAPTER FOUR

Pieter, wake up.

Mary's telepathic shout jolted him out of a sound sleep. As his eyes opened, flashes of blue light filled his room. He turned his head to check the common area between the cells. Arcs of lightning sizzled through the room. *Kakogo cherta,* he thought, watching the dancing discharge.

It's Mike. He's having a nightmare. Mary sounded frantic inside his mind.

Can't you switch him off?

He can't hear me.

Pieter stood and approached the barrier between his cell and the common room. The crackling discharge reminded him of a small Tesla coil his teacher had brought to class. The lightning followed any hand or finger that touched the glass sphere. But this was on a scale he had never seen.

His eyes focused on the room across from his and caught sight of Joan watching the lights. They were all watching, too terrified to do anything to stop it.

Pieter pressed his hand to the clear wall and immediately the blue, static lights flowed to the spot. He felt no pain. The electrical discharge stopped at the other side of the wall, just like the Tesla coil in school. The pops and crackles from the common room made him wary. As he listened, he could hear the electric lock mechanism on his door cycle on and off every few seconds.

Has he ever done this before?

Not like this, Mary replied. **Not this bad.**

Pieter listened for his door to open and pushed his hand against the clear panel. The lock clicked and the door swung away. He eased his way past the frame and into the room. The first cold spark to hit him drove him to his knees. Sharp needles raced up and down his spine and along his arms.

Pieter, what are you doing? Mary thought. **That isn't what I meant.**

Crippling pain lanced through his body. The electrical charge running through him made his muscles spasm and convulse. Every move was an exercise in agony. He could not answer Mary or he would lose his concentration.

On his hands and knees, he crawled towards Mike's room; the inside gave off light like an incandescent bulb. The acrid aroma of ozone filled his head as he got closer. Inside the room he could see Mike thrashing against the confining sheets that had twisted around his body. His hand touched the transparent wall of Mike's cell. The wall was warm to his touch. He slapped the plastic partition. A deep boom like a drum reverberated into the room but the only response was a jolt that ran up his arm, knocking him onto his back.

Pieter rolled onto his stomach and pushed up against the floor. He closed his eyes and took the weight off his arms. His legs refused to work for him. His feet and finger tips became distant, disembodied things. He floated in space while Mike writhed in mental anguish.

As he watched, an empty cup flew past him and crashed into Mike's door. Then a chair rebounded off the clear wall. An invisible hand seized him and pulled him away from the out-of-control human dynamo. From his new position, he could see Billy's hand pressed against his inside wall. Blue lights flashed where his hands touched the surface.

In the neighboring cell, Mary pressed her hands against the partition, attracting an identical aurora. A bright blue glow to his right told him Susan had also pressed her hands to the wall. Farther down the dancing lights surrounded an even larger area on Joan's door.

Slowly he could feel sensation return to his body as the current was diverted. The charge around him shrank to a mild tingle. He nodded to Billy who sat him back on his wobbly feet. Now he could walk to Mike's door and, as he had with his own, listen for the lock to cycle. He pressed his hand against the door and waited. The door swung aside and he was inside the heart of the maelstrom.

Mike continued to thrash in the throes of his private torment. Pieter reached for his nearest limb and grasped Mike's right wrist. The charge that flowed up his arm caused his muscles to seize in place. His knees buckled and Pieter was again driven to the floor.

****

Pieter's body hummed like a giant tuning fork that had been struck by a sledge hammer. Soft fingers caressed his face, giving solace to the throbbing in his head. Slowly the world reappeared out of a blue haze. Joan's face hovered over him and watched his eyes with hope and caution.

"That was a very brave and stupid thing you did," she whispered.

"I am liking you too."

"This isn't Mike's first electrical storm. Until now we just waited it out in our rooms."

"Had to stop…"

"No, you didn't. Our rooms are insulated but the common room and the space where Mike is having his nightmare isn't."

"I feel like guard has beaten me."

"You're lucky you're alive."

"Was just static electricity"

"That could have stopped your heart."

"Where am I?" he asked.

"You're still on the floor in Mike's cell. Susan has already checked you and declared you alive."

Pieter realized he was resting on Joan's lap. His arms and legs felt much as they did in the heavy gravity of home. His head hummed between his ears and his pulse hammered through him. His pain would have been insufferable if Joan's gentle fingers and quiet voice didn't chase it away.

"Hey!" Susan called to Joan. "You guys need to get a room."

Joan laughed, causing her to shake and sending stabs of pain through Pieter's head. "Billy, Mary, give me a hand." Joan spoke to two shadows just outside the door.

Try as he might, he could not stand on his own. Billy put an arm across his shoulder and heaved. He couldn't even lower the pull of gravity on him to help his attendants. Struggles and curses followed before he was dropped on his own bed.

Mary paused at the door and made sure Pieter was watching her. She grinned and winked, then followed Billy out.

"Susan says the effects will wear off eventually." Joan checked his face for fever. "In the meantime, I don't mind staying with you."

****

Susan stood over Mike's bed and pressed her fingertips to his temples. Even semi-awake, he sent tingles running up her arms.

"Sparky? You in there, buddy?" she whispered.

Mike blinked and opened his eyes. "I did it again, didn't I?"

"Fraid so, pal."

"Anyone hurt?"

"You managed to fry some of Pieter's wiring, but he'll be fine. He's got his own personal angel looking after him. I made sure he was still ticking, then I left the rest of his nursing to Joan." She smiled and chuckled. "I wouldn't put it past him to have done it intentionally."

"Could you at least tell him I'm sorry?"

"Tell him yourself. You're not hurt. Your battery's drained but otherwise you're okay. You wanna tell me what's going on inside that brain pan of yours?"

"Bad dreams. I don't remember what about now."

"Look, it would be simple to sic Mary on you and let her take a crowbar to your mind and peel the pain out, but I would rather get you to talk it out."

"I don't need someone to psychobabble me."

"Okay. Have it your way. How about this? I'll show you mine if you'll show me yours."

Mike looked up and flashed a twisted smile.

"Not what I meant and you know it." Susan sat on the edge of his bed and held his hand. "I haven't told anyone about what went on… well, before."

"Before what?" he asked.

"Before this."

"Before this you were a nice girl on a nice planet with a nice home and a nice family."

"I was, until I turned ten and became. Good old Mom and Dad didn't want anyone to see my... deformity. While I was a child, my folks just let my hair grow to cover my ears. I did hear my dad say I should have them clipped but that never happened. A few days after my tenth birthday I was up in a tree with a girlfriend of mine. She got way out on a limb and it snapped off under her." Susan's rolled her eyes, filled with the pain of remembering. "I thought she was dead. I jumped down and went to see if she was breathing. She wasn't. I remember holding her hand and wishing there was something I could do. Suddenly she sucked in a deep breath and opened her eyes."

"Was that the first time?" he asked.

"Yeah, it was." She swallowed. "I was shocked, she was shocked. Then she said her arm hurt. I touched her wrist and I just knew it was broken. But I made another wish and her pain went away. The next thing I knew she was on her feet and running for home."

"Sounds like happily ever after to me."

"You would think so. I thought so. But the next day my friend showed up at our house with her folks. Next thing I know they're asking me questions and asking my folks and on and on. They must not have been happy with the answers because the next day the police showed up and it started all over again."

Mike chuckled, "There's an old saying about no good deed going unpunished."

"I thought we were done, but a few days later some people from the government showed up. This bunch wanted to put me through some test, so we loaded up and went to a hospital. They showed me people who were sick or injured and asked me to do what I did for my friend."

"Tell me you didn't."

"I was a kid. I did what I was told."

"That was stupid."

"As I found out, people can't keep secrets. Word got out. Researchers showed up to study me, draw blood and so on. So many people started showing up at my house the government moved me to a "secure location". I was safe, but my family had to move away."

"At least you had a roof over your head and three meals a day."

"I was a prisoner. They called it a safe house, gave me a new name, and had people go with me everywhere I went. Somehow someone still found out where I was. One day this woman walked up to me on the street and shoved her baby in my hands. It looked like a baby, mostly. The top of its head was all caved in and it was dead."

Mike eyes widened. "Oh my God," he whispered.

She was crying and begging me to bring her baby back to her. I tried but there was nothing I could do. I can heal, but I can't resurrect. I said I was sorry and handed her back the body. She started screaming and calling me a fake and a witch. I never went outside again, until this ship showed up to take me away."

Mike stared into his own hands. "I get it. I thought I was the only one to have it rough until Pieter showed up beat to hell. But I guess we all got our horror stories."

Susan reached for his hands and covered them. "Yeah, even Billy and Mary. So, what's your story, tough guy?"

"I ran away from home as soon as I could. I was like eight. My dad wasn't exactly father of the year material. I got tired of being his personal punching bag."

"Where did you go?"

"Parks, under bridges and culverts, wherever I could stay dry. And I wasn't alone. Our colony brought Prime's problems with it. No, actually; there were two colonies on my world. The very rich lived like royalty while everyone else fought over their table scraps. In my case the fighting for scraps meant just that. If you had a nice dry flop, someone could come and take it from you."

She put her arms around Mike's shoulders. "Mike, I'm sorry. I didn't know."

"It was the way it was. Didn't do any good to whine about it. Life got easier after I started figuring out what I could do. Guys stopped trying to steal my stuff or beat me up for giggles after I smoked a couple. That was two years after I ran away from home."

"It's amazing that you survived that long."

Mike reached for his collar and tugged his shirt over his head. Sue gasped at the lacework of scars on his chest and back. "Mike, what the hell? Where did you get them?"

"My old man gave me about half of them. He liked to use the buckle end of his belt," Mike's fingers traced the lines and connected the dots made on his deeply marked skin. "The rest came from fighting for my place to sleep, or a scrap of food, or just because I was a kid and someone bigger felt like working off their problems on someone who couldn't fight back. Some of those are where I got cut and some are where I got stabbed," his hand mimed the movements, "I know you all hate this place, but compared to back home this ain't so bad."

Sue threw her arms around him and kissed his cheek. Mike's hands found her face and drew her lips to his. Her fingers moved quickly and blocked his kiss. Instead she kissed his forehead and sat back on the bed.

"What the matter?" He asked. "I thought…"

"I know you did. It's not your fault. I want you to know that. It's just that I'm not really attracted to men. I like you a lot, Michael, too much to mislead you."

"What do you mean," Mike's eyebrows arched as understanding dawned. "you're… not attracted… to… ohhhh."

"But I still want to be friends, if that's okay

with you.”

"I don’t see why not. Who else knows?”

"Just you and Mary. And I would appreciate you keeping my secret for now.”

Mike held out his hand with just his little finger extended. "Pinky swear.”

CHAPTER FIVE

The 64 squares on the board were drawn on the table between Pieter and Mike. Nuts, bolts, and washers did duty as pawns knights, bishops, and other pieces. Bob's synthesized voice broke Pieter's concentration. "I am sorry to interrupt the game; however, orbit is imminent."

Billy raised his bare arm and looked at the back of his empty wrist at a watch that was not there, "215 days, 16 hours and 23 minutes; right on time."

A green and blue marble appeared in the viewer. Asgard was more Prime-like than the gravity-rich Steppes. As it filled the screen, coastlines that looked like they were gnawed and gouged by some huge, mythical sea creature came into focus. Pieter sat, gape-mouthed, watching the lush blue and green ball come closer by the minute. He remembered his own dark, rocky world, and a pang of envy gnawed at him.

The engines powered up in braking mode, and soon the wheels touched down at the planet's only spaceport. Perhaps port was a stretch for a single slab of reinforced cement strong enough to permit a vertical landing or take off. They were allowed to view the outside world through the ship's external cameras. A single concrete building surrounded by lights dominated the view. The remaining nightscape was filled with views of towering trees surrounding the fence line.

A few hours passed before the ship's mainframe alerted the unwilling passengers to the approach of Captain Jack Blue and the last exile to be taken back to Prime. Pieter watched a cluster of men in the same uniforms as those who captured him, wheeling a cargo platform to the ships loading ramp.

Pieter felt the rage uncoiling in his gut. These men worked for the same masters that took him from his home and family, beat him, spit on him and sent him into exile. He could kill them from here. It would be easy.

And what then? Mary asked. Her now familiar whisper in his mind damped down the fire in his soul.

Then we escape?

And how many people will you have to kill to do that, Pieter? You're not a murderer. Would your Confessor want you to become the monster they think you are?

The mention of Brother Mykel made him pause. She was right. If he unleashed the beast in his heart, he would only confirm the fear and suspicion that set the wheels of this plan in motion. As they rolled their human cargo onto the loading ramp, he lost sight of the group and his chance passed by.

Pieter took several slow, calming breaths then spoke to Mary again.

And who is prisoner?

Mary's voice echoed softly in his head, *I can't reach him.*

The door to their menagerie opened and a team of technicians rolled a coffin-sized device into the last available space. Tanks of compressed gases and a vessel like a large thermos were rolled in along with it. Both they and the Captain ignored him and the other residents of their prison.

The last cell was directly across from him. He watched as Jack Blue signed several pages of paperwork, then listened with obvious disinterest as one of the technicians explained the workings of the cryo coffin. His eyes rolled and his arms crossed as he stood with his chest puffed out.

Again, Mary spoke to Pieter. *He's in cold sleep. What does he do that they need to keep him in cold storage?*

Blue ushered his visitors out of the holding area leaving Clair Jones to inspect her new charge. Pieter's view was momentarily blocked. He stood and watched the eyes of the other inmates. The door across from his closed with a clink, and Miss Jones walked slowly toward the corridor.

As on his own planet, he felt and heard the main engines spooling up for departure. He continued to stand and watch the slim, dark haired girl across from him as long as she remained in view. A smile flickered across her lips and her fingers rested for a moment on the glass. A red light flashed a final warning, sending them both to their respective chairs.

An hour later the pull on their bodies slacked off as artificial gravity took over, and the doors opened, allowing the group to gather in the room with the cryo chamber.

Joan pitched her voice upward, "Bob."

From a speaker in the ceiling the synthetic voice replied, "Yes, Joan, how may I be of service?"

"Is there anything on this boy?"

"Very little, I am afraid. His name is Loki. He was born on Asgard and they have instructions not to revive him. He's to be turned over to the genetics research unit on Prime as is."

"Do the records give any indication what his ability is?"

"No, they do not. They simply state that he is to be kept in cryo stasis for the duration."

Billy whistled and knocked on the casing. "Hey, you in there, what makes you so bad they gotta keep you on ice?"

Leeann leaned over a small view plate and used her sleeve to wipe away a coating of frost. "Oh!"

Sue and Mary crowded in from the other side and peered in as well. Mary smiled, "I agree."

"He's really not my type, but not bad," Sue added.

"I wish I could see his eyes." Leeann whispered as a pinkish glow colored her cheeks.

Mike leaned against the wall holding his hands over the control panel. "I can shut it down, but I have no idea what would happen to him if I did."

Billy rapped on the casing. "If we're going to get out of this with our skins intact we could use a guy with some serious mojo."

"And you are saying none of us has this... mojo?" Pieter asked.

"Hey, we all got some special skills, but he's the only one they put in the freezer."

"So, getting him out is priority. But we need help. And we need what you call a get-a-way car."

Joan giggled under her breath, drawing Pieter's attention. He looked up and caught an impish grin. "You find me amusing?"

She glanced away and answered, "I think the way you talk is kinda cute. I love your accent."

Pieter returned her smile. "To me, you are one with accent."

Sue leaned against the wall and sighed, "Well, the gang's all here, more or less; what now?"

Mike sat on the floor near her feet and looked down. "I've been in this fishbowl so long I can shave now. I'm sick of being stuck in here." He held his hands up and blue flashes of lightning danced between them.

The pall of despair filled the room. They were all silent. Only the soft beeps and clicks of the cryo unit echoed from the walls.

Leeann still stared into the face behind the glass. She glanced at Pieter and Joan for a moment then back into the machine. "What's going to happen to us?"

Sue snorted, "You know damn well what's going to happen if we get back to Prime."

"The question is, what are we going to do about

it?" Joan's question was a whisper, but they all nodded.

"Ptitsa v kletke." Pieter whispered. "We are all birds in cage."

"We have time to think of a way out of this." Joan did her best to sound hopeful. "It's a long trip back to Prime. Anything can happen."

****

Pieter sat with his back to the wall and spoke softly. "Steppes is hard world. Winters are long and gravity is strong. We were last planet opened for settlement by Golden Door. Life is still primitive compared to some of your worlds."

Billy's eyes narrowed, "Did you ever consider the possibility that your people were being ripped off?"

"I am not understanding this 'ripped off.'"

"As in sold a pig in a poke, swindled, robbed blind, cheated."

"Please explain."

The way I heard it told the living conditions in Russia were worse than almost anywhere else on Prime. Your people would have been desperate to make a deal to find another place to live."

"This much we all knew."

"I'm just saying Golden Door is not known for their generous nature. They wouldn't let a little fudging the facts and figures get in the way of making a profit."

"I am curious about your home world, Beely." Pieter turned the conversation as he sat across from the young kinetic.

"I was picked up on Kepler 186f. We just call it Kepler. It was one of the earliest colonized planets. It's less than 500 light years from Prime, so it's almost across the street, in galactic terms. My folks worked at the bio-dynamics station helping to develop adaptable strains of Prime plants for terraforming projects."

"How old were you when ship comes for you?"

"Ten. I was just ten years old. I was eight when someone reported me to Prime. How do you tell an eight-year-old boy not to be himself? There was no struggle like you. They came to my school and took me. My parents never knew until I was long gone."

"And Mary?"

"Mary was already on board when I got here. She was actually happy to have someone to talk to after being stuck in here for a year by herself."

"A year alone?"

"Well, not entirely. She tells me Miss Jones came to keep her company almost every day."

****

There were no windows or portholes in their holding area. Even if there had been, they would only have seen the painfully slow passage of alien stars as they made their way to a distant world none of them had seen before.

Three times a day, military ration packs dropped from a slot in their food processors into a heating tray. A few moments later and their meals were ready. As on most days they ate around a table in the common area between the rows of cells.

Pieter watched Joan carefully cut her artificial meat substitute into equally sized pieces and nibble slowly through each bite. He observed the girls all ate with some decorum. Mike stabbed at his plate as if were something to kill. Billy refused to use utensils at all and simply ripped his food to pieces and floated each bite to his mouth.

"I hope it isn't a waste of time to ask, but has anyone anything to suggest?" Pieter spoke softly but with careful articulation.

Billy spat a piece of food from his mouth and watched it float in midair. "Yeah, I suggest this food tastes like my shoe. No, wait, my shoe is better."

Mike smiled and added, "He's right, his shoe is better than this."

Sue swallowed and mumbled, "I bet they're not

eating this crap."

"All the more reason to come up with a way out," Joan wiped her lips on her paper napkin and stood. "To that end, I have extended our control of the ship's mainframe. I've had to work slowly so I don't give myself away."

Pieter looked up into her obsidian eyes. "Do we have enough control to take over the ship?"

"Not yet. But I'm making progress. The computer is simple enough, but the military are a distrustful bunch, so there are pass codes and firewalls every time I open a file. You boys have any brilliant ideas how to get the Captain off the ship?"

****

The prisoners gathered around Joan in the lunch room to witness a week's worth of her handiwork. Joan pitched her voice to the ceiling again, "Bob, can you override navigation?"

"At your command, Joan," Bob's flat, computer voice replied.

"Does that answer your question?"

"Da, ochen' khorosho," Pieter replied.

"What?"

"Very good," He translated. For a moment, he reverted to his old self as he spoke. "Beely, Maykl, we must make plan to take ship. That means getting

Blue to get off."

Billy smacked his hands together and affected a reply, "Aye, Cap'n Blood, say the word and the scurvy dog walks the plank."

For a moment Pieter's face was frozen but then explosive laughter filled the room.

****

Jack Blue leaned back into his well-worn Captain's chair and scanned the monitors on his display. He thought about the bonus he would get when they made landfall and what he would do with the money. He even considered giving the regular space force a try with a solid recommendation from Golden Door in hand.

The cameras monitoring the holding room revealed all seven of his prizes were busy doing nothing in their individual cells. The eighth room was a whisper of electronic hums and clicks as the cryo coffin held his last passenger. Everyone was a paycheck waiting to be banked.

Clair Jones smirked as she set a coffee cup next to Blue's elbow. She didn't bother to speak and he didn't bother to thank her. He treated her like she was his personal maid and waitress and enjoyed pointing out that he outranked her.

Jones looked up at the same screens he was watching and delighted in her smug sense of satisfaction. Each time she saw him do this she was tempted to tell him what an idiot he was and that their charges had free run of the common space. But to do so would deny her the pleasure of watching him.

"Beats the hell out of me how they do it," he drawled.

"Do what?"

"Spend that much time in those little rooms and not go crazy. If it was me I would be chewing the paint off the walls by now."

Jones had to catch her lower lip between her teeth to resist the urge to laugh. "Maybe they're just stronger than we are."

"Nahh, it's gotta be some kinda mumbo jumbo, hocus pocus with these kids. Hell, we've watched some of them grow up on this ship."

"I check on them every day, give them a once over with the medical program once a month and make sure they're not swinging from the rafters. That's the best I can do." Clair Jones stared into her lap and twisted to corner of her napkin and her frustration bubbled over. "But honestly, I wish I could do more for them. They were children, most of them, when we took them. Even Pieter is barely half way through puberty. I would be crawling out of my skin by now."

"We don't have rafters, Jones." Blue grinned at

his own joke, then returned to his earlier train of thought. "What are you gonna do with all those credits?"

"I'm taking mine as credit against passage to somewhere far away from Prime."

"I didn't take you for the colonist type. Where you wanna go?"

She closed her eyes and settled back into her seat. "Somewhere I can still see the stars at night and breathe the air without a mask and drink the water without filtering it and boiling it first."

"A back to nature babe; I would never have picked you for the type."

"Oh, I'm full of surprises."

"Don 't be stupid." Blue used a playing card to pick the remains of his lunch from his teeth. "Pick a place that's at least third or fourth wave. Unless you wanna work a plow and live in a place with no electricity and running water."

"It's not the Wild West anymore, Blue; settlements have power and lights and water from day one."

"Not me. I'm a Primer born and raised. I'm gonna get me a place above the smog where I can kick back and enjoy the good life."

****

Bob's voice hissed from the speaker, "Joan, we

are six hours from the Lagrange point."

Pieter turned and nodded to both Mike and Billy then retreated to his room.

Billy called out, "Everyone strap in; it's gonna get bumpy."

A chorus of clicks echoed through the room as everyone buckled themselves into their chairs. Mike reached out and placed his hand against the bulkhead. Seconds later the entire ship shook and lurched.

"Inertial dampers and gyros off line," Mike shouted. "Shutting down main power grid. Gravitational rotation slowing."

The high pitch whine of the motors that spun the center section of the ship wound down to a deep hum. They gave each other sideways glances, trying their best to look brave despite their fear.

The ship floated in space with no power and no control. Emergency lights flickered on in the room and the corridors beyond. Red lights flashed and a distinctly female computer voice spoke, "Life support failure in five minutes, warning, life support failure in five minutes."

Anything not locked down floated free, including Jack Blue who thrashed in midair, reaching for something from which to push off. A free-floating chair provided a bit of mass to nudge him towards the door of the command deck. He grabbed the nearest leg and pushed the chair away in the direction away from the door. Isaac Newton helped him to his target. From somewhere down the corridor he could hear hysterical screams.

Near the door was a large red button with a placard that read, "In Case of Emergency". Blue's left palm smacked the button firing the emergency rotation thrusters. Seconds later and he, along with every other floating object, fell slowly to the deck.

"Are we okay?" Jones screamed. "Is everything back to normal? Are we going to live?"

Blue picked himself up from the deck and called, "Calm down, Jones. We need to get to the escape pod and wait for rescue."

Somewhere, in the back of his mind, Blue calculated, "One pod. two people, six months. What if it takes longer? Shit! I need to lighten the load."

As he reached Jones' cabin the overhead female voice spoke again, "Warning, life support failure in four minutes. Warning, life support failure in four minutes."

Blue reached for Jones' trembling hand and led her down the corridor towards the escape pod. In his mind, an idea took shape. "We've got to hurry and get off this ship now."

"What happened?"

"Lady, do I look like an engineer to you? How the hell do I know what happened? It's an old ship.

It was headed for the bone yard before it got this reprieve. It's a shame about those kids."

"What do you mean?"

"They'll have enough air for a few days, maybe a week. But the computer is offline, so no food or water. Not a nice way to go either way. "

Jones hesitated and slowed her pace, forcing Blue to slow as well. "The worst thing may be that they'll all die alone, locked in those little rooms. I'd sure hate to go that way."

He knew the overhead voice was the same as before but now it seemed to possess additional urgency. "Warning, life support failure in three minutes."

"Jack, we can't just leave them like this. We have to get them out."

His face beamed with concern but inwardly Blue enjoyed a private grin. "Okay, you go get them and I'll warm up the pod. But for God's sake, Clair, hurry."

They separated and Blue cast a last glance over his shoulder as Jones turned the corner heading for the containment rooms. He grinned and sighed. A split second of regret colored his thoughts and then was gone. He hurried down the empty corridor.

The pod was standard issue for cruisers this size. They were intended for use in fleet situations with room for up to fifteen. This was the only one of the original complement of three still on the ship. Fifteen men could survive several days in a pod waiting for a sister ship of the fleet to pick them up.

Alone in deep space it could take as long as a year for a ship to pinpoint his beacon. The door closed behind him and the outer door spun into the void as the pod floated clear of the ship before a short-burst thruster sent the pod a safe distance from the cripple. The exit of the pod sent a shudder through the ship and Newton's Third Law pushed the helpless vessel off its trajectory.

In the corridor, a few steps from the "quarantine" room, Clair Jones stopped as the reality of the moment sunk in. Fear and anger filled her throat even before her voice filled the corridor. "Blue, you son-of-a-bitch," she screamed. She sank to her knees and gasped for air, as if the precious resource were about to run out. As she trembled with knowledge of her certain doom, the lights flickered to life and the door ahead of her opened.

Pieter emerged from his cubicle in time to watch Mary push open the door leading to the corridor. A few random objects that had floated free in the common area were scattered on the floor. He followed Mary out into the passageway. Clair Jones huddled on the floor, her back pressed to the wall as she wept. She did her best to tuck her bare feet under the hem of her nightgown and several strands of her tightly controlled hair rebelled across her face.

Mary stopped and watched the woman cower in fear and desperation. Her eyes were squeezed shut and her lips trembled.

Don't be afraid, Miss Jones. The small elfin girl approached her. *We knew you wouldn't abandon us, no matter what. You'll be safe with us. I promise.*

Jones looked up and stared at the child, then noticed her lips weren't moving. She recoiled and put up her hand as if to ward off a demon.

You don't have to be that way, Miss Jones. None of us will do you harm. We know you were just doing your job, but you weren't cruel to us or neglectful like the Captain.

"Blue," the name spit from her lips. "That bastard left me to die."

He left us to die with you. He's a coward. We were counting on that when we staged the power failure.

Her eyes became wide and she drew a sharp breath. "You staged the whole thing?"

We're sorry if you were frightened, but it was necessary to get him off the ship. We were hoping you would stay.

We want to revive the boy in cryo. I think you know how that's done. Am I right?

"Yes. But how could you..." Her eyebrows pinched as the answer appeared to her. "You've been reading my mind."

This time Mary's lips moved. "Not all the time. Just enough to know a few things for sure."

"Such as?"

"That you never meant us any harm, that you were concerned about us."

"And that I know how to operate the cryo unit."

"Well, yes." Mary's grin grew.

Clair Jones floated up from the floor until she could stand.

Mary smiled. "That was Billy."

"I want you to know, I was never in favor of locking you up. Some of you have been confined to that room for years already, and there's another three-year trip home ahead of us. That was inhuman."

Mike leaned against the door frame. "It's all right, Miss Jones, we know. But I don't think Prime is our next stop any more."

Leeann touched her hand. "Please, can you help us get the new boy out?"

Pieter made his way to the front of the gathering and held out his hand. "Pozhaluysta."

"I don't know what that means, Pieter, but I'll do my best. They downloaded a set of emergency instructions on to my reader. It's in my room."

Mary smiled and offered her hand. "Let's go get it then. We can talk on the way."

Pieter watched their backs retreat down the corridor and around the corner. He had to resist the temptation to follow them. Billy's hand clasped his arm. "Give her some room. You gotta trust Mother Mary to do the right thing."

Mary followed Clair into the personnel quarters set aside for her. The room was sparse and devoid of any personal touches. Without the clothes and neatly made bed, it would be hard to know the room was occupied.

Mary stopped and looked around the room. "No pictures?"

"No family. My parents died when I was young. I'm an only child. And I've never been married."

"I'm sorry. I didn't mean to make you sad."

"I'm not…"

"Yes, you are. It's okay. We all understand. We know what it's like to be alone, to be shunned by everyone because you're different."

****

Joan keyed in the instructions as Clair read the procedure from rows of digital text on her hand-held. "Set core temperature to zero degrees Celsius. Now we wait."

Leeann sat and watched as the machine followed the latest orders. Pieter sniffed the air and caught a strange aroma that made his mouth water and his stomach suddenly complain of neglect. In a moment, Billy and Mike entered the room with a large, round, flat platters in each hand. Steam rose from the surface, and a viscous layer bubbled, beckoning him to come to the table.

Chairs floated in from separate rooms at Billy's beckoning, and soon everyone but Leeann was gathered around the table. Sue tugged on a bite and let the cheese draw out in a thin strand leading to her mouth. Her eyes rolled with obvious delight. No one talked as the treat was consumed with relish.

"I know its frozen pizza, but it's still better than what the automated system has been feeding us," Mike said between bites. "Billy and I found them in the main commissary freezer."

"He's right. There's a ton of food in there," Billy added as he passed out foil drink packs.

Pieter raised the hot wedge of pie to his lips and slowly nibbled the edge of the crust. It tasted a lot like his mother's toasted flatbread. He had helped his father build a tandoor oven so she could cook the crusty treat. He slid the point of the pizza into his mouth and bit down as a sharp acid taste bathed his tongue with sweet overtones. Then the melted cheese bridged the gap between his mouth and the remaining slice.

Clair listened to the moans of pleasure. "Say what you will about Golden Door, they feed their people well."

"I thought it was the Prime Republic Assembly that wanted us picked up and brought back," Sue posited.

Clair nodded again, "It is. In particular, the Genetic Research section of the defense department wants to find out what makes you tick. It's Doctor Mills' pet project. But they contract out jobs like this with Golden Door. As I understand, the contract would let the company keep this ship once delivery is made."

"What about Captain Blue?"

Jones snickered. "He was a wash out. The regular space fleet busted him out for insubordination. He got a job as crew making milk runs for Golden Door. This was his first command ever."

A chime interrupted the meal. Leeann ran in from Loki's room. "Sue, Miss Jones, come quick. There's a red light flashing and the machine is beeping like crazy."

Clair Jones checked her watch and rose from her chair. "Calm down, Leeann. Everything is on schedule. His core temperature is above freezing so it's time to warm up his blood and pump it back into his body while we pump out the frog juice."

Leeann turned on Clair, "Frog juice?"

Joan answered for Clair, "Years ago, when space flight could take a lifetime to get from one star to another, the only way to get humans to their destination was to put them in a freezer like this. But they needed a way to keep the cold from damaging their bodies. Turns out there's a little frog that could freeze solid and then revive over and over without damage. The frog made its own antifreeze. They synthesized the compound for people. Someone named it frog juice and the name stuck."

Miss Jones smiled at the girl. "I'll bet you won all the science fairs back home. Yes, we warm up his blood and use it to replace the antifreeze. Once his blood is back in his body and his internal organs are warmed up, we can restart his heart."

CHAPTER SIX

Clair Jones and Leeann both leaned over the clear panel poised over Loki's face. The hum of the self-contained heart/lung machine filled the room with background noise as it circulated his blood. His pale skin gradually took on a pinkish glow. Clair Jones' finger hovered above a glowing spot on the control panel.

"Everyone stand back," she ordered. Her finger pressed the red dot. Loki's body tensed and went limp several times as a series of electrical pulses stimulated his heart. Then a steady blip appeared on a monitor above the control panel. Another switch slowly shut down the heart/lung machine.

"His heart is beating and he's breathing on the ventilator," Jones said. "We'll monitor his vitals and let him continue to warm up. He won't come around for a few days." She touched Leeann's hand to get her attention. "I better warn you: he could be anything from grumpy to delusional when he wakes up. He's likely to be a bit nauseous for a while too. That's what's called a frog juice hangover."

Leeann's hand touched the window. "What do you know about him?"

"Not very much, I'm afraid. I have no idea why they wanted him kept in cryo."

"I mean about him. Not what he can do but about what he's like."

Clair smiled at Leeann's girlish curiosity. "Not much there either. But I can tell you he was raised on Asgard. It's a bit of a strange society that keeps its distance from everyone. They say they want to avoid contaminating their culture. They live by Old Norse traditions. They speak an ancient Scandinavian dialect and worship Gods out of mythology. They live off the land and depend on their own handicraft. This boy is a Viking."

Mike asked, "What's that?"

"The history books say they are a warrior culture. They believed that they should die in battle with a sword in their hand if they want to get into Valhalla. That's their heaven."

"What about him?"

"Hard to say," Jones held up her hands. "They dropped off a few personal possessions for him.

They're in Blue's room."

Joan stood and spoke to the group. "I hate to bring this up, but now what?"

Billy answered, "What do you mean, now what?"

"She means what do we do now that ship is ours and Blue is gone," Pieter answered in his low, purposeful, accented voice. "We can't drift forever. There is food for years but, sooner or later, ship will need fuel and we must re-supply."

"Genius plan, Billy," Mike barked. "We're stuck out here with no place to go. We would have been better off getting to Prime."

Billy stood chest to chest with Mike and returned, "I didn't hear you offering any brilliant ideas when we started this, Sparky. You want some of me?"

"I'll fry your ass where you stand!" Mike's hand came up with blue arcs of current flowing between them

Pieter shoved them apart and shouted, "Ostanovit' yego!"

Billy puffed out his chest and shouted back. "Who the hell put you in charge of me?"

Sue stepped between them and faced Billy. "He's right. If we start fighting among ourselves now, we'll never survive."

"I'm doing the best I can to keep us alive, but I

need your help, Beely. You too, Maykl. On Steppes, men would embrace and kiss cheek, but you can shake hands."

Billy extended his hand toward Mike, but pulled it away when a tingle ran up his arm.

"Maykl, you will please to make friends."

This time their hands locked and shook vigorously.

"Where can we land that we won't be arrested again?" Sue asked. "And if we need fuel and supplies, what do we use for money?"

Billy replied, "When I was in the lock up back home, there was a lot of loose talk among the guards. One day they got to talking about several tribute shipments heading for Prime that were hijacked. To hear them talk, there is an organized group of what they called pirates working from a place called Dragon."

Mike whispered, "It's probably just a legend, but they say it's outside the control of the Republic and Golden Door. They said it's a safe place for these raiders to operate. Like Port Royal or Tortugas back in the days of tall ships. I mean, it's the kind of place you would need if you were raiding some of the eight worlds and freighters in space."

Pieter put a hand on Mike's back. "Did they say where is ghost planet?"

"Just that it's a secret. Isn't that why it's called a secret base?"

Joan sat next to Pieter and added, "It would be great if we could find a place like that. Getting money is easy. I can hack exchange computers all over the network and tap a little from a lot of accounts. That way we'll have all the Golden Door credits we would need."

"So, all we need do is find planet that doesn't exist and isn't on charts." Pieter sighed.

Mary spoke up, "What if we could hang around near some of the major shipping lanes, quiet and dark and invisible while we listen for a pirate to come along."

Joan nodded and added, "We'll need to take out the emergency transponder."

Billy asked, "What's an emergency transponder?"

"It's a circuit that's hardwired into the ship that helps rescue and salvage ships find it. But we don't want to be found."

"How do you know we have one?"

"There's always an emergency transponder, sometimes more than one. I'm just saying, once we take out the emergency transponder," She glanced at Mike who nodded. "We should be invisible."

"And I can listen for anyone in the area." Mary tapped her head.

"How far?" Jones asked.

"I don't know, really. A few million kilometers, I guess."

Mike whistled. Pieter rolled his eyes up to look at Clair.

"That could work," he said.

Billy asked, "What do we do while we wait for someone to come close enough?"

"Take inventory," Pieter stood and replied. "We need know what is left on ship that could be useful. Let's split into teams and start looking in every corner and closet."

"What are we looking for?"

"Anything we can use to our advantage."

****

Mike walked into the dining hall and tossed a thin rectangular object on the table among the plates where Sue sat enjoying a wedge of pie. "We are officially off the grid. I found it right where Joan said I would."

Sue picked it up, rubbing carbon black between her fingers. "What was it?"

"The emergency transponder," Mike answered. "I didn't have to cook it, but I like to make sure."

"Are you sure there aren't any more of these?"

"Hey, if it's got juice running through it I can find it. How's Viking boy?"

"Still sleeping it off."

"That explains where Lee is."

"And Miss Clair. He's been breathing on his own for four days. How long before he wakes up?"

"Clair says it could happen any time now. She has me on standby. Joan and Pieter are on the command deck. Where's Billy?" Sue asked

"Rummaging through every piece of the ship, room by room. I haven't seen anyone having that much fun in a long time."

"And Mary?"

"With Billy, where else."

"Don't those two seem to have hit it off?"

"They were the first two to be picked up. They spent a lot of time alone."

Pieter's voice echoed through the ship's loudspeakers, "We are to restart main engines. Find comfortable place to strap in and get ready for extra G's."

Mike and Sue both reached for their seat restraints and waited for the feeling of acceleration to push them back into the cushions. They shared a private smile like kids on an amusement park ride. Instead of the jolt associated with takeoff, the push was slow and gentle as they gathered speed and turned toward a spot near the interplanetary shipping lanes.

****

Mary relayed the urgent call from Clair, "Sue, Clair needs your help with Loki. He's trying to wake up."

Sue raced into the room set aside in the ships infirmary for their comatose passenger. Moving the curtain aside, she found Clair and Leeann pulling the feeding tube from Loki's throat. In the bed Loki coughed and gagged as the tube was extracted from his stomach. His eyes blinked and rolled and his hands clinched as they reached for thin air. The screen above his bed flashed with a frenzy of activity that showed his heart and respiration spiking upward. Another readout showed a sudden uptick in his brain activity.

Sue stepped close to the bed and placed her hand on Loki's brow. Instantly his thrashing subsided, and his rapidly beating heart slowed to seventy-five beats a minute. The feeding tube slipped easily from his mouth and his eyes blinked several times. He glanced first at Sue then at Clair Jones before they focused on Leeann.

"Uff da! Hvem fanden er du?" His voice croaked from disuse and the effects of the tube.

His eyes rolled and blinked. His hands reached for the bed under him as he tried to push himself up. "Hvor er jeg?" he shouted.

Leeann glanced from Sue to Clair, "What is he

saying?"

Sue grabbed his hand and tried to push him back onto the bed. "I have no idea. Can I get some help here? He's stronger than he looks, and he looks pretty strong."

The blond man-child struggled against his confusion and disorientation. His cerulean eyes darted from face to face. He pushed against the bed until his thick arms bulged with well used muscle.

Clair and Leeann each grabbed an arm and forced him back into his pillow. Sue slapped a hand on his forehead and whispered one word.

"Sleep."

In an instant Loki's eyes closed and his breathing settled into a regular deep rhythm.

Clair folded a muscular arm across Loki's chest. "I warned you he might be disoriented and delusional."

Leeann took a step back and replied, "I guess I might feel the same way if I woke up in a strange place with people I didn't know and no one understood a word I said."

Clair nodded, "Not to mention they forced his family to give him up, took him from his home, knocked him out and stuck him in that... thing."

The unmistakable sounds of choking and gagging drew their attention. Sue snatched up an empty trash can and managed to turn his head in time to catch a watery, greenish discharge from his mouth. As she lowered the can to the floor and wiped his lips with a moist towel she looked up at Leeann. "We'll have to restrain him before he wakes up again." Sue tossed the wet cloth into a laundry hamper, picked up another and dipped it in warm water. Before she could wipe her patient's face, Leeann reached for the cloth and ran it across Loki's brow, cheeks, and neck.

"It would help if we could communicate," Leeann sighed.

She continued to swab Loki's skin, softly swabbing across his deep chest. Sue and Clair slipped soft, padded restraint straps around his wrist and chest before anchoring them to his bed rails.

Mary entered the room. "Joan had Bob ran the audio from this room through the mainframe. There isn't an exact match in the translation file. Bob says it's a dialect called Old West Norse. Try these." Mary held out her hand and offered three small cone shaped objects. "Put one in your ear."

"Who's Bob?" Clair asked.

"I am, Miss Jones." A mechanical voice responded in her ear. "Joan decided I needed a name. If you need assistance simply touch the earpiece to activate, say my name, and state your question."

"Can we find a way to talk to him next time

he's awake?"

"I will do my best. Old West Norse was the root language for most of the Scandinavian dialects. The closest match is late 18th century Danish, which I happen to have in my data banks thanks to some literature from that period. There will be some words that will be different, but there should be enough commonality to hold a reasonable conversation."

"I hope so," Leeann whispered.

"Except for dead languages such as Latin and those that are resistant to change, all languages evolve and change over time. Separated by time and distance, the same language may not be recognizable."

Leeann smiled, "Bob, how do I tell him my name?"

"Try saying, Mit nave er Leeann."

Leeann repeated, "Mit nave er Leeann."

"Correct. I shall be monitoring your conversation and adjusting as quickly as possible. Be patient, and remember this will be by trial and error until I have built up a working vocabulary."

Leeann looked to Sue and Clair. "It's been over 72 hours since we started his heart, how much longer should we let him sleep?"

Sue answered, "Let me get some restraints on his legs and we'll let him sleep until he's ready to wake up again." She winked at Clair. "I'm starving. Anyone else want to grab a bite before Leif Erickson here wakes up?"

Leeann was quick to volunteer. "I'll stay with him until you get back." She took a seat next to Loki's bed while Mary, Sue and Clair left for the lunch room. She lowered the safety rail on that side and leaned her arms across the top. She idly stroked her fingers through his hair and brushed it back to reveal the peaked top of his ear. "So you really are one of us," she whispered.

His head rolled to face her and his eyes blinked open again. He did not speak but the question in his bright blue eyes was clear. Leeann touched the bud in her ear. "Bob, how do I tell him he's okay and we won't hurt him?"

"Tell him, Du er fint. Ingen vil skade dig."

Leeann repeated the message in a quiet voice and smiled. Her patient took a deep breath and smiled in return.

"Hvem er du?" He asked.

Bob's voice whispered in her ear, "He's asking your name. Remember what I told you earlier."

Leeann sat up and touched her chest with her hand, "Mit nave er Leeann."

"Tak Oden," he smiled. "Jeg troede, Jeg var død , og du var den Valkyrie."

In her ear, she got the translation. "He says he

was afraid he was dead and that you were a Valkyrie come to take him."

"Hvor er jeg?"

"Tell him he is on a ship in deep space."

Leeann relayed Bob's reply. "Du er på et skib i det ydre rum."

"Should I send for the others, Miss?"

"I think we're okay right now, Bob. Let's not spook him with a bunch of people in here."

"As you wish, Miss."

Leeann's fingers brushed her hair back, and she turned her head to reveal her ears to him. As she looked back, he was smiling and nodding his head as if to say he understood. Her fingers slipped into his hand and gave it a squeeze.

****

In a dark corridor, deep in the lower holds of the ship, Billy focused his mind on the locked door in front of him. The pins were old and rusty, but Billy would not be denied. Pops, grinds, and scrapes echoed down the hall.

"Open, dammit," he hissed under his breath. He brushed away the dust obscuring the stenciled numbers on the door and tapped the switch to the com-link in his ear. "Bob, any idea what's behind door 3-23-A?"

The voice that answered was still a digital

reproduction of a human voice but sounded more human by the day. "I have no record of contents for that locker."

"Do you have the combination?"

"I am sorry, Master William, I do not."

"Bob, what have I told you about calling me that?"

"You have threatened me on four separate occasions with various forms of destruction and demolition. To which threat were you referring?"

"Bob, is there anything on board that I can use to blow this door?"

"If by 'blow' you mean the use of explosives, Master William, I am sorry but there are none on board."

"Explain to me why everyone thinks you are so damn helpful."

Billy's foot lashed out and kicked the steel door. Hinges creaked and the door swung open with great protest. Billy raised a light stick above his head and peered inside. The hull of a tracked machine revealed itself in the gloom. A rectangular casing rose above the tracks surmounted with a spherical shell.

Billy's whistle reverberated down the corridor.

****

Mike mused as his hands ran over the shell of the seven-foot-tall robotic machine. Its outer shell gleamed with polish and a fresh wax job. The open access panel revealed several rows of glowing lights. The circular top piece carried an array of sensors. "I'm impressed. Not bad for a week's worth of work. What are you going to call him?"

Joan answered, "My first thought was Robbie after a movie robot. Then I thought Bob because most of his programming is linked to the ships mainframe. But when I remembered the condition Billy found him in, I decided on Scarecrow."

"I don't get it."

"His control computer was missing so I built him a new one."

"Oh, now I get it." Mike grinned and nodded.

"Pieter made some mechanical repairs and got him running again. He has a communication link, radar, infrared and a non-lethal defense component."

"So he can kick ass."

"Yeah, but not to kill. He can also transport several hundred kilos and do a lot of repair work on this ship. I think that's what he was designed for in the first place."

"Cool."

****

Dr. Mills glared into the face of Jack Blue, who had just explained again why he abandoned his ship, leaving the caretaker and all eight of his prize specimens to die. There were three officers of the TRSC (Terrain Republic Space Corps) in attendance to clarify why they had failed to find a ship floating dead in space, even with coordinates recovered from the escape pod. The air in the room was laden with the smell of sweat and fear.

"Let me tell you what I think, gentlemen. I think Mr. Blue here is both an idiot and a coward. Those brats found a way to knock out the power long enough to frighten him into jumping ship. I also think he's a blatant liar. I don't think for a second that Clair Jones was taken prisoner by that gaggle of freaks." Mills bent at the waist until he was nose to nose with Blue. "I think you simply found a way to give her the slip long enough to get away with your yellow skin intact." Turning on the officers he continued his rant. "And you, gentlemen, apparently are incapable of finding your collective asses with a map and a torch."

Mills' fist slammed into the top of his desk. "By God, by the time I'm through with you you'll be lucky if you're not cleaning latrines on some ball of ice in a forgotten backwater of the known galaxy." His voice thundered between the richly paneled walls. "Get the hell out of my sight, all of you, before I organize a firing squad."

Blue and the trio of officers hurried for the corridor and disappeared into the labyrinth of bureaucratic offices. Mills returned to his luxurious leather chair and inserted an ear piece into his right ear. A tap activated the secure com link. "Call Golden Door, Charles Radcliffe." His fingers drummed on his desk while the private link was activated. "Charles... Yes, it's me... Who else calls you on this line? Shut up and listen, Charlie. You're going to help me with a little problem... Because if you don't I'll yank your cash cow monopoly in a heartbeat... That's more like it... I need you to find a missing ship for me... It's one of our decommissioned class two cruisers. One of your officers was running a little errand for me. Standard contract, you were supposed to get the ship at the end of the run... Yes, the same one that's gone missing... No, I don't know where it is, you idiot. If I knew that I wouldn't be talking to you, would I? ... Capture if possible, destroy if not... Hell no, Chuck, this whole thing is strictly off the books. I don't want to know the details. I just want results. I'll have specs on the ship and what information I have on its last known whereabouts and its current crew relayed to your office"

Mills closed the line and relaxed back into his

chair. He opened a drawer on his desk and took out a richly embossed volume. He opened the book to a carefully marked page and began to read.

Witchcraft not only gives that honor to the devil which is due to God alone, but bids defiance to the divine providence, wages war with God's government, puts his work into the devil's hand, expecting him to do good and evil. By our law, consulting, covenanting with, invocating, or employing any evil spirit to any intent whatever, and exercising any enchantment, charm, or sorcery, whereby hurt shall be done to any person, is made felony, without benefit of clergy; also pretending to tell where goods lost or stolen may be found, is an iniquity punishable by the judge, and the second offense with death.

CHAPTER SEVEN

Loki sat at a table, elbow to elbow with Leeann. Both stared at a book. Leeann spoke at a measured pace, "Now, sound out the word."

"The gray cat wa..t.ch..ed th' ye..lo bird."

"Very good."

"Your lan..guige is hard."

"I can't argue with you there. So many rules and too many exceptions. Be patient. It's only been a few weeks."

"I want thank you."

"You're welcome. May I ask you a question?"

"Ja."

"Where did you get your name? Does it mean something?"

Loki smiled, but his brows knit together. "When I was child I had different name. When boy becomes warrior, he is given man's name. But when I do trick they call me Gud fortræd; ummm, God of mischief. They say I am trickster, like ræv… fox. So, I called Loki, for God of mischief."

"Do trick?"

A soft pop was followed by a crack like thunder as Loki vanished from his chair and reappeared behind Leeann, slipping his hands over her eyes.

"Oh my God, you can teleport."

"Jeg er Loke, Gud fortræd."

"Yes, you certainly are Loki, God of mischief." Leeann's hands closed on his before he could pull them away. "Tell me about the place where you grew up, Loki."

Loki sat on the bench next to Leeann facing away. He leaned his head back and closed his eyes before answering, "Asgård er smuk. Vi lever simple liv."

"English please. Think of this as practice."

He spoke slowly, searching for the right words. Her hand felt warm and comforting. "Asgard is beautiful. We live simple lives."

"I heard you were raised as a warrior."

"Ja, children are trained to use sword and ax and bow and spear to fight like Viking. But there is no one to fight. No war. We are farmers and hunters. We learn to forge steel and carve bow and build long boats. I train with my father and my brothers, but mostly I plow and plant and herd sheep."

"You can use a bow and a sword?"

"Ja. I know is silly in age when people fight by pushing button, but my father says it is harder to make war when you must look man you kill in eyes and see he is man like you."

"Have you ever…"

"Killed?" Loki finished her question. "For meat on table, yes. In anger, no. Who would I fight? Our colony…small. Everyone knows everyone. We must work together to survive. We all have our swords, but blacksmiths make more plows and shovels than axes and shields."

"You have a sword?" There was a hint of awe in her whisper.

"Yes, and bow and ax. My father promised to send them with me but I don't know where they are."

Leeann whirled in her seat and reached for his hand. "Come with me."

****

Pieter rubbed his eyes and stretched before settling into a chair on the ship's bridge. He keyed a switch on the panel and asked, "Bob, inventory query, please."

"Yes, Pieter, how may I be of service?" Bob's synthetic voice had become a nearly perfect simulation.

"How long can we remain here before we are forced to find place to land and re-supply?"

"Given our current rate of consumption, eighteen months, three weeks, and four days, if you intend to return to the nearest colonized planet."

"Chjort," he shouted.

"I'm sorry if my report disturbed you, Pieter."

"Is not you, Bob. But if we must to sit here and do nothing for eighteen months we'll all go Choknutjy."

"I understand your concern, sir. I wonder if Master William hasn't already gone, as you say, Choknutjy."

"Where is Mary?"

"She is in her quiet room, listening. If I might observe, sir, she is spending an unhealthy amount of time in isolation."

"I know. And that may be big part of Billy's problem."

"I have come to the same conclusion, sir. She has shut him out and he is quite lost without her."

"I wish I could help."

"I know, sir."

"Where is Joan?"

"Miss Fujimori is in astrogation."

"Spasibo, Bob."

"A pleasure to be of service, sir."

Pieter rose from the command chair and slid down the railing on the ladder leading to the deck below. The astrogation computer projected a chart of local stars against a transparent dome. Joan's nimble fingers rolled the control ball making the plots between stars and planets swirl against the dome in a three-dimensional display. Pieter's hand settled on her shoulder. She shrieked, spun, and lashed out with an open palm that cracked across Pieter's left cheek.

"Oh my God, Pieter, I'm sorry."

Pieter rubbed his scarlet tinged face. "Nyet, I should have knocked first. I scare you."

Joan's hand reached up to cover the rising red mark on Pieter's cheek. "It's this waiting and doing nothing; it has us all on edge. I was focused on trying to figure a way to get Mary within hearing range."

"And did you?"

At first Joan was reluctant to remover her hand from his face, but then she turned her attention back to the holographic display. "The best I can do is put us in the most likely spots for a strike on a tribute ship. The way I figure, those ships carry whatever a colony has to send back to Prime. Some of it is precious metals, but a lot of it is agricultural produce. Those ships head back after the growing season. So, if we know when that's likely to take place on a particular planet we can park somewhere along that route and wait. That has to improve our odds."

Pieter smiled into her dark eyes. "So, I was right. You are smart one."

****

From the debris and disarray, it was clear that the former Captain's quarters had been thoroughly pillaged. Clothes, toiletries, photo frames, empty boxes, ship models, and every sign of past habitation littered the floor and bed. Leeann and Loki rummaged through the carnage.

"Who would do this thing?" Loki asked.

Leeann stood with her hands on her hips and a scowl on her face. "I have a good idea." She tapped her earpiece. "Bob."

"Yes, Miss Leeann, how may I be of service?"

"Bob, where is Billy?"

"Master William is in the dining room consuming his second pizza of the day."

"Would you put me through to 'Master William' please, Bob?"

"Certainly, Miss Leeann."

Leeann's greeting was sharp, shrill, and direct. "Where is it, Billy?"

"Where is what, Lee? I have no idea what you're talking about."

"Don't play stupid with me, Billy."

"What makes you think I'm playing?"

"The box with Loki's stuff, where is it, Billy?"

"Stuff covers a lot, Lee. Can you be more…?"

"Ax, bow, sword, see anything like that?"

"You know, now that you mention it, I may have seen something like that."

"Where is it?"

"I was just keeping an eye on it for you. Didn't want that kind of stuff to go missing. Why don't you meet me at my room?"

"That's where we're headed now."

Billy shoved the half-eaten piece of pizza into his mouth and hurried out the door. The lift doors opened to find Leeann and Loki standing outside his room. Leeann's arms were crossed over her breasts and her foot tapped a rapid beat on the floor.

"Honestly," Billy said as he tapped his pass code into the lock. "I was gonna give the big guy all his stuff as soon as Miss Clair said it was cool."

His door slid back into the bulkhead and the overhead lights came on. The room was filled with stacks of open boxes, bits and pieces of machine parts, electric cable, a case of drinks, food wrappers thrown haphazard on the floor. Everything was in chaos except for the bed. Billy's bunk was neat and carefully made. On top of the tucked blanket was a gleaming broadsword, a long-handled bearded ax, an unstrung longbow with a bundle of arrows, and a few pieces of jewelry.

Loki gasped, "Tak Odin, Legbiter!" He dropped to his knees and raised the sword across both hands to his lips.

Billy and Leeann stood and watched as Loki clutched the sword to his chest and tears flowed down his face. Loki's right hand reached out and stroked the meticulous engraving on the cheek of the ax. Swirls of interlocking knots and mythical creatures embellished the artwork. The long, curved handle shone with use. Finally, his fingers caressed his bow. Almost as long as the bed it rested on, it was stout through the midsection, and the bow's face was layered with sinew.

Leeann stepped close and placed a hand on his shoulder. "I can tell they mean a lot to you."

"Legbiter was my father's sword. He passed it to me when I came of age. To my people this is a Viking's soul. Tak, William. Thank you for looking after them for me."

"Hey, no problem," Billy replied, "Any time."

"If there is anything I can do to repay you…"

"Well, actually I was wondering if you could teach me…"

"To fight?" Loki leapt to his feet and clapped

Billy on the back. "Uff da! Ja, William."

"Hey, I'm not a big strong guy like you."

"Strength will come, William. But strength is not enough to win. You must be… what are words? Hurtig og adræt?"

Leeann translated, "Quick and nimble."

"Yes, quick and nimble. If you are that and have skill, you will conquer."

Loki gathered his prizes in his arms and hurried from the room. "Come, Brother William, we will train."

Billy looked up at Leeann. "I'm going to die, aren't I?"

"Quite possibly."

****

It began as an itch he could not scratch because he could not locate the spot. Then he realized the buzzing was a whisper inside his mind. Pieter's eyes blinked open, peering into the darkness in his room.

Pieter, Pieter… Mary's mental voice whispered.

You don't have to whisper, Mary, I'm up.

I'm entering a set of coordinates into the navigation computer. I think we've found them.

Are you sure?

Someone just hit a tribute ship inbound to Prime. This is where they were going after transferring the cargo.

Do you still have contact?

Yes, but we need to hurry.

I'll be on bridge in five. Give everyone shake and tell them to be ready. We move now.

Yes, Pieter.

Mary?

Yes, Pieter?

Good job. Another three months and I would be going Choknutjy.

Pieter discovered he wasn't the first to reach the command deck. Joan, Mike, and Billy strapped in as he gave the order to the ship's computer to fire up the main engines and make for the location Mary entered.

Mike asked, "Do you think this is really the place we're looking for?"

"You can't fool Mary," Billy answered. "You can't hide from her and you can't lie. She can tell what you're thinking even if you know she's doing it and try to block her."

"That sounds like the voice of experience."

"Take my word for it: never play poker with her."

Thrust from the main engines spooled up slowly, pressing the passengers into their seats. The aging ship accelerated in steps to near light speed before making the final leap to the Faster-Than-Light drive. The third generation Alcubierre Drive began to warp the time space fabric around the ship. The ship caught the leading edge of the temporal wave and surged past light speed. Stars in the forward view screens took on a bluish cast while the Doppler Effect gave the retreating bodies a reddish hue.

"What is ETA, Bob?"

"Three months, twenty-two days, eleven hours, and forty-five minutes, Pieter."

Billy whistled, "Guess that's why they call it space."

Joan slapped the latch releasing her chair restraints. "We keep busy, in the meantime, and make plans for when we get there."

Pieter warned, "You do realize we're going to be dealing with a bunch of pirates?"

"You mean like 'Arrr there, ya scurvy knave. Heave to and come about?'"

"No, Billy, like they'll kill you for any reason at all. We'll need to be careful. And we're going to need currency, lots of it."

Joan giggled, "Money, please; Golden Door's central bank is a kid's piggy bank to someone like me. Bob? What's in the kitty so far?"

"To date, Miss, we have thirty-two million, six

hundred, thirty-three thousand, seven hundred and sixty-seven credits in the… kitty."

"How the hell…?"

"The bank and the Prime Republic are just huge bureaucracies with their hands in each other's pockets. All I had to do was download a little virus that implanted a new tax record that skimmed a few cents on every transaction. There are billions of transactions every day. I'm like a mouse gathering up crumbs in a bread factory."

Pieter blew a gust of air that made his cheeks bulge. "How long have you been gathering crumbs?"

"Since you said we might go to this place."

****

Lee stood behind him, separating his long blond hair into separate strands. It recalled a time, many years ago, when she did the same for her younger sister. Six years later she never imagined a boy wanting braids. It didn't matter to her that it seemed strange; it gave her an excuse to be alone in his room with him.

"Let me know if this is too tight," she spoke almost directly into his peaked ear. The braid would hold his hair away from his face and leave his ears exposed. She looked up into the mirror screen to see him sitting with his eyes closed and a grin on his face.

Her fingers brushed his broad, muscular shoulders as she ran a comb through his hair. Her stomach fluttered and she took a deep breath of his freshly showered skin. "I've never asked how old you are."

She could feel his voice rumble up from somewhere deep in his chest. "I have seen sixteen summers in my father's long house."

"Then we're the same age."

"Sixteen. And you have no husband?" He sounded surprised.

"Is that unusual?"

"On Asgard a woman your age should be married and training her children."

"Sixteen was too young where I come from. Besides, I was several months short of eleven when they took me."

His right hand reached up and trapped her fingers against his shoulder. "Forgive me for saying such foolish things. It must give you pain to recall being taken from your home and family."

"No more than anyone else, even you." She hesitated. "Can I ask, are all the boys on your world like you?"

"What do you mean, like me?"

"You have strong arms and shoulders." Her hands brushed down his shoulders to his thick upper arms. "I've never see a boy your age with your strength."

"When I was ten my father apprenticed me to village grovsmed. How would you say… black smith? I would have been master smith by my next birthday."

"Blacksmith?" She could see him in her mind's eye, back-lit by the glow of a forge and a shower of sparks from his hammer and anvil. "You mean like with a big hammer and a forge and all that."

"Ja. And train with sword and ax. In spring, I plow ground with my father."

"You were a farmer too?"

"How did you eat on your home world?"

"We had farmers, to be sure, but most people bought their food at the market." She focused her eyes and hands on the tasks of weaving his braids. Hand over hand she drew together three long strands of hair.

"Yes, we traded at market as well. The extra that we grew, the things I made at my forge, cloth my mother made at her loom."

"I looked up Vikings while you were still asleep. The clothes they wore were very colorful. Did your mother make clothes like that?"

"Yes. She was master in her own right. She knew which plants and roots and flowers make dyes. She made clothes for all of us and cloth for market."

"That is something I would like to learn. I'll ask Joan if there's anything in the database."

Loki sighed and nodded. "I spent many nights watching my mother turning wool into yarn, yarn into cloth and cloth into clothes. I could build you a loom, but we have no wool for yarn or plants for dyes. If we make it to the other side of this adventure, perhaps Pieter would take me home again."

"Perhaps he would, if we asked him nicely."

A glint of light caught Leeann's eye. She saw two chains with pendants hanging against his chest. A finger found the chains where they traversed the back of Loki's neck. A gentle tug was all it took to draw his hand to his chest.

"What are these?" she asked.

"When I am learning to work metal, my master gives me small bits to practice with. So I make necklace. This one..." His fingers lifted a shining anchor shaped with intricate engraved markings. "This is Thor's hammer. It is a charm for strength and courage." Loki then lifted a simple round piece of bronze. "And this is me."

"I don't understand. How is this you?"

"You see this mark?" Loki held the charm so one side faced Leeann. Lee stared at the rune; a simple line with a 'vee' pointing to the right. "This is also a sign for Thor's hammer. It is for strength and luck." He turned the charm to show her the other side with a more intricate mark. This one looked like two boxes stood on their corners with a line through the center. The bottom box lacked the final line on its left side. "And this is my wish for peace."

Then Loki turned in his chair to face her. He looked up into her eyes and took her hands in his. He whispered, "Jeg ville gøre et hjem for dig med mine to hænder."

Leeann took a sharp breath and smiled. "Would you, Loki? Would you build a longhouse for me, with a loom of my own?"

Loki's eyes grew wide and his brows arched.

Leeann laughed and cupped her hands against his ears. "Don't look at me that way. I've been learning a new language too."

Loki stood and faced her. His fingers found the soft peaks of her ears and touched them. "Du er for smuk til at være alene."

"Do you really think I'm beautiful, Loki?"

She felt his hands caress the back of her head, then slowly bring her lips to his. His warm breath bathed her face and her heart raced. A tiny whimper of delight escaped as she felt his body move closer. Her knees nearly failed her. She slid her arms around him to hold herself up and in so doing pulled him tighter against her.

For all his strength, his touch was gentle. His lips teased her then pressed softly. She sagged against him and let him bear her weight. His hands slipped slowly down her back and held her. There was heat in his touch but no urgency, no demands. Finally, he released her lips and her face turned to rest against his bare chest. She could hear his heart pounding and his breath rumble in her ear.

****

Mike took a turn at chairing the weekly progress meeting around the lunch table. "Is there any further business?"

Mary raised her hand and waited to be recognized. Mike stood next to her and pretended to look past her raised hand. "Anyone, anyone at all," he teased.

The toe of Mary's shoe cracked solidly against his shin. "Owe, Damnit!" A split second later a halo of blue light flashed around his body then faded as quickly as it appeared. "The chair recognizes Mary for new business."

Mike sat and bent to rub his wound. Mary stood and cleared her throat. "Thank you, Mister Chairman. Members of the crew, I rise to address a huge oversight in our family order. Through our shared experience and our common... physical abnormalities, we have become a family of sorts. Brothers and sisters bonded as one. There is, however one person I believe deserves special recognition and inclusion in our family. Miss Jones, would you please stand?"

Clair Jones stood to the sound of applause. She glanced at Mary and then at Pieter. She brought her hands to her cheeks and felt them fill with heat.

Mary continued, "Clair Jones, it is the decision of this family that you have shared our hurts and struggles. From the time we were given into your care you did what you could for us and treated us like human beings instead of cargo. You never abused us or did anything to add to our misery. You could have left us behind and fled with the captain, but you came back for us. You wouldn't abandon us to die in space. And for that we thank you. You have become the adult we look up to and lean on when we need a shoulder. You are as much a member of this family and crew as any of us. Therefore, it is by unanimous consent of this family that you be adopted as our Aunt, and for those of us without family, which is all of us, that we recognize you as our guardian."

Pieter and Loki moved to embrace the older woman and kiss her cheeks. Mary wrapped her arms around Clair and hugged her close. In an instant, she was walled in on every side by warm hands and smiling faces. Leeann's face was awash with tears. They cheered and hugged and clasped her hands and called her Aunt Clair.

Billy floated a large tray in from the corridor and set it on the table. It was a simple sheet cake, given their resources; yellow cake with white icing and that had been held in cold storage for the occasional special event celebrated by the ship's crew. A few small candles burned brightly. It was dry and nearly tasteless and could only be consumed with plenty of liquid to wash it down. No one seemed to care, least of all Clair Jones. It was like a birthday party celebrating her new life and her new family.

****

Charles Radcliffe, CEO of Golden Door Corporation, stood to shake hands with each of the dozen or so men and women ushered into his office by his private security detail. Smartly tailored uniforms with their Mother of Exiles badge set them apart from the grunts who worked the odd jobs among the real-estate. Tables were set out around his spacious suite with a pair of chairs, shot glasses, and bottles of liquor at each. The mercenaries sorted themselves among the comfortable seats before Radcliffe poured himself a drink and stood at the front of the room.

"Ladies," his head inclined toward the corner of the room occupied by the four female trackers, "and gentlemen." A short burst of laughter interrupted his comments. He stood in the front of the room and scanned his invitees. They were as advertised, heavily inked, even branded. The room was heavy in the aroma of pre-game hormones. "I've asked you all here today because I have a… special job for you. Several months ago, a decommissioned class two government cruiser disappeared while on a contracted mission. It was presumed lost to a systems failure."

"Its captain..." He was again interrupted by derisive laughter when Blue's face filled the screen behind him. "Its captain, one Jack Blue, took the only available escape pod and abandoned ship. He was tracked by his emergency beacon and picked up after spending several weeks adrift. However, all attempts to track and recover the Corsica have failed. We must assume the emergency transponder was intentionally disabled. It is now believed the system failure was a ruse by its passengers to get rid of the captain and take over the ship. If you will refer to the files I have had transmitted to each of you, there is a record of each of the suspects in this mutiny."

Radcliffe paused to give his guests time to call up and review the files. He braced for their anticipated reaction. Ripples of laughter spread through the collection of hardened mercenaries. A large man seated near the front of the room stood and tossed his reader onto the table.

"Now I understand why you're trying to get us drunk, Radcliffe. These are the dangerous felons you want us to track down? They're a bunch of snot-nosed kids. There's not a shaver in the bunch. What's the catch?"

"Do not take these... people lightly. They are probably a step up on the evolutionary ladder from all of us. They have developed special abilities that the government would like to investigate. Dr. Mills has taken a special interest in this matter, if you catch my drift? Let me remind you that both you and your highly illegal base of operation have benefited greatly from our mutual self-interest. I am quite certain that Doctor Mills' gratitude would be worth much more than the substantial bounty."

"I don't work for Mills and I don't work for you, unless the price is right. This warrant is dead or alive. Are these freaks so dangerous that you and the Doc are willing to kill the whole lot to keep them from getting away?"

Radcliffe stood face to face with the self-appointed spokesman. "The bounty in generous and the warrant is good. It's exactly what it says; alive if possible, otherwise deadly force is authorized."

"Why do you need so damn many mercs to track down this ship?" the bounty hunter asked.

"Do you remember why they call it space?"

CHAPTER EIGHT

Pieter fretted as he paced on the ship's bridge. His new set of clothes already felt confining. A search of ships stores and the crew lockers had not turned up anything larger. He felt it most across his chest and shoulders. He stared up into the bridge monitor and its camera. "Hey, it doesn't have to do anything. I am only going to hold it in front of camera. Just make it look large and deadly."

Pieter's requests were played over the speakers in the hastily assembled machine shop. Billy held an odd amalgam of tubes and pressure vessels together for Mike to spot weld into something resembling a gun.

"He could have asked for this three months ago," Mike complained under his breath. "I hate working under pressure."

"Come, Brother Michael, wherefore is thy sense of adventure?"

"You have got to stop hanging out with Viking Boy. You've taken one too many hits to your head."

"Nay, Brother, though I be small, I am quick and nimble."

Mike's hand snapped out and slapped Billy's shoulder. Billy cringed, grabbed his shoulder, and dropped to the floor.

"Owww!" Billy screamed. "What the hell? That hurts." He glared up at Mike.

"Quick and nimble, right, how's that working for ya?"

Billy continued to rub his shoulder as he stood. "If he doesn't kill me, I'll be fine."

"You shouldn't let him hit you like that."

"Is that your suggestion, don't let him hit me? What do you think I'm doing in there, dancing?"

"I know what you were thinking. You thought you would get to play with his sword and ax and look all badass. Now you just look black and blue."

"I'm getting better."

"Good. Otherwise you might die. Sue tells me she's cut you off. Better not break anything."

"Say what you will about Loki, he loves to train."

Electricity crackled from Mike's fingers.

Current ran through several pieces of metal tubing, heating the solder and locking them together. The heat disappeared as soon as Mike ceased running current through it. He hefted the fake gun in his hands and admired their handiwork. He held the faux firearm up to the camera. "What do you think, Pieter, does that look evil enough?"

An hour passed before Pieter stood in front of the camera on the ships bridge. Joan stood in his shadow with her hand on his back. His body shifted and morphed growing taller, adding bulk. His features rearranged themselves into a brutish visage with a heavy brow and thick lips. He lifted the fake firearm into his hands and scowled.

Billy offered a suggestion, "I still say he would look tougher with an eye patch."

"How do I look on camera?"

Sue chuckled. "Like a bloodthirsty thug I wouldn't want to mess with."

"That's what we want." He turned to Joan. "How long can you keep me this way?"

"Standing this close I can do it forever. If I have to do it over distance you'll start to change back after about thirty minutes and if I lose both contact and focus you'll revert instantly."

"That should work." He nodded toward the elfin telepath. "Okay, Mary, let's say Hi."

Mary's eyes closed for a moment, then blinked

open. Her fingers punched in a set of numbers into a radio keypad on the control panel attached to her seat, "We are knocking on the door. Let's see if anyone answers."

On the screen near Pieter's face an image appeared: a coiled winged serpent with flames spouting from its mouth. Then a man followed, rumpled gray hair and thick stubble on his face. It was hard to tell from his eyes if he was sleepy or bored.

"Who the hell are you and what do you want?"

Pieter cleared his throat before he answered. His voice was deeper and fuller since the day he was taken. He let his thick Russian accent color his reply, "Is that any way to say preeveet?"

"I really don't give a damn what you think. State your business or be vaporized."

"Name is Thatch, Edward Thatch. I hear this is the place to come if you want to refit a ship… no questions asked."

"Who told you?"

"A little bird. What does that matter? I need some work and my wallet is thick. Can we do business?"

"Show me your fat wallet."

Pieter held up a card that displayed a long number in Golden Door credits. "Fat enough for you?"

"Where the hell did you get that?"

"Can you keep a secret?"

"Sure."

"So can I. Well, can we do business?"

The image faded for a moment then reappeared. "Fine, smart-ass, I'm transmitting the landing zone and the flight path. You get off that path by so much as an eyelash and you and your fat wallet will be cooked. Understand?"

"Perfectly," Pieter affected a crooked grin. "Have your crew chief standing by when we park. I have a long list of repairs for him."

"No problem."

"Pleasure doing business." The screen went dark. A second later Pieter's body quivered then reformed in his normal shape.

"Oh my God!" Joan squealed. "How do you do that? That was amazing."

Pieter turned to face her. "Let me sit. My knees are shaking."

Bob set the navigation computer to the transmitted coordinates and fired a burst of the engines to begin their approach. "Well done, Pieter. That was an award-winning performance."

"Thank you, Bob, but I am to be doing this live and on fly very soon. Any advice?"

"I would tell you to be yourself, but that would defeat the purpose."

Joan's hand settled on his shoulder. "I'll be with you the whole time. Whatever happens we'll get through it."

Bob's voice whispered in Pieter's ear, "Speaking of getting through this, don't you think it's time you had the procedure?"

Pieter frowned. "Is this necessary?"

"It would be unfortunate if someone found the bud in your ear. A surgical implant is simple, quick, and quite painless. Miss Fujimori has already undergone the procedure."

"Really?" He sneaked a quick glance in her direction.

"Yes, this morning. As you can see, she is in no pain. Miss Luscinia and Miss Jones will meet you in your room."

"Isn't there another way to do this?"

"It is a very simple procedure, sir. The components are simply injected under your skin."

"I understand, Bob, but," Pieter paused and lowered his voice. "I'm not fond of needles."

"I see, sir. Would you prefer to be asleep for the implantation?"

"No, I can't do this."

"Perhaps a sedative, Sir?"

"Did Joan have one?"

"No, Sir."

"Then neither will I."

"I shall tell Miss Luscinia and Miss Jones to expect you presently."

"Sure, Bob. Tell them I'm on my way."

As Pieter turned to leave the bridge, Joan's hand slipped into his as she fell into step with him.

"You don't have to go with me."

She smiled and squeezed his hand. "I know, but I want to be there to lend a little...support. I had mine done earlier. It didn't hurt a bit."

"So I'm told."

Joan stopped and turned to face Pieter. She pushed his back against the wall and stared into his eyes. "Do you see me?"

"Da."

"Do you feel my hand?"

"Da."

"Good. When we go in there you are going to look me in the eyes and I am going to hold your hand tight."

"But, but..."

"I know. You're a big tough guy who's not afraid of anything. I get that. I just want you to know I'm here."

****

A day later the stolen ship and its new crew entered orbit around a large asteroid in a field of debris orbiting a dwarf red star.

"No wonder it's hard to find."

"I agree, Master Michael." Bob's computer voice was piped onto the bridge. "Rather like hiding a pebble on a beach."

Mary stared at the image from the forward cameras. "Dangerous place to live. How do they keep from smashing into other asteroids?"

"They are generating a significant containment field around the body. It appears to serve the purpose of warding off impacts from outside while maintaining an atmosphere inside."

"How do we get in?" Pieter asked.

"The instructions I have been sent call for a well-timed approach at which time they will lower the containment field for a moment then raise it again once we're inside."

"And once we're inside how do we get out again?"

"I suppose we shall cross that force field when we come to it, Sir."

"Thank you, Bob, I feel much better." Pieter touched his earlobe, activating his new communication link. "Everyone strap in; we're heading for a landing."

The containment field appeared as a shimmer in the forward view. Bob's autopilot followed the prescribed path down until the shimmer disappeared. The breaking thrusters stirred up dust on the landing field. They came to a stop outside a large hanger and settled to the tarmac. As the gangway lowered, Joan stood behind a completely morphed Pieter in the doorway. His face was now scarred and sported a short, black beard. Behind them the robot called Scarecrow prepared to disembark.

Three men, two with guns, approached the bottom of the gangway. In the pool of light cast by the ship's flood lamps the unarmed man turned out to be the same person Pieter spoke to on the com-link.

"Alright, smart-ass; welcome to Dragon. No weapons allowed."

Pieter leaned on the top railing and glared down. "What about them?" He pointed to the two armed men.

"Just here to keep the peace."

Pieter raised his arms and turned to show he wasn't carrying anything. "Satisfied, or do you wanna frisk me?"

"Who is she?" The man pointed to Joan.

"She's my, uh…secretary."

"Ain't she a little young?"

"I like my secretaries young."

Below them all three men gave a nasty chuckle. Pieter rubbed a spot next to his eye where a livid scar appeared.

"Anyone else on board?" the man asked.

"I got a few guests. No one you need to worry about."

"And what about him?" He pointed at Scarecrow.

Pieter chuckled. "My, uh, secretary plans to do a little shopping while we're here and I ain't carrying her bags. You the guy gets the repair list?"

"Yeah."

Pieter dropped a silver disk into the air. It floated slowly in the slight gravity of the asteroid. The man below held out his hand and let the tiny disk settle on his palm. It fit neatly into a reader and several pages of repair orders scrolled past.

He scanned the list and whistled. "You do know you could probably buy a new ship for what this is going to cost?"

Pieter's hand slapped the hull. "Let's just say I have a sentimental attachment to the old girl."

"Where'd you get her?"

"Salvage. Found her drifting in space. Dead to the world."

"And the crew?"

"Must have bailed and took all the pods. That's on the list too."

Pieter and Joan began the descent down the steps, their feet nearly floating in the low gravity. Joan clung to Pieter's jacket. The sky overhead was perfectly black with a reddish glow on the horizon. The darkness revealed spinning objects just beyond the shimmer. "Rooms?" Pieter asked.

"That way, Mr. Thatch." The older man pointed to a two-story building to the left of the hanger.

A set of rollers popped out on either side of Scarecrow's tracks, exactly the width of the gangway, and the robot rolled down to meet Pieter and Joan.

"You'll let me know when you have an estimate of how long this is going to take."

"Could be three weeks, could be six; depends on how many men I can put on the job." Gray Hair's voice was oily with greed.

Pieter turned to face him, "Look, I don't need to stay on rock any longer than absolutely necessary. Places to go, people to kill. You know how it is. Put as many men on it as you need. Hell, I'll even throw in a little extra bonus if you can cut the time in half." Pieter turned and led Joan and Scarecrow toward their lodgings.

The Hotel was a reinforced cement building with airlocks for doors and wall sized view screens showing a choice of digital outdoor images. Pieter suspected the structure could maintain an atmosphere for some time if the containment field were lost. The walls were splashed with an assortment of bright colors and odd stencil work to imitate the look of a grand hotel.

A man, who could have been Gray Hair's brother, slouched against the raised desk and eyed Pieter suspiciously. A salacious leer crossed his face as he got a glimpse of Joan.

"Is this best flop on rock?" Pieter demanded.

"It's the only flop on this rock. Two rooms?"

"One will be fine," Joan countered as she signed the register.

The clerk pointed at their Robot. "You can leave him outside. They make some of the… clientele nervous."

Pieter touched the micro switch in his earlobe and addressed the seven-foot-tall automaton. "Go wait outside, but stay on alert."

Scarecrow rolled outside the door and turned to put his back to the wall. His sensor array retracted within the main body and his lights dimmed.

"Is okay?" Pieter asked the clerk.

"Whatever, here's yer key, Thatch. Room's one flight up on yer left."

The stairs offered little challenge in the low gravity. Even their bags weighed only a few grams. True to the clerk's word, room two-oh-four was just off the stairs to the left. Their key fit an old-style padlock instead of a traditional door lock. The inside of the room was in keeping with the rest of the facility: windowless, painted concrete walls with a small closet; a dingy bath with a shower; and a single bed.

Pieter closed the door behind them and padlocked it from the inside. "You take bed. I'll bunk down on floor."

"Oh, come on, Pieter," Joan cooed, "we can share. I trust you. You're my knight is shining armor."

"Bed's not that big. Besides, I'll be more comfortable on the floor."

"What are you trying to say?" Joan exaggerated a pout and batted her lashes at him. "That you're too shy to share a bed with a girl?"

"No. I'm just not ready to share bed with you."

"Pieter, you're blushing."

He looked into the discolored mirror on the wall and saw his own face with a deep tinge of red. "It's just…"

"You're very sweet," Joan whispered into his ear. She stood behind him and brushed his ear with the tip of her finger. "I appreciate that you respect me that much. But what happens if someone comes to check on us and you're sleeping on the floor while your young secretary is in the bed alone?" She flashed a coy smile and batted her eyes at him again.

Pieter smiled back. "I appreciate what you're

trying to do, but the door is locked from inside and there are no windows."

"You're taking all the fun out of this."

Pieter sat on the edge of the bed and patted a spot next to him for her. Joan sat and put her arms around his neck. Pieter gave her a serious look and pulled her hands into his lap. "I was raised in the Russian Orthodox church. I was raised to believe it was my duty to remain pure until I take a wife."

"So, you're a virgin?"

"That's not dirty word."

"No, that's not what I mean." She glanced down, her cheeks flushed scarlet. "So am I."

"I'm glad. You're my best friend, Joan; let's promise to stay that way for now."

She leaned closer and kissed his cheek.

CHAPTER NINE

Even at half normal gravity, the game was deadly serious. Billy ducked the heavy ball as it whistled above his head. They were training weapons, no sharp edges, no points, no spikes. That wasn't to say they didn't hurt when they hit you, especially when Loki's muscles powered them. Billy shoved off against the wall and rolled away from the follow up blow. He sprang to his feet in time to see Loki's padded training ax pass an inch in front of his face. He wore a safety helmet they borrowed from the welder's locker, but if Loki made solid contact his head would ring like a cheap bell.

He ducked and lunged for Loki's legs, but the big Norseman jumped above the arc of his padded sword. Applause and cheers echoed off the mess hall walls. From a bench at the far end shouts of encouragement reached them both. All three girls on board were there to witness his humiliation. Sue, at least, was there just in case. Mary spent much of her time with her eyes covered by her palms. Leeann stood and cheered on the object of her infatuation.

Billy's chest hurt and breath was hard to draw as his stamina slowly ebbed. Sweat ran down his face and stung his eyes until he could not blink the salt away. Blinded and gasping, he waited for the blow. The padded ball that stood in for the ax head landed with a thud in his back, sending him sprawling on the floor.

Mary was on her knees and at his side in a heartbeat. She cradled his head and pulled away his helmet. As bad as he felt, her smile made him feel better. In the background Sue called out for the ship's AI, "Bob."

"Yes, Susan, how may I be of service?"

"Turn off the artificial gravity please."

"Yes, Miss."

The mechanical rotation of the center section of the ship slowed to a stop and the pull on his body fell to the infinitesimal amount that was normal on the asteroid. Sue's hands pressed against his back and stomach, easing his pain.

She scowled down at him. "I shouldn't do this,

you know. I should let you lie there and hurt and swell up. It's what you deserve for making Mary worry."

Leeann helped Loki remove his helmet and wiped what little sweat he had from his face. Loki grinned and offered Billy a hand.

"Tac, Brother William. It is good to train, yes? You are getting stronger and quicker by the day. Do not be discouraged."

"I'm not discouraged, Loki." He locked hands with the huge man child. "One day, I swear, I will beat you." Everyone shared a laugh before he let Loki lift him back to his feet.

"I have something for you, my brother." Loki reached behind his neck and unlatched a silver chain. He pulled it from under his shirt to reveal an intricately carved bronze casting that looked much like an anchor. He spun Billy around and draped the chain around his neck.

Billy cupped the pendent in his right palm and stared at it. Interlaced knots ending in wolf and dragon heads decorated the bronze casting. He turned and looked up at Loki. "What is it?"

"It is Thor's hammer; a mark of a brave Viking warrior. You and I are now truly brothers."

Billy wrapped his arms around Loki and hugged him close. "Tac, min bror."

****

Mary's arm felt warm around his waist as they made their way down the corridor, past teams of technicians and shipbuilders already working on the refit. The sound of heavy equipment reverberated up through the deck, and he was aware of many suspicious eyes watching them everywhere they went.

Loki and Leeann stopped and punched in the pass code to Loki's room, leaving him and Mary alone in the passageway. "Do you want me to come in?" she asked.

"Do you want to?"

"Yes," she didn't hesitate.

Billy entered his pass code and waited for Mary to go in. His room had undergone a transformation since her last visit. It was neat and tidy, with all the extraneous trash removed. He asked for two cold drinks from the processor and stepped into his small bath. The shower made him wonder if Loki had to get in a piece at a time. Small as it was he could stand under the stream of hot water and feel his aches and pains disappear.

Your drink's ready.

He was used to having Mary in his head nearly all the time. They had no secrets, how they felt toward one another the least of them. He stepped out and the water shut itself off instantly. He toweled off a bit and slipped into a pair of loose fitting shorts.

Mary was waiting for him when he opened the door. She handed him his drink and stood on tiptoe to kiss him. Her lips felt warm and pliant, and her breath was always sweet. In the low gravity, he could lift her with one arm and set her on the edge of his bed. He sat next to her and felt her arms slip around his neck.

"Say it."

"Say what?" he teased.

"You know what. Just say it."

'Why should I have to say it when you already know?"

"Because, a girl likes to hear it aloud every now and then."

"Okay." He paused and let his lips brush hers. "I love you, Mary."

****

Joan's eyes blinked into darkness. A whisper tickled the back of her mind like distant echoes. *Joan, can you hear me?*

"Mary?"

Yes. Don't say anything, just think it. I've been trying to wake Pieter but he's sleeping too soundly.

Deep rumbling thrums rose from the darkness

on the side of the bed nearest the wall. In the perfect darkness Joan grinned and thought, *Confirm that. Why didn't you try the implant?*

Too noisy. It's also a transmission and that may be risky.

Is there something wrong?

Hard to be sure, but I think someone has been trying to get into your room.

A thief?

Can't say, but what I'm picking up is someone wants to keep an eye on you.

A spy?

More likely. I got images of someone trying to bug your room, maybe put a camera in through a hole in the ventilation, microphones too.

Camera's not gonna work in here, it's too dark.

Infrared. Where's Pieter?

"Oh gosh…" Joan exaggerated a stretch as she sat up in the bed and looked from side to side. Then she spoke into the darkness, "Edward, baby, where'd you go? Come back to bed." Leaning to the side of the bed she gave Pieter's shoulder a firm shake. "There you are, Edward. My goodness, did you fall out of bed again?"

Pieter mumbled, "What…"

"An important man like you should never sleep on a cold floor. Come back to bed." And to Mary she thought, *He's awake, fill him in and tell him to play along.* Joan's hand snaked out and transformed Pieter back into Edward Thatch before he could stand. She held the blanket back and waited for Pieter to slide under the thin cover. "That's a good boy, Eddie."

The bed shifted and shook as Pieter climbed in under the blanket. Her fingers traced the lines of his shoulder blades and felt a tremor as she did. He was warm to her touch and gave off a strong, spicy smell. Her hand slipped around his shoulder and fell against his chest. His heart beat against her palm and his breathing was deep causing his ribs to rise and fall.

She inched closer and rested her ear against his back, listening for the steady thump, thump from within. Joan let her weight, slight as it was, settle against him. It made her stomach flutter, but was calming at the same time.

It's for show, Mary's inner voice reminded her. *If someone is watching you need to keep up appearances.*

****

Loki walked the ship's busy corridors. The low gravity took time to adjust to; his feet barely skimmed the deck as his hands slid along the safety rails anchored to the walls.

After months of near silence, the hum of power tools and the constant chatter of workmen was unsettling. None of them had behaved badly, but he saw the way they looked at Sue and Lee. He had no intention of actually hurting anyone, but he wanted them to know someone was watching.

He wore his one-piece open to the waist and tied the arms around his middle like a belt. His thin undershirt did little to conceal his thick muscles. *I must remember to thank Brother William for helping me restore my strength. Training is always better with a friend.*

He turned into the dining room on the crew deck. Lee was already there with a pair of covered trays fresh from the food processor. The food was still spat from an automated machine that knew little about what taste good.

"I know it's not real meat, but it's supposed to have lots of protein for a growing boy." Lee smiled and helped Loki peel the plastic cover from his dish.

Loki cut a piece of his "meat" and sniffed it before letting it fall back to his plate with a plastic on plastic clack. "And you are saying this is better than food from captivity?"

Lee giggled and spooned a bite of reconstituted vegetables into her mouth. Loki reluctantly forced the brown mass on his fork between his lips. He chewed slowly with eyes pinched shut. He swallowed and put his fork back on his plate. "Brother William swears he will eat only the pies of pizza."

Lee laughed and answered, "And at the rate he's going through them, we'll run out soon."

"Den let us hope Sister Joan remembers her mission."

****

The windowless room gave no clue to the hour. There was no sunrise on a tumbling chunk of rock in space, only the clock chime at the hour they set last night. Pieter rolled to the side of the bed and sat up, both relieved and disappointed to be out of Joan's arms. His fingers tapped the clock and shut off the alarm. Another tap and the lights flickered on.

Joan yawned and stretched. "Do you want to shower first?"

"No, go ahead. I'll..." Pieter paused as he got a look at his morphed self in the mirror. The strange features made him look away. "I'll see to our grip first."

Joan's hand settled on his back for a moment, making sure Pieter remained Edward until she got back. The lights in the bath were harsh and off-color. The towels were thin and a shade of white trending toward gray. Her kit included a bar of ship's soap, shampoo, and a tube of toothpaste plus a comb and a toothbrush. The temperature setting for the shower included a notice that read, "Showers are limited to five minutes. Any additional time will be charged to the bill."

Even set to thirty-eight degrees, the shower felt tepid at best. She hurried to rinse and get out before the time expired. Joan's wardrobe was limited to standard, ship's fatigues, consisting of a dark blue, one-piece jump suit. She dragged a comb through her damp hair, then bound it into a long tail down her back, making sure her ears were covered.

When she pulled the curtain back, Pieter was laying out several objects on the bed. Among them were a few knives, a dozen or so small round balls, and a brace of metal tubes arranged neatly on the blanket.

Pieter looked up at her. "What are you comfortable with?" Instead of waiting for her answer, he tossed several items her way. "Good choice. Give me a minute in the shower and we'll go look for Ship's Stores."

On the bed in front of her were a packet of the small, round, balls and a pair of objects that looked like old fashioned writing pens. *It's all non-lethal,* Mary whispered inside her mind. *In case you were wondering, the balls are small flash/bangs and the pens are shockers. Pieter doesn't want you walking around this place completely unarmed.*

Behind the curtain the shower started running. Joan thought back to Mary, *What do I do with them?*

If you're cornered, take one or two of the little balls and throw them at the floor or the wall, then cover your ears and close your eyes. A bright flash and loud pop will disorient anyone in range and give you a chance to get away.

And these? She held one of the pens.

Point and click. It fires a jolt of electricity into whoever it's pointed at. Back on Prime they were named for a pulp novel science fiction hero named Tom Swift.

Where did Pieter get all this?

Where do you think? Billy, Loki, Mike. It's a guy thing, but it's not a bad precaution, considering.

Joan was jolted from her mental conversation by the curtain opening and Pieter walking out in full Edward Thatch mode. She knew the illusion was of her own making, but preferred the reality it masked.

Pieter's jump suit was tied around his waist, leaving his upper torso bare except for the towel draped around his neck. He turned to face the bed and took a moment to strap the knives to his forearms before tucking the remaining items into his pockets. A few stray drops of water ran down his back. Joan caught her lower lip between her teeth and resisted the urge to take a towel and dry him more thoroughly. His arms slipped into the full sleeves and a tug of the zipper covered his upper body.

Pieter returned the heavy lock to the hasp facing the hallway and looped an arm around Joan. At the lobby desk, he leaned over the day clerk and spoke one word, "Stores?"

"Yes, Mister Thatch; the quartermaster is expecting you. Your line of credit has been transmitted. Warehouse is three hundred meters to your left as you exit the front door."

Instead of backing away Pieter gave a malicious grin. "One more thing, and let me make myself clear on this: I really don't like anyone snooping on me. I mean, I really hate being spied on, by anyone. Do you understand?"

The clerk swallowed hard and looked up into Pieter's narrowed eyes and hateful smile. "Perfectly, Mister Thatch," he replied.

"Good."

The sky beneath the shimmer was unchanged

since they arrived, revealing no clues to the passage of time. They walked, half bounding, down the tarmac in the direction of the warehouse. A number of ships sat on the flat, paved spaces between the buildings. Several were surrounded by portable lights and teams of mechanics.

At a door marked "STORES" Pieter turned, taking Joan with him. Inside the door, a shriveled little man sat at huge desk. His crevassed features were interrupted by a pair of wire framed glasses perched on an ugly knob of a nose. "Ah," his voice was high and nasal, "…you would be Mister Thatch," he took a second to nod toward Joan, "…and associate. I was alerted to your impending arrival."

Pieter planted both hands on the edge of the desk and leaned over the clerk. "We need to re-supply. I assume you deliver."

"Indeed we do, sir. If you have a list we will be happy to see to your needs."

It was obvious that their line of credit had preceded them. The clerk was oily in his fawning as Joan handed over a disk similar to the one Pieter gave the crew chief. The clerk grinned as he read. "Yes, yes. I see. Yes, Mister Thatch. We have a number of styles of uniforms; if you would care to follow me?"

Instead of standing, the clerk rolled from

behind his desk in a chariot-like chair. He trundled onto a ramp that delivered his chair into the front of a cart. With a hand gesture, he directed Pieter and Joan to sit on the bench behind him.

"I wasn't always like this. I used to have my own ship until it got blown out from under me. I was known as the best ship builder in the free company. But I have this job now."

Pieter leaned closer to hear the old man and whispered back, "God bless you, father."

The old man laughed. "Say that after I cheat you."

The shelves were built such that Pieter need only stand to examine the goods. His hands brushed over many different color uniforms before settling on a deep, royal blue with a high neck collar.

"I see you have a good eye, Mister Thatch. Those are formal Republic Navy. We have a variety of rank and other insignia for your crew."

Pieter nodded. "My secretary has a list of sizes. I also believe she has an additional list for some off-duty items."

Joan tugged on Pieter's sleeve, "Edward, don't forget about Cook."

"Oh yes. I realize this may be impossible, but do you have any fresh produce?"

"Produce, sir?"

"Vegetables, fruit, meat, eggs, grains, rice,

flour. After a long time out here, my crew and I would favor a change."

The old man nodded, "Very good, sir. Agricultural produce are regular items on tribute shipments. I'm sure we can see to your Chef's needs."

"And I have one more special request from a member of my crew." Pieter slipped the man a note.

The old man's eyes first looked over his glasses at Pieter, then carefully at the paper. "Easily done, Sir; this sort of gear finds its way onto nearly every outbound colonial shipment."

"So, father. Is there a galley here about where we could try some of that produce?"

"If you're meanin' a restaurant of sorts, I can't recommend any such place on this here rock. What they call food wouldn't pass for swill on my ship. But if it's fresh food you're after, that I can do. Let me call ahead and let the cook know to set the table for two more."

"We don't mean to intrude."

The old man waved a bony hand in front of his face as if brushing away a fly. "A pleasure to have a gentleman such as yourself, Mister Thatch. One of the perks of being the Quartermaster here is I get first pick of whatever's brought in."

"Then we're grateful for the invitation, Mister...."

"Picard, Auguste Picard. You're not the ruffian you pretend to be, are you Mister Thatch? Ya needn't worry, I won't tell a soul. Better to scare away than to fight off, 'eh?"

"You're a very astute man, Mister Picard."

"I may not look it now, but there was a time I was the best ship fitter this side of Prime. It will be a pleasure to have someone with intelligence to make dinner conversation."

****

You managed to spook whoever was trying to bug your room.

Pieter stood and stared into empty space but he could feel Mary's grin behind her spectral voice. *So we're clear?*

As far as I can tell. Several skimmers showed up with the first loads of supplies. Oh, and Loki says thanks.

How does the fresh food look?

It looks great, but there's nothing to cook it on in here. Ask the crew chief if they have a kitchen module to fit this ship.

Anything else?

Yeah, a cookbook would be handy.

Pieter grinned. *Are you telling me there's no*

one on board who can...?

Sorry, boss, no one asked. Aunt Clair says she can, a little. Mike says he'll take a whack at it and Loki says he can, but only over an open fire.

His laughter caught Joan off guard but then he continued his silent conversation. *No open fires, please.*

Oh. Mary's spectral voice had the hint of laughter, her mental imagery carried scenes of Billy and Mike parading through the halls. **Pieter, the uniforms were a nice touch. Mike and Billy are strutting around like peacocks but Loki's was a little tight through the chest. Maybe they have one that's a bit bigger?**

We'll do what we can. What is progress on refit?

The ship is crawling with tradesmen around the clock. The fish tank has been ripped out and a common room has been put into its place. Three new pods are all locked and loaded and they've installed the new rails.

Good. I hope we never need them, but you know what they say about better to have and not need. Any trouble?

A few looks and the occasional rude remark. One of the workers made a pass at Sue and got a new hairdo for his trouble.

I don't follow.

Michael hit him with enough voltage to make his hair smoke and stand on end. And Loki walks around without a shirt and huge hammer over his shoulder. He calls it Mjölnir, whatever that means.

The room was undisturbed, except that housekeeping had made a stop to make the bed and swap out fresh towels. The twenty-four hour chronometer read twenty-two fifty.

It had been a very long day.

Joan released Pieter and let him slip slowly back to his normal shape, rubbing her eyes, and swaying on her feet. Pieter caught the motion out of the corner of his eye. He moved with the speed of a big cat to catch her before she collapsed to the floor. He scooped her up and deposited her on the bed.

"Joan." His voice bordered on frantic. "Joan, are you okay?"

Her eyes blinked and she turned to face him. "I'm just tired. Turning you into that thug took more out of me than I expected. I just need some rest.”

Pieter closed his eyes. *Mary*!

Yes, Pieter.

I need Susan, now.

A boom filled the enclosed space as Loki appeared with Sue in his arms.

“What’s wrong with her?” Pieter asked.

“At least give me a chance to give her a once over, will ya?”

Sue’s hands caressed Joan’s face before touching her chest. “She’s very tired. Exhausted, I would say. Best thing you can do is let her sleep.” Sue placed a palm on Joan’s forehead and closed her eyes.

Pieter sat on the end of the bed and let his head sag, his palms covered his eyes. Sue put a hand on his back. “Relax, Pieter. She’ll be fine. Just don’t make any all-day appearances as Captain Thatch for a while.”

“Thank you, Sue. I asked too much of her.”

“No, you didn’t. We’re all learning our limitations. I recommend you get some rest too, glorious leader.” Sue stood and hooked her arm in Loki’s. “Home, James.”

If their arrival was like a thunder clap their departure was a puff of displaced air. Pieter watched Joan as she slept peacefully. He stared until his eyes threatened to close of their own accord, then got up and moved to the side of the bed opposite Joan. He pulled the blanket over her then slid into bed. He rolled to face her and continued to watch her sleeping until he succumbed.

****

Pieter's com link to the ship crackled in his ear with the voice of the ship's mainframe. "Pieter, are you there?"

He pressed a finger against a spot in front of his earlobe and answered, "Yes Bob, I'm here."

"Pieter, we may have a situation."

"What kind of situation?"

"I have been monitoring off planet communications, as a security precaution. Nothing caught my attention during the first seventy-two hours, but now I am picking up transmissions between some locals and several ships a few days out on an inbound course."

"So? That's what they do here, Bob. If the communications are friendly, they can't be government ships."

"They are not, per se, government ships, Pieter, but in the course of their communication they sought information about a stolen class two cruiser. And they offered remuneration for information."

Pieter sat up, alert to everything around him. "How far out exactly, Bob?"

"Two, perhaps three days at their current speed. Pieter, they know we're here."

"Have they asked the locals to prevent us from leaving?"

"Not yet."

"Can you transmit an order to begin refueling?"

"Fueling has already begun, Sir."

"Thank you, Bob. Are our supplies loaded?"

"At least ninety percent. Should I ask for the rest to be delivered now?

"No, refueling is normal, but a rush delivery might look suspicious. I would have liked to give the refit crews another day but we're going to leave as is. Otherwise, normal orders according to the Admiralty. Get everyone else ready to leave the minute refueling is complete. I'll get Joan and return to the ship."

****

Reflections of gauges and switches shone brightly off the metal rails and control surfaces of the mercenary ships bridge. The ship was built for speed and could give a good account of itself in a fight. A pair of figures stood shoulder to shoulder in silhouette against the lights. "Shouldn't we warn the locals and have 'em lock down the ship?"

"And split the reward? Screw that. I got a few friends on Dragon. I can have them slow 'em down long enough for us to close in. Then we'll take 'em up here, when they manage to take off." The mercenary captain was a beastly man with sallow skin and almond eyes from Asian ancestry. The corner of his left eye marked the end of a scar that trailed down to his cheek. The eye milky and useless, narrowed at the suggestion of cutting in the locals. "Is that damper field generator ready?"

"If the instruction manual they sent with that thing is correct, it should be up and running."

"Good. That bunch of delinquents is not going to get the chance to do anything once we have them rounded up. Remember, stun only. Make sure everyone gets that order."

The lackey inclined his head and replied, "Aye, Captain. But I don't see why we don't just make 'em cold and bring 'em back in the meat locker?"

The captain laughed. "You're an idiot, Cribs. If those freaks are worth that much to Mills dead or alive, imagine how much they might fetch on the open market, alive. My grandfather always told me to do my fishing with live bait."

"So you're gonna double cross both Mills and Radcliffe?"

"That's why I'm the captain and you're an idiot."

****

Joan threw her kit into her shoulder bag and tugged the zipper close. "What exactly did Bob say?"

"Ships, several of them, all headed this way and asking about a stolen class two."

Joan shifted Pieter before they headed out the door. Their bill was settled and their bags were transferred to Scarecrow. They walked quickly toward the hanger where their ship was waiting. Pieter touched his ear. "Bob."

The shipboard entity answered, "Yes, Pieter."

"How is the refueling going?"

"I had to do a little bluffing but we're nearly topped off. How far are you?"

"Five minutes, Bob. We'll pay the toll and be on our way."

"Sir, my cameras are picking up a number of unsavory individuals in the hanger. Facial recognition does not register any of them as among the workers who performed the refit."

"Copy, Bob. Tell everyone to buckle up and be prepared for a fast exit."

"As you wish, Pieter."

As they approached the hanger the man Pieter knew as Grey Hair appeared out of the gloom and fell into step with them. "Mister Thatch, good to see you again."

Pieter looked his way but never broke stride. "We were on our way to pay our bill, if that's what you were wondering."

"Oh no, Sir, I weren't worried about that. I has it on good word that you're as fine a member of the Gentleman's Court whatever captained a ship. I just wanted to give you your new papers."

Pieter stopped and turned to stand face to face with the man. In his hand, he held a thick envelope which he handed to Pieter.

"Your ship's registry, under its new name."

"I don't recall asking to change the name."

"Nevertheless, Sir, the man what runs this here shipyard asked for the change shortly after meeting you. He said you were a decent man and you didn't complain when he cheated you on the price a bit. He said you treated him with kindness and respect."

"You're telling me that old man at ship's stores…"

"This is his asteroid. He's the boss, and he said rename that ship The Phoenix."

"Why?"

"He said the Corsica didn't suit ya, Sir. He said with your accent you might appreciate a ship named after The Firebird. Oh, and he said to give you this too. Although he said why a star cruiser would need a ship's carpenter and a smith is a bit strange." He handed Pieter a roll of cloth with ties at each end.

"These are for your crew, Sir."

Pieter nodded and shook the man's hand before continuing to the hanger. They paid for their fuel and repairs while Scarecrow went up the gangway ahead of them. The ship looked like it was freshly out of space dock. It gleamed brightly in the hangar lights. The pair of warp rings bore fresh coats of paint that included the ship's new name and a rendition of the Firebird from Russian legend, head high and turned to one side, wings spread and bright flames in gold, red and orange.

Finally, they turned to make their way up the gangway only to find their path blocked by a group of six heavily built men.

"Where the hell do you think you're going?" The group's spokesman addressed Pieter.

"Anywhere we want; you have issue with that, suka blyad." Pieter stood as tall as he could and puffed out his chest and he came eye to eye with the bald-headed thug.

"Ah, Russian; I haven't heard talk like that in years. Here's how this works, Black Beard. You gotta pay the exit toll first."

"There's no such thing," Joan shouldered her way between Pieter and the shake-down goon.

"If I say there is, there is. Besides, we got some friends on the way who wants to meet you, so why don't you stick around?" Slowly they found themselves surrounded. The goon bent down to get nose to nose with Joan. Pieter locked eyes with him and bared his teeth. The cudgel seemed to appear from thin air and cracked a glancing blow across the back of her head. An instant later Edward became Pieter as Joan sank to the floor. Pieter watched as a pool of blood collected under her head.

"What the fuck," the goon in front of Pieter swore. "They're just kids." He laughed at Pieter, drawing echoes of laughter from his comrades. Then he lashed out, striking Pieter across his face with an open palm. His head moved only an inch or so, then he returned his gaze to Joan who lay at his feet.

"What have you done to her?" Pieter's voice was remarkably calm, even as the man who struck Joan and the one who struck him both crumpled to their knees. A crack like thunder filled the service hanger as Loki appeared at Joan's side. He scooped her into his arms and a soft pop marked his disappearance as air rushed in to fill the void.

Pieter bared his teeth and closed his eyes while the men around him slowly went from their hands and knees to lying face down against the concrete. When Pieter's eyes opened his rage shone in them like cold fire. He turned and put his hands against the railing, glaring down on his captives. Memories of his torment flooded through him. In his mind, he relived each kick and punch from his jailers. For the first time since he was taken, Pieter loosed a scream of anguish that echoed through the hanger, sending onlookers running for exits.

Before they could muster a scream the six thugs on the floor felt the air squeezed from their lungs. Seconds later, the sound of bones shattering echoed off the metal walls. Pieter walked calmly up the ramp while the men on the floor were reduced to flattened blots of crushed flesh and bone. The hatch closed and the ramp disappeared into the hull.

Where is she? Pieter asked Mary.

Infirmary. Loki took her there directly. Sue is with her, Pieter. She'll be fine. I'm more worried about you. What did you do out there?

I made sure those men would never hurt anyone again. I can do more than make gravity go away, you know.

So it would seem. You should talk to Joan. Tell her how you feel.

She was my responsibility.

Responsibility didn't make you just kill six men, Pieter. I'm not saying they didn't get what they deserve, but Joan isn't the only one who's going to have scars. That wasn't you out there. I know you, maybe better than you do right now.

Pieter's face was stoic. *Get everyone strapped in, Mary, including you. We're getting off this rock now.*

CHAPTER TEN

"Pieter." The voice in his ear was urgent.

"Yes, Loki." His answer was flat and devoid of emotion, almost mechanical.

"Pieter, they're not opening the hanger doors."

"Billy, are you there?" Pieter called out.

Billy answered over the ship's intercom. "Yes, my Captain." There was a clear edge of excitement in his voice.

"Billy, I think it's time we showed them who they're playing with. Do you understand?"

"I understand, Pieter; my pleasure." Billy closed his eyes and bent his will against the object blocking their path. Steel hanger doors rattled and flexed, but then inexorably bent and buckled from the middle outward until they were a crumpled mass of sheet steel hanging tenuously from the ends of their overhead tracks. The gaping wound between them was more than enough to permit the Phoenix to leave the hanger and roll out on the tarmac.

The radio crackled with a frantic voice, "Phoenix, you are ordered to return to the hanger. You are not, repeat, not cleared to taxi."

Pieter blinked but still showed no emotion. "Mike?"

"Yes, Pieter."

"That noise in my ear is really bothering me. Would you mind?"

"My pleasure, Captain."

Flashes of light were seen and screams could be heard coming from the control tower. Similar events followed in a chain reaction until every electrical device at the port was a smoking piece of junk.

"Thank you, Michael."

"Anytime, Captain."

"Everyone strap in, this is going to happen quick." Pieter touched the switch relay by his right ear. "Bob, get us out of here now."

"Yes, Pieter."

Pieter had only seconds to strap himself in before the main engines throttled up to full power and sent the Phoenix hurtling toward space.

Michael asked, "Do you want me to take out their containment field?"

"Don't destroy it. Just turn it off until we're clear.

"Aye, sir."

"Course and destination, Captain?"

"Maintain this course for now, Bob. We'll figure out where soon enough."

"Aye, Captain. Steady as she goes." Bob's AI voice sounded completely human and strangely excited.

The instant the ship stopped accelerating Pieter released his restraints and made to leave the command deck. He walked like a man with a purpose until he found the infirmary. Just inside Sue attended to Joan, strapped into a hospital bed. Sue was belted to a stool attached to the bed, with her hand resting on Joan's forehead. Billy and Mary stood on the other side. Inside his mind Pieter heard Mary's voice.

She'll be fine, Pieter. She had a fractured skull and a severe concussion, but Sue is almost done making her as good as new.

Joan reached for Pieter's hand as he came closer. "What happened, Pieter? I felt a pain in my head and then I woke up here?"

"One of those men hit you. But I took care of them. You'll be fine now. We'll all be fine."

She could feel a tremble in his hand and a

wavering in his voice she had never heard before. "What do you mean, took care of them? Pieter, what did you do?" Her voice was urgent and her grip on his hand tightened.

Billy interrupted, "Ever drop a sledge hammer on a grape?"

"That's quite enough, Billy," Sue jumped in. "You're not helping."

"Pieter, what does he mean? What did you do?" Joan gasped.

Pieter looked at his shoes and hesitated before he spoke. "They hurt you."

"Yes, I know. But I'll be okay now."

"They hurt you. They nearly killed you and they laughed about it. I was angry. You were only there because I needed you for the mission. You were my responsibility."

"Don't be angry with him, Joan." Mary spoke aloud, something she did less and less of late, but her voice was soothing. "I saw those men's minds. They all had blood on their hands. They were nothing more than a pack of wild animals preying on others. And if Pieter hadn't put them down, they were going to turn on us next."

"He sure put them down. I mean down flat."

"Billy, stop it." Mary's sharp voice brought him up short. Billy closed his mouth and stood with his eyes down like a boy who's been scolded by his teacher.

Mary continued, "Pieter has been holding in a lot of hurt and anger for a long time. He never talks about what was done to him before we knew him." Pieter blushed and looked away. "And he cares for you more than he knows."

Sue released her harness, stood, and kissed Joan's cheek. Mary took Billy's hand and led him from the room following Sue down the hall. The door slid silently closed.

"Is all that true, what Mary said?" Joan asked, squeezing Pieter's hand.

Pieter blushed again and stammered for words. "I didn't ask to be in charge. It just happened. It was the first time anyone ever trusted me to do anything, so I was determined to do my best. And you were so helpful, so steady. Every time I was afraid I wouldn't be good enough, you were there."

Joan sat up on her bed, listening carefully to every word.

"And then I got word from Bob that there were ships a couple of days out and they were looking for us. I shouldn't have been caught by surprise that way. And then that son-of-a-bitch hit you." Pieter started to shake as he recalled the incident. "And I looked down and you weren't moving and there was blood all over you, all over the ground under you. I got scared." He looked into Joan's eyes and wiped his tears away. "More scared than I've ever been in my life. And I just wanted to hurt them back. Oh my God, I killed them, Joan. I could hear their bones breaking and their bodies being crushed, but I couldn't stop."

Joan slipped her arms around Pieter. He wrapped his arms around her and began to sob hard racking tears into her shoulder.

"Oh my God, Joan, I killed them, I killed them."

Her arms consoled him as he purged himself of his guilt and fear. If anyone had tried to enter the room they would have found the door sealed and all the monitors dark.

An hour later Pieter and Joan emerged from the infirmary without fanfare. A few minutes later they walked onto the command deck. Loki, Leeann, and Mike stood as they entered the room. Pieter stood straight but his eyes were red, and his face still held deep lines where smooth boyish skin had been. They all watched him carefully as he took his place at the command chair.

"Status, Loki," his voice was flat and devoid of feeling.

"Sir, we are monitoring half a dozen vessels at the outer edge of our scanner range. They appear to be following, but not closing on us."

"Weapons status," he shouted.

Mike thrust his chest and chin. "Sir, rail guns are loaded and ready, Captain."

Pieter settled in the Captain's chair and opened the ship-wide communication link. "I won't sugar coat it. Someone is chasing us. There are six ships out there following us, and I have a feeling they're not alone." Pieter paused and drew a long breath before speaking again. "I killed some men today. I was not raised to kill. I was always told that killing is wrong. I feel terrible for what I did, but I was given no choice. I know most of you were also raised to believe that it's wrong to kill. But we may not be given that choice. We can only hope that they were paying attention to our departure from Dragon, and that they know they would do well to keep their distance. Pieter out."

****

Leeann stood in the darkened corridor and pressed her ear to the door. She waited and listened but heard nothing. *What if someone comes down this way?* She thought. *Don't just stand here in your nightshirt, stupid, punch in the last number.*

Her finger shook and nearly keyed in the wrong digit. The door slid open with no more sound than a gasp of air. She stepped into his room, invading his space uninvited, but still closed the door behind her. What would Mary say if she looked for her right now? What would the others think of her? She wasn't raised this way. Her mother didn't raise her to act this way, but this was beyond her control. Her heart thundered in her chest and breath eluded her in the darkness.

She tried to count the steps between the door and Loki's bed but her shin told her sharply that her count was off. Loki stirred and snorted in his sleep. She could not restrain a giggle. She reached out and found the bed and slid slowly onto the edge.

Her fingers found the round shape of his shoulder and traced that line to the void between his shoulder blades. She pressed the flat of her hand against his broad back and thrilled to the feel of his heart beating. Leeann leaned over and kissed the side of his neck.

Loki rolled to face her on the darkness. He whispered, "What are you doing?"

"Vær ikke vred," she replied in his native tongue.

"I'm not angry. Why would I be angry?"

"Jeg har bare brug for at være i nærheden af dig."

Loki reached out with his hand and softly brushed her hair to reveal her ear. He caressed her distinctive tip and kissed her softly. "You can stay if you like."

Leeann burrowed against his chest and inhaled,

enjoying his scent of soap and man. His arms closed around her and she felt safe for the first time since she was taken aboard the ship. She knew there were men in the ships out there that meant them harm. But in his arms, no fear could reach her.

****

With the fingers of her other hand, Joan absently toyed with her new collar pins. One was a golden casting of the firebird and the other a leaf over crossed swords. The roll of cloth had contained insignia for many different jobs on the ship and a golden Phoenix for each of them.

How is he? Mary's voice was still a whisper even inside her head.

Finally asleep, Joan answered. She lay next to him, as she had at the close of every duty watch since their escape from Dragon. He was still restless behind his shuttered eyes. He didn't sleep more than an hour or two at a time before the nightmares would come for him.

Let's hope the sedative Sue slipped him kicks in and he gets some rest. Speaking of which, you could use a few hours yourself.

I'll be fine. Joan resisted the dragging weight of fatigue. *I just want to keep an eye on him for a few more minutes.*

She ran a hand across his face, feeling the short stubble that hid the weight he had lost. He slept with his fingers wrapped around the silver cross that hung around his neck. She sometimes listened to him pray in his native Russian. She could not follow everything but she was learning. More to the point, she thought he prayed like a little boy saying his bedtime prayers.

He's still in shock, Mary reminded her. *He's never had to kill someone before, and killing six at once was just too much.*

Joan wiped a tear from her cheek and answered, *Isn't there anything I can do? He needs to forgive himself. He needs to get it...*

... out of his system. I wish I could tell you he'll be fine, but he may get worse before he gets better. Goodnight, Joan.

Pieter's breathing settled into a deep, steady rhythm. Her arm rested across his shoulder. He still felt the way he did on Dragon: strong, solid, and reassuring. His skin smelled slightly spicy and damp from his shower. She curled herself against his warmth and surrendered to the need for sleep.

****

Sounds of water running stirred her eyes open. Pieter was already up, standing at a steaming basin of water and massaging soap into his face. She watched him shave for the first time in days. He ran his fingers over skin turned pink by the hot water. He watched his beard sluice away down the drain and wiped himself clean with a wet towel. Finally, his eyes took notice of her propped on one elbow, staring at him. He smiled at her reflection and drew a comb through his damp hair.

"Are you going to stay there all day?" he asked.

"Day, night, what's the difference?"

"None, really. It's just that we have our watch to stand in about an hour and we need to eat."

She smiled to herself at his mention of food. Meals had been something he skipped more than not of late. "Breakfast sounds good to me. I've been working on learning how to make biscuits."

"Don't trouble yourself. I'll just call up something from the processor."

She sat up on the edge of his bed and watched him slip into his shirt and tunic. His muscles stood out under his skin, but his ribs were too exposed. "You need to eat better than that."

"You sound like my mother."

"Your mother would say the same thing if she were here, and then she would scold me for taking such bad care of her boy."

He sat next to her to pull on his trousers and socks. His face pinched at the brows. "You're not my mother, and I can take care of myself." His voice had an angry edge.

"Pieter, I didn't mean..."

"You need to stop worrying about me and take care of *your* self. You can't stand watch looking like that. Go change and pull yourself together."

He stood and walked quickly from his room leaving her to stare after him as his door closed. She pushed herself onto her feet and made her way down the hall to her own room. *He didn't mean it that way,* she thought. It was the stress talking. She sat on the edge of her own bed, still neatly made. Warm salty tears ran into her hands and into the corner of her mouth. She shook with her private pain for several minutes.

When she emerged from her room, she was freshly showered, with neatly brushed hair and a few touches of powder and makeup. She followed the corridor to the lift and went down one level to the floor with the mess hall.

Lively sounds of chatting friends found her as she approached the open door. Even closer and the aroma of food wafted down the corridor as well. She paused at the door and scanned the room. Loki and Leeann sat close to one another at a table while

Mary shared a booth with Billy. Sue sat alone picking at a dish of processor rations. Inside the door, she turned to see Pieter asleep at a corner table, food pushed to one side, head resting on his folded arms.

She resisted the urge to sit next to him and instead got her bowl of "oatmeal-like" breakfast cereal and took a seat opposite Susan. "Did he eat much?" she asked.

"A few bites at the most. How are you?"

"Tired, angry, worried. We had words before he left the room."

"I thought he was over the worst, but now I wonder," Sue replied and shook her head. "Mary's worried too. She's keeping a close eye on him, if you catch my meaning."

"What did you find in the ship's medical database?"

"He's depressed, of course, and trapped in some sort of cycle where he keeps reliving the incident. He's also flashing back to how horribly he was treated by the people who captured him on his home planet."

"The nightmares are more frequent," Joan's voice broke as she choked back a sob. "I don't know what to do."

"I'm not sure there's anything any of us can do. If it was a physical injury I could help him, but this…"

"We need him, Sue. I need him."

A clatter from across the room ended the conversation. Loki jumped to his feet and ran for the corner where Pieter had been sleeping. Screams and shouts in Russian and Norse filled the room. The clamor rose as Loki fell to his knees and shouted in agony as he was pressed, face down, into the deck.

Leeann ran to Loki's side and raised a hand as if to ward off a demon. Joan rushed to see Pieter, wild eyed and screaming, trying to stab himself with a kitchen knife. Suddenly a thick black fog enveloped him and floated above the table where he sat.

Loki gasped as air rushed back into his lungs. Muffled sounds escaped from the dark sphere holding Pieter. Slowly they faded to sobs and Lee let the bubble become clear.

Joan's hands touch the energy separating her from Pieter. Pieter turned to face her, his face wet and swollen. His fingers reached for hers and pressed against shimmering energy. Pieter's head shook and soundless words appeared on his lips.

"What is he saying? I can't hear him," Joan pleaded with Leeann.

Mary answered, "He's saying he's sorry."

Joan turned to see Mary standing in the

doorway. "Sorry?"

"Yes. For failing you, for killing, for becoming the monster they said he was."

A pinpoint of spectral light appeared inside the bubble. Pieter stared at it as it became brighter and larger.

"What's he doing?"

Mary approached Joan where she stood. "He's trying to kill himself. He's focused his power to create a tiny black hole inside the bubble. When it's built up enough, he'll be sucked into the gravity well."

Joan began pounding her fist against the bubble, screaming frantically into the void, "Pieter, no. Don't do this please. I need you. We all need you." She turned to Leeann, "Lee, let him out."

Lee pressed her hands to her temples and replied, "He could kill us all if I do. Someone do something quick, he's drawing my energy field in on itself." She slowly settled to her knees and released a wail of pain into the room.

"I can stop him," Joan cried. "I can stop him. Please don't let him die."

Sue took up a stance near the bubble opposite Joan. "Keep him looking at you, Joan."

Joan hugged the sphere and pressed her cheek to that side. Pieter looked down and pushed his fingers against his side where her face should be.

Sue spoke quietly, "Lee, I need to get my hand inside. I need to make physical contact with him."

A dark blot formed on the sphere where Sue's hand rested. As it went black her hand passed through. Air whistled around her wrist as she grasped Pieter by his ankle. She whispered one word, "Sleep." Pieter slumped against the wall of Lee's bubble and his eyes closed. Instantly the bright point of light winked out of existence. Leeann's bubble settled and disappeared like dust in a breeze, leaving Pieter on the floor asleep.

****

"Where the hell are they going?" A short, wiry man sitting at the navigational console of the lead mercenary ship let his inner monologue out onto the bridge.

"How the hell should I know? They don't seem to be heading anywhere." The Captain rubbed his index finger against a scar next to his blind left eye.

"Maybe they have a secret base somewhere."

"And maybe your mother was a whore on Prime."

"We could still split 'em open and pick up the bodies."

"No. I still want 'em alive."

"You're the Captain."

"Don't forget that, Cribs."

****

In a dark fog, he heard a voice. "Here he comes."

The voice was soft, concerned and female. The fog began to lift, and light filtered in between his eyelids. A hand rested on his and gripped his fingers. His eyes opened, revealing a dimly lit room. To his left Sue sat watching him intently. It had been her voice he heard. The hand squeezing his fingers belonged to Joan.

He tried to sit up only to find a padded restraint across his chest. As he reached for it he found his arms were similarly bound to the bed. He inhaled sharply and thrashed against his restraints.

"Stop, Pieter, please," Joan spoke to him as she put her hands on his chest. "It's for your own good."

"My own good?" He spat the words and flexed his arms against the padded straps. "How would you know what is for my own good?"

Joan fell across his chest and gripped his hands. "You killed them for a reason, remember? You killed them because of what they did to me. That makes me as responsible for what happened as you."

"You didn't do anything."

"I butted in and got in the way. I should have trusted you to talk your way past them, but I stuck my nose in where it didn't belong and got my head cracked for my trouble."

"You didn't kill anyone," he whispered.

"What I did set you off."

"No. It's my sin to carry, not yours."

"Those men weren't worried about God or anything else. They were ready to kill us all before they let us escape. You saved us all, Pieter." She felt his arms relax under her hands. He exhaled deeply and sank into the bed beneath him.

"You could have let me go."

"No, we couldn't. We need you. You are the Captain of this ship by unanimous consent. Everyone is ready to follow you, Pieter."

"Loki could…"

"Loki is very brave, but even he agrees he would rather follow you than lead us into a fight."

****

Pieter's room was comfortable, with a chair and a desk where he could keep his dark thoughts at bay by reading or playing chess against the ship's computer. Even as he sat, his fingers passed the beads of his Chotki from one to the other as he whispered his prayers.

A tap on his door told him it was lunch time. "Come," he spoke aloud to the door. It opened and Joan stepped into his room with a tray in her hands.

She set the tray on his desk and pulled a chair up to sit next to him. "I wish I could tell you it's delicious, but I haven't tasted it yet."

Two bowls contained what appeared to be a mixed fruit salad and identical plates held sandwiches. She held a fork out to him and waited. He sighed and accepted her offering. "Fork, spoon, disposable plates and cups; nothing I could hurt myself with."

"Leeann prepared everything. You can't blame her for being cautious."

"I'm tired of being treated like a child."

"I don't treat you like a child, do I? If you really want a knife I'll bring you one. I can see you're back in touch with your faith, Pieter." She reached into her pocket and brought out a rosary with scarlet tear-shaped beads in sets of seven, divided by round icons and a silver cross. "They're called Mary's Tears; a gift from my mother. They were the last thing she gave me when I was taken. She said I could pray for miracles with them. I'll pray with you if you like."

Pieter hung his head for a moment then reached for her hand. "I don't deserve you. Just when I think there is no way out of my darkness, you shine a light for me."

Mike's voice whispered into his ear through his implant, "Pieter, we've received a transmission I think you should see. It's a little degraded, but you can still make it out."

"Put it through to my room please, Mike."

A grainy picture of the man he knew as Quartermaster on Dragon coalesced on the screen. He was smiling in the way Pieter remembered. "Greetings, Mister Thatch, or whatever your real name is. I apologize that it's taken this long to send this message, but someone managed to burn out my radio array and nearly every electronic component on my asteroid. You wouldn't know anything about that, would you?" The old man laughed. "I must tell you, you remind me a lot of my son.

"I understand why you appeared as the ruffian that you did, but I know from sitting at our dinner table and having the time to speak with you that you are not what you appeared to be. Now I also understand that you are some sort of shape shifter. Amazing. I hope at least that you are human.

"By now you know I changed the registry of your ship, and I hope she is treating you well. I really wanted to say I'm sorry for what happened to you in the hanger. Those were not my men, and we have rounded up several more in the pay of Golden Door who were part of the plot to capture or delay you. More to the point, they broke my laws and will be dealt with accordingly.

"I also wanted to say that I found you to be a

fine, well spoken, intelligent young man and I would be honored to have you as a member of our Gentleman's Court. The life of a Privateer is not an easy one, Mister Thatch. I wish you good sailing and may you find a sweet, safe harbor to call home."

Pieter smiled.

****

The half-eaten bowls of stew were cold, like the cook pot on the stove at the far end of the dining hall. The acquisition of fresh produce and meat, plus the addition of a retrofitted cooking module, led to impromptu cooking lessons from Bob, courtesy of his extensive data base. The stew was a group project between the computer, Mike, and Billy. Mike was capable, but it was Billy who demonstrated a real gift.

With a mind of its own, Joan's right hand reached out to cover Pieter's. She asked, "Pieter, what do you think they're doing out there, those six ships?"

Pieter looked up into her dark, almond eyes. "I remember watching a nature film from Prime when I was about eight years old. It was about how wolves would hunt caribou...when there *were* still wolves and caribou. Some of the wolves got in behind the herd and ran them until a straggler dropped back. Then they took turns chasing the straggler until he was too tired to run. Finally, they would chase him into a trap set by the rest of the pack. I think that's what they're trying to do to us. Keep us running until we exhaust our fuel or until we run into another bunch of ships somewhere out there ahead of us."

"You've been thinking a lot about this."

"Six weeks and they haven't gotten a click closer. They're not trailing us for our health. They also haven't called for help, so they don't work directly for the government on Prime. It's like having an itch I can't scratch. I almost wish they would do something."

"Like?"

"I don't know, something, anything. I'm just sick of waiting."

Mary's inner voice broke in. *They're scared, Pieter. You were right. They got reports of what happened in the port on Dragon. They even got visuals of your fight in the hanger and our escape up to the point when Sparky fried the electronics. They're afraid.*

"Mary says they're afraid. I'm impressed. I had no idea she could read them from this distance."

I have discovered that distance is

nearly irrelevant, Pieter.

Pieter paused and pinched his lower lip between his thumb and forefinger. His eyes glanced right and left but really looked at nothing. His brow creased and wrinkles appeared at the corners of his eyes. His fingers played across the covers of several books that littered his table. One was open to the most recent read page on his chess table. It was the first time she had seen him so lost in thought.

Joan's hand settled on his again, just enough to draw his attention. "Pieter, what's wrong?"

"Nothing. I know what we have to do; I just don't know how to do it. I've been reading everything I can find on how to command, how to lead people into a battle. I've probably read Sun Tzu six or seven times. I've studied Drake, Morgan, Teach, and Nelson. I need to know what they knew."

Joan's hand squeezed his and made him stop. "You doubt yourself. I guess that's only natural for what you're going through. You're not even nineteen and here you are trying to lead your friends into a fight. That's crazy. No one can expect you to know what to do."

"But if I get it wrong, people are going to die."

"That's always a possibility. We know that, all of us. We don't expect you to be perfect, but we're all ready to follow you into whatever comes, especially me." Her hands grasped his face; He made to pull back, but she held tight and pulled him close enough to brush her lips against his.

His arms circled her slender waist and pulled her close. He could feel the warmth of her lips and her moist tongue. Her fingers teased the peak of his ear, as if to remind him how different they all are.

"I wish you could transform me into a brilliant leader who knows just what to do to get us through this in one piece. I'm afraid. I wasn't this afraid when I was in a holding cell back home. Even when they beat me and spit on me and cursed me, I wasn't this afraid."

Joan cradled his head in her arms and whispered. "That's what I'm trying to tell you, Pieter: you already are that man. You can't go by the book on this. There's never been a crew like us before, so there *is* no book. The rules have changed. Just believe in yourself and in your friends and we'll get through this."

"I wish I had your faith."

"But you do, Pieter."

He was startled when her hand slid into his shirt. Her warm skin glided across his chest until her hand closed on his hidden treasure. She withdrew her hand, revealing his Chotki beads and three-bar cross.

"Who gave this to you?" Joan asked. "Was it

your mother?"

"Nyet. It was my confessor, Brother Maykl. He told me it would bring me peace in times of trouble."

"Do you believe what he said?"

"Yes, I do. He also told me I was a young man of strong faith."

"I believe him. You should believe him too."

Pieter's hand closed over Joan's hand holding his cross. He sat up and seemed to remember. "Brother Maykl told me a story from the Bible, about a man going into battle against a giant, armed only with his faith and a few river rocks."

"Did he win?"

"Of course he won. What would be the point of the story if he lost?" Pieter's eyes grew wide and he sat up straight. "Of course! I get it now. We're not the caribou, we're the big bad wolf. At least we are in their minds. I think it's time we huffed and puffed a little." He touched the key at his ear. "Bob."

The AI spoke softly in his ear, "Yes, Pieter, how may I be of service?"

"Bob, I have a crazy idea and I need to know if it could work."

"I shall endeavor to do my best to answer your questions."

He took Joan's hand and left the mess hall for

the forward area of the ship. As he walked he touched his com implant. "Loki?"

Loki answered, "Yes, boss?"

"Get to the gunnery station right away."

"Yes, boss." His reply was tinged with excitement.

They arrived at the bridge to be greeted by Mike and Mary. Both stood as Pieter took his seat in the command chair. He turned to Mary and gave her a wink.

"Everyone find a seat and buckle up. Prepare to come about, Mike, 180 degrees, maintain this aspect."

"But Pieter," Mike's voice wavered nervously, "That will take us directly at the people chasing us."

"Exactly." He touched the implant again. "Loki, make sure everything is loaded."

Joan's face had a wicked grin when she heard Pieter's orders. She looked at Mike and whispered, "They've got us right where he wants them."

"Hunh?" Mike's brow pinched and he ran his palm across his short, sandy hair. "Pieter, we've still got a problem with this turn. We're way past light speed in a big, heavy Class Two Cruiser. It'll take several days to slow down enough to do a slow turn, let alone a sharp 1-80. And if I slam it into reverse we'll rip the warp rings off the hull. It's just not possible, Captain."

"Stop thinking like a normal human, Mike," Pieter said as he flashed a feral smile. "Those ships out there are still bound by the laws of physics, but not us. With this crew, anything is possible." Pieter touched his com link. "Billy, report to the bridge."

Billy's high-pitched voice replied in Pieter's ear, "Aye, Captain."

"Mike, begin deceleration."

Mike pulled the tandem engine levers back, first into the null setting and then into reverse. The ship shook against the sudden change in the temporal wave around the ship. Pieter closed his eyes and concentrated. Speed fell off rapidly as the gravity well around the ship dropped.

"The closer we get to zero gravity, the faster we slow down. When we hit zero mass, cut the engines."

"Aye, Captain," Michael paused and looked up at Pieter. "I hate to sound stupid but how will I know when our mass is down to zero?"

"You'll know when you and everything on this ship becomes weightless." Pieter shouted, "Billy?"

Billy exploded into the bridge, breathless. "Here, Pieter."

"Remember what Joan said about the speed of any object with no pull of gravity?"

"A little, yeah."

"I'm bringing our mass down to zero; flattening

out our gravity well. Mike is going to cut the engines in just a second. When he does I want you to gently turn this ship around without going backward or forward. Understand?"

"I think so, Pieter. What are you up to?" Billy asked.

"Just be ready." Pieter settled in his seat and pulled his straps tight. "Everyone strap your selves down tight, this is going to get bumpy. Sound off when you're ready."

One by one they all checked in. He nodded to Billy and the ship turned to face the distant fleet.

"Okay, Mike. I'm going to count to three and I want full power. Got it?" Mike nodded and returned the controls to null.

"One, two, three."

Mike threw the thrust wide open and the ship instantly bolted past light speed, skimming along the temporal wave surrounding the ship. Only Pieter's control of gravity kept them from being crushed into their seats.

Joan smiled at Mike. "I don't think they're expecting us to do anything like this."

"Neither was I."

****

Chaos erupted on the bridge of the lead bounty hunter. "I'm telling you they just came about and charged. No slow down, no big arching turn, nothing."

"Son-of-a bitch," the Captain screamed. He thumbed a button on his ship-to-ship radio. "Everyone spread out. Give 'em room."

"Captain, he's coming straight at us and at this closing speed they'll be here in minutes."

Again, he pressed the communication button. "Gunners to your stations. Shoot to cripple. I repeat, shoot to cripple. I want these brats alive."

Five small blots of light took up flanking positions ahead of the command ship. In the dark silence of the airless vacuum they waited. Second by second the blip on their scanners closed the gap.

****

Pieter watched as their former pursuers spread out like a net, waiting for them. "Maykl," Pieter called out, adding the accent for fun, "Can you make a burst of electricity in the middle of their formation?"

Mike stared at the images on the screen, "Something like an EMP? I never have, but I don't see why not. You want me to knock out their electronics?"

"Exactly," Pieter's grin was wild.

Mike focused his eyes on the forward view screen. "Say the word."

"Tell me when you're in range."

"Aye, Captain."

"Loki, how are the waist guns?"

"Loaded, Pieter, but unmanned."

"Can you pull the trigger from where you are?"

"Yes, but I can't aim them. They'll just fire straight out on either side."

"That's all I want. Standby on the waist guns."

****

A scoundrel watching the scope on the lead ship looked up at his commander. "They're not slowing down. Captain, it looks like he wants to play chicken."

There was a brief, bright flash and a crackling shock wave swept through the formation. Instead of turning away, the approaching cruiser began to rotate around its longitudinal axis, spinning faster and faster until its track looked like a tightly wound corkscrew. As the shock wave passed, electronic systems on the mercenary ships winked out.

"Son-of-a-bitch! Shut everything off and reboot fast." The Captain bellowed. "Brat's smart. Hit us with some kind of EMP!"

****

"Loki, now." Pieter's voice was calm but firm.

The new rail guns, mounted on either side of

the ship, began spitting slugs of spent uranium in all directions. Pieter's control of gravity made his crew immune to the effects of the tight spiral of the ship. On his screen, he watched as the heavy slugs tore away pieces of their pursuers, sending the shattered bits floating off into the airless void.

As they passed the cone of compromised vessels Pieter spoke softly. "You can stop the roll now, Billy."

The Phoenix stopped spinning and continued straight away from the bounty hunters.

****

"God dammit," the Captain screamed from the bridge of his crippled ship. He shouted into his radio, "Did anyone even get off a shot?" Nothing returned but static. Then a single voice emerged from the white noise. "… limpet… hull. All… could manage. Lucky shot."

"What's the package?" he asked, referring to the explosive.

"Twenty meg nuke," was the reply.

"How long?"

"Under ten minutes and counting."

"Dammit!" He looked at his flickering bridge instruments. He was still blind, with several breaches venting air into space. His thumb opened a channel. "Anyone who can make way, run at best speed or get caught by the shock wave."

****

On board the Phoenix the celebration began the moment the ship stopped spinning and sailed past the damaged pursuers. Exiles, giddy with discovering their power, jumped, shouted, and hugged. Then the celebration was cut short by Bob's voice, "Pieter, we have a problem."

"What's wrong, Bob?"

"As we were passing their formation one of the ships managed to fire a device at us that is now attached to my hull."

Pieter held up his hand and every voice went suddenly mute. "What can you tell me, Bob?" Pieter asked.

"It is a magnetic mine, of some sort. I believe it has a thermonuclear warhead and it is counting down from under seven minutes."

CHAPTER ELEVEN

There was a long minute of silence. An aroma of ammonia permeated the bridge. Finally, Pieter cleared his throat and spoke. "What can we do to get this thing off, Bob?"

"I do not know, Pieter. It has firmly attached itself to my outer hull. First with magnets, but now several barbed projections have worked their way past my outer skin. I am searching my database for any possible solution."

"Can we cut it off?"

"There is not sufficient time, Pieter."

"Can you jam the mechanism?"

"I have already attempted that. It is heavily shielded. I do not believe even Michael could penetrate the workings."

Pieter glanced at Michael who was hunched

over in his chair, rubbing his temples. His skin was pale and dotted with beads of sweat "What about it, Mike?"

"No can do, Pieter. There's some kind of charge on the skin of that thing and it's got me locked out."

"Bob?"

"Six minutes and counting."

In the gunnery station Loki listened to the tension building on the bridge. He closed his eyes and concentrated, but not on the bomb. Mary's mind touched his. *Loki, it's too dangerous.*

It's the only way. Don't worry. I'll be back so quick you'll never know I was gone.

Pieter won't permit...

Pieter can't know, Mary. Where's Leeann?

Strapped into a chair in the rec-room.

Thank you, Mary.

There was a pop as Loki vanished from the gunnery station. A crack of thunder and a pressure wave rippled through the rec-room. Leeann looked up, startled and wide-eyed. Before she could speak he grasped her arm and they both vanished. Deep in the ship they reappeared in a room surrounded by thick bulkheads and heavily shielded walls. Leeann landed on her backside in the same sitting position she was in when they winked out.

"Loki, what are you doing?"

"There's no time, Lee." He helped her to her feet. "They somehow managed to attach a bomb to our hull and there's no way anyone else can get it off before it explodes."

"What do you mean 'anyone else', Loki? Don't you even think about what you're thinking."

"I have to, Lee. I can teleport it off the ship and get back before it goes off. If I don't, you and everyone else are dead. This room has the heaviest shielding on the ship."

"Why do I need to be shielded?"

"It's a nuclear bomb, Lee."

Leeann reached for Loki and hugged him tight. "Don't go. Please don't leave me. Someone will figure a way."

Loki glanced at his watch. "Bob, seal the door. Do not unlock it for fifteen minutes. Do you understand?"

"Yes, Loki. May I express my hopes for a successful outcome?"

"Thanks, Bob." Loki looked into Leeann's eyes and smiled. Suddenly she pulled him down to her and kissed him. For a long moment, he cupped her face and held her close. He took his charm from around his neck and draped it around hers. "I will be with you, always."

With another soft pop of displaced air, he was

gone. In the cold void, he grasped the rim of the bomb and willed himself and it onto the bridge of a bounty hunter ship.

Thunder rocked the bridge of the crippled mercenary ship. The men standing around him stared in disbelief. Loki let go of the heavy bomb that landed at his feet with a loud clang. He closed his eyes and willed himself to return to Leeann. He opened his eyes only to see the same men standing around him, but now they panicked as they recognized the device he brought with him.

No, no, no. This can't be happening.

The ship's captain watched him close and open his eyes and he laughed. "You can't get off the way you got on, can you freak? You're trapped here with us. Well, at least I have the satisfaction of taking one of you with me. You're gonna die with the rest of us."

****

Bob reported, "The device is gone, Pieter."

"How?"

"Perhaps you should ask Master Loki, sir."

"Is that where he went, Mary?" Pieter's voice was angry and frantic. "Did he just teleport that bomb off our hull?"

"Yes, Pieter." Mary flashed Pieter a worried look. "Loki believed that he was the only one who could get it away from us. But he hasn't returned, and I'm having trouble finding him."

"Where did he take it?"

"I think he took it to one of the other ships. But I can barely feel him. He's in trouble. I can hear him. He's trying so hard to reach me. He wants me to give a message to Leeann."

"20 seconds, Pieter," Bob announced. "Pieter, we're not far enough away to escape the shock wave."

Mary focused all her will on Loki. "She's listening, Loki."

Deep in the ship Leeann was rocked by the force of Mary's mental contact. But the voice in her head was not Mary's.

Lee, I am sorry. I promised I would come back, but now I can't. I wish we had more time but there are only a few seconds left. Be strong, Lee. I love you. I will see you again in Valhalla.

Loki, no! Leeann reached for him in her mind. *Don't leave me, Loki. I love you.* But her contact with him was gone. Leeann's cry of anguish echoed through the engine room. From one metallic surface to another it rang through the ship's hull into the cold vacuum.

Far behind them there was a bright flash as the bounty hunter ship vaporized. Seconds later the shock wave struck the other five ships, flinging their scattered parts into deep space.

"Bob, can we outrun that blast?" Pieter asked.

"No, Pieter. We cannot."

"How long do we have?"

"At our current rate of speed, approximately one minute and fifty-three seconds."

Looking back, he spotted Mary in her seat, her hands covered her eyes as tears ran down her cheeks and through her fingers. "Mary, what's wrong?"

"He's dead, Pieter. Loki's dead. He got trapped on that ship. He was still there when the bomb went off."

A long, stunned silence was slowly replaced by sniffs and sobs. Only Pieter remained silent, deep in thought. He released his seat restraints and walked to Mary's side. "Mary." At first, she appeared not to hear him. "Mary." This time he touched her arm and considered her face, wet with tears. "Mary, I need Leeann."

"She's locked in the engine room for at least another ten minutes. Loki put her there to keep her safe."

"Can you talk to her?"

"Pieter, she…"

"I know, Mary. So are we all. But if I can't get Leeann to project the strongest bubble of her life, we're all in a lot of trouble. Do you understand?"

Mary wiped the tears from her eyes and then closed them. On the floor of the engine room Leeann could hear Mary plead with her.

Leeann.

Leave me alone, Mary. In the private world of her mind Leeann was a hot sea of pain, grief, and anger. She lay on the deck and pounded her fist into the metal. She screamed and tore at her clothes. *How could he do this to me? He's gone and I'm alone again. It's unfair!*

I'm sorry, Leeann. Mary's quiet whisper touched the troubled waters and Leeann's inner storm became still. *I'm so sorry for Loki, but Pieter says if you don't put a very strong bubble around this ship in less than a minute everything Loki did will be meaningless.*

"What do you mean?"

The explosion sent out a shock wave and it's coming for us now. Pieter thinks if you can put a powerful force field around us, we might have a chance to survive the shock wave.

I don't think I can, Mary.

Do it for him, Leeann. Do it for Loki, so his sacrifice won't be for nothing.

You don't understand, Mary. I loved him. I loved him so much and now he's gone. I don't want to live without him. Lee sat up and drew her knees to her chest, wrapping her arms around them and rocking against her pain.

I know, Lee. I know how you feel. If it were me; if it were Billy, I would be the same way. And I know he loved you too. That's why he put you where you are. But we all need you now.

Outside the ship, a shimmer of energy wrapped itself around the Phoenix. It coalesced from a thin mist, to a foggy gray, to a dark, steel-like color. Huddled on the floor, Leeann focused her power as never before. The shock wave struck her bubble, which rippled, shook, and distorted in the face of the wave. She pressed her hands to her ears and screamed into the darkness of her cell. Outside the wave parted and slipped around the ship, fading into the endless vacuum.

Lee, Mary's spectral voice caressed her mind. *It's over now, Lee. You saved us all.*

Pieter stood and looked at his young crew. They were shaken and pale. Billy gripped the arms of his chair and wept. Tears tumbled down cheeks all around him until his own dripped to his tunic. He wiped his face on his sleeve and made his way to the door. One by one they all followed him into the heart of the ship.

Pieter waited until he heard the lock click and pushed against the heavy metal door to the engine room. He followed the sound of sobbing to where Leeann lay. Her face was hidden by her hands and her body curled in on itself. Blood covered her upper lip and parts of her face where her hands spread the flow from a nosebleed.

Pieter knelt and scooped Leeann into his arms. He hugged her to him and whispered into her ear, then carried her to her room and set her on her bed. Before he released her, he knelt and kissed her cheek. For a moment Lee released her grip on Loki's charm to return his embrace.

Clair Jones waited with a first aid kit and a wet wash cloth. As soon as Pieter stood, she hurried to Leeann's side and wiped her face clean. Then she cleaned Leeann's bloody hands and examined her briefly.

"I think she's fine. Just a bleed from the strain."

Sue put her hand on Leeann's brow. "She's right. But she's used a monstrous amount of energy. I can stop the bleeding and repair the damage, but what she needs is rest."

As Sue moved aside, Mary took her place, speaking quietly in Leeann's mind. **We're here** for you Lee; we all share your grief, sister. We all feel his loss.

One by one the others stepped close to her bed and said goodnight, leaving Mary and Leeann in peace.

Leeann rolled into a fetal ball on her side. "My whole life was filled with being alone. My mother died giving birth to me. My own father could hardly bring himself to touch me. But I wasn't a freak with Loki. We were the same. We touched, we held…. we kissed. He was so sweet and gentle, Mary. But in the end, he was the brave warrior he was raised to be."

Mary climbed into the bunk behind Leeann and held her close. "He had no fear, only disappointment that he could not come back to you. His last thoughts were of you, Lee." Absently, Mary's fingers touched the curved upper arch of Leeann's ear.

"What do I do now, Mary?"

Mary's fingers were warm and calming. Mary pulled her closer and cuddled like a mother with a frightened child. Leeann wondered where Mary had learned to use her instincts so well. She drifted slowly towards sleep, then Mary whispered.

"You live for him, for both of you."

Three days passed while Sue and Mary took turns caring for Leeann. Even Billy sat with her, reading to her and trying to cheer her up. On the fourth day Leeann joined everyone in the dining hall for lunch. Joan, Mike, and finally Pieter each shared an embrace before being shooed away by Mary.

"I'm okay, Mary. You don't have to keep mothering me."

"And who do you think you're talking to, young lady? You forget I know more about what's going on in there than you do yourself." Mary playfully rapped on Leeann's forehead with her finger.

Mike delivered a tray to their table with bowls of steaming beef and noodles. "Bob calls it stroganoff, but it looks like stew to me. The noodles were actually pretty easy to make."

Leeann looked up into his grinning face. "You made this?"

His eyes grew wide and he placed a hand to his chest as if stricken. "Don't look so shocked."

Mike took the seat opposite Mary and waited for a response from Leeann. She lifted a spoon to her lips and inhaled the steam before sipping cautiously. The tip of her tongue licked her lips then let the spoon pass. A stray noodle was slurped into her mouth and she smiled.

Leeann called out. "Sue, I think you should keep this one."

It was the first laughter to be heard in days.

214

CHAPTER TWELVE

Pieter woke with a jump when a hand settled on his shoulder. He pushed himself up straight and passed a hand across his face. He looked up to find Clair Jones smiling down at him.

She spoke softly, "Pieter, go to your room. Get some sleep."

"I'm fine, Miss Jones," he replied, clearing his throat and sitting upright in the command chair.

"Are you, really? You're not sleeping well. You're jumpy. You even snapped at Joan when she pointed it out to you. That's not 'fine' Pieter. Not by any sense of the word." She stared into the man-child's dark eyes. They looked too old for his face. "It's not just you either. They're all waiting for something and they don't know what they're waiting for."

"What do you mean?"

"They haven't really had a chance to mourn, Pieter. It wasn't just Leeann who lost Loki. You lost him. You all lost him. There aren't many of you to begin with, and to lose someone like that was traumatic. Leeann had a chance to cry but she's still holding so much inside. Mary's in an awful state. The poor little dear came to my room last night. She's having awful nightmares and is near to hysteria. She was in contact with Loki when…. well, you know. It's still echoing in her mind, that last second of his life, of his link with Leeann. She absorbed all of that, Pieter. I did what I could to comfort her, but it's not enough."

"What can I do?"

"For starters, you can stop calling me *Mizz* Jones. Mary calls me Aunt Clair. I think you should too. That was a very sweet thing you all did for me. You took me in like an old stray cat and made me family. But I'm the only real adult on this ship. You're all trying so hard to be older than you really are. You're a wonderful boy, Pieter, but still a boy none-the-less."

"All right, Aunt Clair. What can I do?"

"Nothing alone, Pieter, this has to be all of you together. You need to grieve. And then you need closure. You need to honor Loki for the hero he is and then let him go."

****

"Is this what he would have wanted, Lee?" Pieter asked as he placed Loki's sword, ax, and bow into the metal tube.

"He told me about his people and what they believed. The last thing he said to me was that he would see me again in Valhalla. That's their version of heaven. It's a Viking belief, so I have to think this is the right thing to do."

Dinner was more raucous than usual. Everyone told stories about Loki. Things he did with them, for them, to them. How he loved to play pranks, how unnerving it was when he appeared out of thin air and what a good friend he was to everyone. There was no alcohol to consume, but they managed to be rowdy without it. There were tears and songs and hugs all around. Billy burst out with a song in Loki's native tongue that silenced the entire gathering. Finally, with the Phoenix in a parking orbit around a white dwarf star, they gathered around the tube with Loki's personal effects. Each of them put a hand-written note and some personal item for their friend into the tube.

Billy was last and with his note he placed a piece from his chess board, a white knight. He spoke in Loki's native tongue, "Farvel, min bror.

Indtil vi mødes igen." He looked up at Pieter with tears on his cheeks. "Well, he was, wasn't he?"

"You and Loki were the most unlikely pair. But you let him be himself and became his best friend. No, really, in your own way, you became his brother. We should all learn from that. We're not just a bunch of random people thrown together on this ship. We are all brothers and sisters in a family of our own. We can never forget that."

Pieter nodded and the tube was sealed. He cleared his throat and took his long string of beads out from under his tunic. He grasped the crucifix in his hand and spoke. "Loki was the last to join us, but that hardly mattered. He was a good friend. He was our hero. I can't pretend to understand everything he believed. Lee knew him best. I can only hope that the Valkyrie have come to take him home."

The tube was loaded into the rail gun, waiting to be shot into the white-hot ball of fire. Leeann clung to Pieter's arm and loosed a torrent into his shoulder. Mary hugged her friend. Leeann's finger trembled as it pressed the firing button. There was a whoosh as the magnetic coil accelerated the tube to high speed, sending it into the Chroma-sphere of the star.

Before the gathering dissolved, Pieter raised his hands. "I think we have two choices in front of us.

We can't just drift through space forever. Despite doing what we could to change the ship, we must assume Mills knows what we look like now. Eventually we'll have to land somewhere. I think we either have to return to one of our home worlds and ask for asylum." There was a rumble of disagreement and a shaking of heads at the suggestion. "Or we find a new world to call home. I've already asked Bob to start looking. We can scan any systems we pass for a suitable planet that could be settled without much in the way of terraforming. Don't vote on it now. Let's give Bob a chance and see what he can come up with."

Mary, Sue, and Leeann gathered for a group hug before going their separate ways. Billy and Mike stared out the gunner's port into deep space with the glow of the white star fading behind them.

"A world of our own, Pieter?" Joan slipped her hand into his. "We're not equipped to settle a frontier world. There are so many basic things we would need, even if we can find an Prime clone somewhere Golden Door hasn't looked."

"When Europeans arrived in North America they were not really equipped for what they found. But somehow they found a way."

"True, after most of the first wave died of disease and starvation and their first winter."

"If we can find a place to live we'll find a way

to get what we need. Mills and his goons can't be everywhere."

"No, but they can be anywhere we might try to land and look for supplies. I think we've worn out our welcome on Dragon."

Pieter stopped walking and pulled Joan aside. His fingers cupped her chin and he stared into her dark eyes. "I am trying my best to give them hope and a purpose. We need a reason to hope."

"But I agree with you, Pieter. We need a place to call home; somewhere to give this new species a chance to take hold. We just have to be very fussy about what kind of place that is."

****

Michael sat at his duty station finishing off a crusty sandwich and a glass of cold tea. "I swear this is the most boring thing I have ever done in my life."

"I can't argue with you," Sue answered with a yawn.

"Six months of searching and nothing."

"Patience," Bob's AI presence emanated through the speaker above them. "What you call Goldilocks planets are few and far between. We knew that when we decided to start looking."

"Where are we?"

"Joan says we're officially 'way out in the

boondocks'."

"And that would be…"

"At least two years travel time back to any colonized planet at best speed."

"How much further can we go?"

"Pieter and Joan have been talking about a point of no return. We will either find a place to land or we have to turn around if we wish to make it back."

Mike wiped a bit of cheese from his lips and returned his sandwich to his plate. "I've been reading an old book about traveling through space and having adventures and such. Only it's hysterically funny. And in this book, there are these funny sayings that actually make sense once you stop laughing." He paused and glanced at Susan to make sure she was still listening. "Anyway, one of them is, 'In an infinite universe anything is possible.'"

****

The distance between the stars grew as The Phoenix continued to follow a tapering spiral arm on the outer edge of the galaxy. The ship rode the temporal wave from system to system. The Doppler Effect made even the red dwarf stars ahead of them glow with a faint blue light.

Bob spoke to the crew on watch, "I do not wish

to cause a stir, but the data is in from the last system we scanned a few days ago."

Sue keyed into the conversation. "You have something to tell us, Bob?"

"I may have, Susan. I was examining the data from our long-range scans of a planet I located in that system. I believe it may be worthy of closer examination."

"Should we wake Pieter?" Mike asked.

"He appears to be sleeping quite soundly, Michael. You and Susan have the watch. If both of you tell me to do so we can alter our course and make way for that system. I will advise Pieter of our change in course when he awakens."

"Pieter would want to be in on that decision," Mike argued.

"Are you saying it looks good, Bob?"

"I need more data. We can only get that by making a much closer pass to the planet in question. But yes, Susan, I am saying it looks promising."

"I say we make the course change now and tell Pieter when he comes on watch." Sue stood her ground.

"There is an old saying, Master Michael. It is easier to ask for forgiveness then it is to ask for permission."

"Okay, I agree." He ran his fingers through his sandy hair and took a deep breath. "But it better be worth the chewing out I'm gonna get."

Sue smiled at him and ruffled his locks with her hand. "You know Pieter doesn't chew out. Besides, if this planet has potential you'll get a great big at-a-boy."

****

Mary shared some breakfast with Leeann while watching the approaching planet. She rested the plate of sliced fruit, cheese, and toast on the console between their chairs.

"I miss him so much," Leeann whispered. "I really thought I had a chance to be with someone for the rest of my life, and now I'm alone again."

Mary turned to look into Lee's eyes on the verge of tears. "How can you say you're alone? You're surrounded by people who care for you, who love you."

"It's just not the same, Mary. I was just beginning to believe that Loki was someone I could depend on to... I don't know... just be there. He was solid and strong and sweet at the same time. It was the first time in my life I really felt close to someone."

"What about your family?"

"I never knew my mother. She died of eclampsia shortly after I was born. My father couldn't take care of me and work at the same time, so I got passed around among family and friends for years. It wasn't just the feeling of obligation I got from them, it was the pity. Poor girl lost her mother so we better be nice to her. I came to hate that most."

Mary's hand found Lee's and held it tight.

"Loki wanted me for me. Not out of pity or obligation, but because he wanted me. Does that make sense?"

"It does. I know he doesn't look it, but inside Billy is the same way. In his own way, he's just like Loki. I think that was what made them such good friends. It was like they had each found a long-lost brother."

Lee smiled and sniffed back a tear. "They were brothers, in a way."

"Does that make us sisters-in-law?"

****

"The atmospheric drone we dropped is reading O-2 levels four percent above Prime normal. Nitrogen, C-O-2 and trace gasses also very close to normal. Gravity is point nine-five PSG, diurnal rotation is twenty-six hours, solar orbit is approximately 400 days and its axial tilt is 22 degrees, giving it seasons very like Prime."

"What about indigenous life forms, Bob?"

"There appears to be a diverse and complex

carbon-based ecosystem in place, Pieter, especially green plants respiring oxygen. There are a numbers of herd animals taking advantage of the abundance of food. I must assume further examinations will reveal predators as well."

"That's not the big question, Bob, and you know it. What about intelligent native species?"

"There are no indications of civilization at any level of development on any of my scans so far, Pieter. There are only normal background levels of radiation; also, no indication of excessive soot or hydrocarbon emissions. This might be an ideal planet."

"So, we have an ideal planet that's not on the charts. Only we don't have the basic supplies to build a settlement even if we had a way to get down there."

"If I may conjecture, Sir, after what I have recorded and reviewed in our recent encounter with the mercenary ships, I believe that between you and Master William the two of you could set this ship down anywhere you please and not singe a blade of grass."

Pieter rubbed the lines that were taking up residence on his brow. "That still leaves us with the problem of supplies."

"I shall compile a suggested list of necessary items based upon records of previous settlements.

Perhaps, with a bit of luck, a means to the end may present itself."

****

"We've recovered several data modules from the debris field; my best people tell me what that ship did is physically impossible."

Dr. Mills watched intently as a blip on the screen accelerated towards him. A flash in space and the recording ended. "What the hell was that?"

"Best anyone can say is an EMP was fired into the middle of the formation. Keep watching."

The screen filled with electronic snow then cleared. A spinning shape filled the view and then the camera floated free. "So?"

The officer reached around Mills and tapped a few keys. "Watch it again in super slow motion so you can get the full effect." This time the spinning blur became a ship rotating around its long axis. Every second or so bright flashes revealed the waist guns firing, sending shells in all directions. "Rather clever, even if I do say so. Outnumbered and outgunned, they dropped out of light speed, turned 180 degrees, and jumped back to light speed almost instantaneously. Something, I would like to point out, none of our ships, even our most advanced ships, can do. Then they ran through those mercenary ships after disabling their electronics.

And they were spinning at high speed as they flew through the formation firing their waist guns automatically. Finally, it appears someone detonated a nuke and the shock-wave took care of everyone. Ordinarily I would say these youngsters were killed along with everyone else. But they already broke several laws of physics just to launch their attack. That spin maneuver alone should have ripped their bodies apart just from the G-forces. But I cannot say, with any degree of certainty, that is what happened." He switched the POV to another angle from a different ship. At its closest point, he froze the image. He pointed at the renegade ship on the screen. "What I can tell you is that no piece of debris from that ship has been found."

Mills leaned back in his chair, pressed his fingers together and contemplated the news. "So, they could still be out there?"

"Yes, sir, I would say the likelihood of that is very high."

Mills' eyes narrowed and the creases on his brow deepened. "That will be all, General."

****

The good ship Phoenix settled into a geostationary orbit above the candidate planet. The viewing screen was filled with a mosaic of images of vast grasslands below them. Slow, lumbering beasts fanned out and cropped the deep green vegetation. A close-up shot revealed creatures that appeared to be covered with wooly coats and short curled horns close to their heads. A few smaller animals passed in the field of view, moving among the larger grazers on long agile legs.

"They're so beautiful," Sue's voice was quiet but easily heard in the hushed cabin.

"Mike," Pieter called from his command chair.

"Aye, Captain!"

"Cut the engines."

"Aye, sir."

"Billy, let's take her down nice and slow."

Billy smiled and closed his eyes. He could feel the weight of the ship drop. He focused his mind on the plains below them and pulled the Phoenix down into the thin upper atmosphere. Feathery trails of ice crystals formed on the windows as the blackness gave way to a bluish glow. A high-altitude jet stream howled past the ship in the thin upper atmosphere. Billy remained focused on the landing area, but most eyes were fixated on the water rich clouds that rose past the view screens. Once below the clouds the verdant panorama spread out before them. A few of the big grazing animals moved away from the spreading shadow of the ship.

Finally, Pieter gave the order, "Gear down, Mike."

A hum could be heard as the landing gear reached for the grassy hill beneath them. The actual touchdown was so well controlled there wasn't even a thump.

The crew gathered at the main hatch and waited for the gangway to reach the ground. Pieter called out, "How's the air out there, Bob?"

"The atmosphere is suitable for human life, Pieter. The temperature is a pleasant 25.5 degrees with a breeze out of the west. Shall I open the hatch, Captain?"

"Open the hatch, Bob."

The restraints withdrew into the hull and the hatch retracted into the recess. A warm, sweet wind pushed its way through the door and into the corridor. As one they took a deep breath of fresh, unfiltered, un-recycled air; the first they had in many months. It was untainted by anything man-made.

Billy pushed his way past Pieter and Joan at the top of the landing. "Well, are we gonna stand here all day, or are we gonna go exploring?"

"Slow down, Billy," Pieter said reaching for Billy's shoulder. "The only thing we know about this world so far is that the air is nice."

Clair Jones spoke up from the rear of the mob. "Pieter's right. Everyone must be very cautious. Even something that looks cute and cuddly can be dangerous. And these animals have never been exposed to human beings. They won't show fear but they may be curious. We don't even know what is safe to touch; and what about bugs? I recommend long sleeves and gloves with long pants tucked into safety boots."

There was a loud, collective groan but then Pieter answered. "Hey, we don't back-talk Aunt Clair. Besides, she's right. So, everyone back inside until we're all dressed for a hike in this unknown paradise."

Thirty minutes later everyone was gathered at the top of the landing. Billy sat on the deck helping Mary lace up her boots. He wrapped the long trailing laces around her pants, effectively sealing them into her boots. As he stood Pieter was finishing his instructions.

"…and no touching anything, no matter how cute it looks. Remember, we're just looking around the property to see how we like it. Stay with your buddy at all times and let's all be careful, okay."

Joan gave his hand a squeeze. "They got it, Pieter. Relax; we're all hooked up on com-link, and Mother Mary watches over all."

By twos they fanned out into the deep grass in all directions--except for Leeann, who held Mary's hand as she walked with her and Billy.

CHAPTER THIRTEEN

With the nearest mountains many miles away, sunset waited until the huge yellow star drifted towards the far western horizon. Just as the orb touched the rim of the alien world, the air was filled with the calls of millions of small, winged animals. Their bodies and wings were covered with thin, translucent scales that overlapped to give them flight. Flocks of them climbed above the tree line and skimmed the tops of the grasses, catching tiny insects that remained hidden until sunset. Their iridescent scales revealed a pallet of bright colors in the setting sun. A buzz of tiny wings filled the air and brief flashes of bioluminescent light mimicked the twinkling of the distant stars.

In their feeding frenzy, several of the small birds collided with some of the crew making their way back to the ship.

Billy appeared with one of the small fliers cupped in his hands. "I didn't mean to hurt it. We just sorta ran into one another."

Pieter struck his best stern pose. "I told you not to touch anything."

"Hey, he hit me first. I couldn't leave 'em in the grass to get stepped on, could I?"

They gathered around the damaged animal for a closer look. Several of the body scales were broken, as was a single, elongated front-right wing scale. Sue gasped at the jewel-like appearance. "Four wings? Look how fast and agile they are in the air. They're amazing." As her finger stroked the warm body, the small head turned toward her and it opened its sharp, wedge-shaped beak. A trill and a chirp were all the thanks the creature could manage before launching itself into the air again. In his hand, Billy cupped the bright shard of the broken scale.

"Wow, Sue, did you do that or was that him?"

Sue's mouth hung open for a moment while she watched the creature return to its flock. "I have no idea. I just wanted to touch it. Did you see those wings? They remind me a little of birds, but they reminded me of something else too."

Mike looked up from his handheld and showed the whole group a picture. "A dragonfly maybe."

Clair Jones leaned in to get a good look. "Different planet, different answers to the questions put to the animals that evolve to fill different niches. Just like all of you, my children."

"Well, there are our first predators, of sorts. Not very dangerous."

There was a round of chuckles to Pieter's observation.

He added, "There are probably seed and nectar feeding variations of this same design."

Billy chimed in, "And probably a big one with long talons and a nasty, hooked beak."

"It would have to be the size of a shuttle to carry off one of those things." Mike pointed at the large grazing animals.

Pieter noticed the fading light and ordered everyone back inside the ship. Excited chatter filled the mess as dinner was consumed with little notice of what was served.

"Some of the long grass is tough and has a sharp edge to it." Mike commented. "I ran my hand through some and it tore up my glove pretty good. I wouldn't want to run through it without some protective gear. Otherwise, I think this place it great."

Joan was next, "I like it. If this is a sample of what we can expect on this rock, I say we claim this planet now."

"Whoa, slow down," Pieter was quick to jump in. "We need a lot more information about this place before we start putting down roots. We need a full geological survey from space. How stable is this ball of mud? Where would be the best place to build a settlement? And is there anything out there in the dark that's likely to develop a taste for us?"

From the back of the room a high, boyish voice sang, "Every party's got a pooper, that's why we invited you..."

Billy's sharp wit drew a loud round of laughter. Even Pieter chuckled. Clair Jones rose to address the group. "Very funny, William, but you all know Pieter is right. His cautious restraint is admirable."

"Pieter wants to be Admiral now? What happened to Captain?" There was another burst of laughter, but a scathing look from Clair pushed Billy into his seat.

Pieter raised his hand for quiet. "Honestly, I'm as excited as all of you about this place. It is beautiful. But Bob showed me the preliminary list of things we'll need to settle here. It will take some heavy lifting to fill this list, even in a ship this big. In the meantime, we'll be dodging both Mills, who wants our skins, and Golden Door, who will want our planet the second they get wind of it. So, we're going to park a couple of observatory satellites in orbit and head for my home world."

Mike took the courteous route and raised his hand. "Why your home world, not mine or anyone else's?"

"Because the Steppes was the most recently settled world among the eight. It still has most of the equipment we're looking for either in storage or in use."

Mike still held the floor. "And when we get there how are we going to get all this stuff?"

"Because when we get there I'm going to say, pozhaluysta."

"Which means?"

"Please."

****

In the comfort of his plush office Dr. Mills was deep in conversation on his secure line to Golden Door CEO, Charles Radcliffe. "Yeah, Charlie, shame about your bounty hunters and all those ships... What the hell, at least you didn't have to make good on the bounty... Yeah, about that. We swept the entire debris field looking for scraps. Picked up a lot of yours, Chuck, none of theirs..." Mills sat in his overstuffed chair and flicked a trail of cigar ash onto the carpet. "How the hell am I supposed to know? All I do know is they did some major damage getting off Dragon, and then this bunch of snot-nosed brats went through the best you had like a hot round going through drywall without so much as a paper cut…I want them, Charles. Either you get them for me, or so help me you won't have a pot to piss in, as my great-grandfather used to say… Nice chatting with you, Charlie."

****

GJ1214b filled the view screen. The super-heavy planet pulled at the ship as much as his first look at home pulled at Pieter's heart. Billy kept a close eye on Mary as they approached The Steppes, but Pieter was already flattening the gravity well on and around the ship. They repeated their earlier landing on a snow swept plain outside Pieter's home city. Leeann's shimmering bubble surrounded the ship, deflecting any radar that might betray them. Billy's control was even better than his first attempt, letting the wheels kiss the ground with a noiseless touch. Pieter then turned his attention to finding and approaching his parents.

Pieter's hand settled for a moment on Billy's shoulder. "Sorry to make you stay behind, but we both know my home world will be very hard on Mary."

"I'll look after her, Pieter. I always do."

Mary floated in midair above her G-Chair, unfettered by the crushing weight imposed on her by the dense core of The Steppes. "We'll be fine,

Pieter. Billy and I have been together since the beginning."

Pieter and Joan took the gangway down to the snowy surface. Joan's feet drug through the snow from the added weight. Even Pieter took some adjusting to the pull on him. His eyes closed and the gravity around them relented to a more civilized degree.

"Thank you, Pieter." Joan took a deep breath. "How did you ever get around here?"

"When you're born here, you don't really notice. It's just the way it is."

"I suppose that accounts for your particular adaptation. What did Aunt Clair call it? Your answer to the questions the environment asked of you."

"I suppose it is. And I suppose the harder the question, the more extreme the answer."

Squat trees opened onto a rail line bordering the city. Street lamps illuminated the area where locals came to shop and eat at restaurants serving indigenous food. Pieter followed the familiar roads he left behind nearly five years ago. His telltale gene-marked ears were concealed under a hat suited for the local weather. To the same end, Joan wore a knit cap.

Lorries and other ground transports cruised by them as they walked toward a block of residential buildings. In the far distance, near the center of the city, floodlights illuminated the townsfolks' great work. Tall spires rose into the night. Brightly painted onion shaped domes topped most. One was still partially concealed by cranes and scaffolds. At the top of each finished spire was a gilded three-bar crucifix.

Pieter pointed at the church that dominated the low skyline. "St. Basil's. The people here have been donating their labor to build it since the settlement was founded."

"It's beautiful," Joan whispered. Then she noticed Pieter's fingers wrapped around an object hanging around his neck. He brought it to his lips then crossed himself.

"I was baptized in that church, though I was too young to remember."

Neat rows of tidy, cookie-cutter houses lined both sides of the street. At last Pieter stopped in front of one such house. The curtains were open in several rooms which revealed the interior and a few shadowy figures inside.

"Batya," Pieter whispered as a grown man stood and looked in their direction.

"What?" Joan asked.

"Father."

"That man is your father?"

"Yes. He did not want to let the men take me.

He fought them, but they had guns, and he had to protect the rest of the family."

"You have brothers and sisters?"

"A younger brother, Anton. And my mother was pregnant when they took me."

Soon two more silhouettes joined the man at the window. The front door flew open, and a younger version of Pieter ran toward them. Strong, stocky, and dark, Anton slammed into his brother and threw them both to the snow.

"Pieter, Pieter, my God, it is you." He cried out in his native Russian.

It was the first time in weeks she saw Pieter smile and heard him laugh. For an instant, he was a nineteen-year-old boy again. The brothers laughed and rolled on the ground while Joan waited. From the door, a deep male voice called to them.

"Anton, stop being a fool. Bring your brother and his friend inside. The streets are filled with eyes."

Laughing and out of breath, they reached their feet. Pieter took Joan's hand and led her toward the open door. Pieter's father stood like a gate guard, watching for anyone who may have taken notice. Once inside the man gathered his son into his arms and crushed him against his thick chest.

"My God, Pieter it IS you. You're alive!" Seldom-seen tears rolled down his cheeks. A torrent of kisses showered Pieter's face. From a back room, a mature woman, with a child in her arms, hurried into the room. Her arms were added to those already clutching her son.

"Matya," Pieter sobbed into her shoulder. Her eyes were dark and brooding, but filled with tears for her son. At last she turned the child in her arms to face Pieter.

"Pieter, this is your sister, Nika," She said softly.

Pieter grinned, and lifted the girl up to receive a kiss on each cheek. His eyes became wide when her hair fell back and ears, like his own, were revealed. Nika smiled.

"What…" Pieter began to ask.

"We don't know. She hasn't done anything yet," his mother answered.

Pieter's father draped an arm across his wife's shoulder. "And there are others, Pieter. This planet is cursed." His voice had a hard, bitter edge.

"We're not a disease, Batya. We're not a curse."

"Then what are you?"

Pieter stepped closer to his father. "We're an answer."

"An answer, to what?"

"The Steppes has given us new challenges as a species. It's like the planet asking us if we can survive. And to survive we must adapt. It's not just this place, Batya; there are answers coming from all the new worlds."

His mother's eyes settled on Joan's Asian features. "How do you know this girl?"

Pieter removed his hat and nodded for Joan to do the same. Taking it as a sign, Joan drew a finger through her hair and turned her head so that her ear was easy to see.

"What can you do…?" Risa's halting, broken English stopped abruptly as Joan shifted first to a perfect copy of Pieter, then her husband, and finally herself before returning to her natural shape.

"My goodness," she gasped.

"I have come back because we need your help."

"What help can you possibly need from us? You who can do so many things that we cannot."

"We have a place, Batya, a place for Nika and the others. A place where they can be safe from Dr. Mills and those who are spreading fear and lies about us. But we need tools and supplies to break ground, build homes, and make a place to live. You still have most of the things we need in warehouses. Golden Door left them here because it would cost too much to get them away from this world's heavy gravity. But, as you know, I have some ability with that."

"You would take Nika?" he asked.

"I would take you all, Papa. Anton, Mama, and every other family with children like us. I would take you to a safe place on a beautiful new world. It means freedom, Papa. Isn't that what your great-grandfather came here to find?"

CHAPTER FOURTEEN

Hot cups of a steaming beverage were passed around the modest kitchen table. The formal tea cups in their silver holders made a pleasant clinking sound. The fire was freshly stoked and fed, taking the chill off the room. Just as she was about to sip, Joan observed the entire family taking a moment to say thanks for their son's return. The warm, sweet liquid was welcome in her chilled insides.

"It's delicious, Pieter." Joan's whisper was overheard.

"It's called sbiten," his mother answered, smiling. "A very old traditional winter drink. It's not as common these days because some of the ingredients are harder to come by. But it's a special day when the son you were told was dead, returns."

"May I ask what's in it?"

"Honey, cloves, cinnamon, blackberries and a few other things. Blackberries are one of the success stories we can tell here. They've adapted very well. We have bees too. They had a rough time of it at first, but have adapted to our winters, and in the warm seasons they find the berries and the other fruit we have cultivated."

"There were no bees on my home world. No honey either. But there was a plant that made a very sweet sap that we used like sugar."

"Sbiten was always one of Pieter's favorite treats."

"You'll have to show me how you make it." Joan couldn't restrain a blush.

A rare smile formed on the face of Pieter's mother. Under the drone of male voices, she whispered, "You and my Pieter, you are couple?"

"I think so, yes," Joan grinned. "You would be so proud of him. He's our leader. Everyone on the ship looks up to your son and would follow him through anything."

"You must call me Risia." She touched her chest. "Pieter was always a strong boy." She knocks on her head with her knuckles. "Like his father, that one. It nearly killed Boris to have his oldest son taken away. Then some men came one day and said there had been an accident and the whole ship was lost. It is not an easy thing to hear your husband cry, especially a man like that. I am a woman and I may shed tears in the open with the other women. But Boris…"

"Pieter doesn't cry easily either," Joan added, remembering the fallout after the incident at Dragon.

Risia shrugged. "Men."

Pieter's father leaned close to his oldest son. "Your plan is ambitious, Pieter. You need so many things to make a home on a new world. Even if you think you have everything you need, there are always things you can't foresee. It is not spoken of much, especially to the younger settlers, but there were many lost in those early winters. When the second wave arrived, there was talk of abandoning The Steppes and going back to Prime."

"I remember, Papa. The Steppes is a hard planet, Grandpa used to say."

"It's more than just the gravity, Pieter. This planet has a very dense iron core. The electromagnetic field around this word is exceptionally powerful. You have seen the aurora in every month of the year. It can be seen from anywhere."

"The beautiful lights of The Steppes."

"The first children like you began to appear in the third generation." Pieter's face stopped as if turned to stone. He turned to look at his mother.

"You were not the first to be born this way, Pieter," Risia added. "Only the first to survive. Scientist from Prime believed the early mutations were too radical for the children to survive. It was their belief that such mutations would remain self-culling. But then you were born and you were strong and, except for your remarkable ears, quite normal. We hid your differences because we were afraid they would want to understand how you were able to survive, not because we were afraid of what you could do."

Pieter's mouth sagged open, but his eyes were wide with apprehension. "You said I was the first."

Boris draped an arm across his son's shoulder. "You were the first, sinulya, the first to survive. Now there are a few more. Nika is the first time a second such child has been born to the same family. What surprises me more than anything is that tsarist pig, Mills, hasn't invaded us yet."

"But he will, Papa. He'll round you all up and put this whole planet to the torch if it serves his thirst for power."

Joan asked, "How many children like us are there?"

"Not many, perhaps six or seven. There may be more in hiding. It's still not that common," Risia replied.

"We would have room for that many and their families on the Phoenix," Joan pleaded. "If we can find the equipment we need and take off in a few days, there's a chance Mills and his agents won't even know we've come and gone."

Boris stood and pointed out the front window. "You know the way, Pieter. The warehouse district is a few kilometers in that direction. Golden Door calculated the cost of shifting the surplus equipment off this planet was more than the costs to replace it. So they locked it up and gave the keys to Sergey Andropov. Sergey still gets the odd job to run a bulldozer or get out the forklift to help someone move. Mostly he lives off the stipend he gets from Golden Door to keep an eye on their surplus stores."

Pieter perked up at the mention of the forklift. "Is that the same..."

"Yes, the same one Pavel nearly ran you down with."

Pieter turned to Joan. "Pavel is Mr. Andropov's oldest son. He was my best friend. We were playing at the warehouse. Pavel wasn't supposed to be driving the forklift. He didn't see me until the machine knocked me down. I thought I was dead. I should have been dead. But the lift just floated over me; several tons of iron and steel just hanging in midair. That was the first time... Anyway, Pavel started screaming that he had killed me and his father came and saw the lift floating. He knew. Soon the whole town knew. Four years later, ship comes to take me away."

His father's voice trembled, "Forgive me, Pieter. I should have fought harder for you, hidden you somewhere, anything but give you up." Boris threw his arms around his son and crushed him to his chest while tears ran down his face.

"What else could you have done, Papa? They smashed their way into our home with guns. And what if they had not gotten me, they would have cut Nika from Mama's womb. They would have taken you all."

Joan put a sympathetic hand on the guilt-stricken man's shoulder. "If they had not taken Pieter, none of us would be here today. I would not be here today. The ship would not be here to take you all to safety."

"We need these supplies, Papa. Can you help us get them?"

"Andropov has the keys. We have not spoken since he reported you to Mills."

"Let me speak to Pavel. He will help us."

"Pavel is missing."

"Papa, we all have a chip to keep track of us by satellite. No one can just go missing."

"Nevertheless, Pavel has not been seen or heard from in several weeks. Nor have his remains been found."

"That's not possible."

"You are not possible, my son. And yet here you are."

Pieter's mother stood and gathered the empty cups and their silver holders and put them on the counter near the sink. "Pavel is only the latest to go missing," she added. "Three other young people have disappeared in the last few months. Same as Pavel, no remains, no return from their chips."

"Is that why there are so few people on the streets, Papa?" Pieter asked and was answered with a sullen nod. Across the room Pieter and Joan locked eyes. "Are you thinking what I'm thinking?"

"If you're thinking no one can hide from Mary, yes."

"Who is this Mary?" Risia asked.

"There were eight of us, Mama, one from each of the settled worlds. Mary was already on board the ship when they came for me. She is a girl, younger than Joan, with remarkable telepathic abilities. Every one of us is different. Sue can heal anything that is alive. Billy is telekinetic. Mike can do things with electricity; Leeann can project an energy bubble around herself or the entire ship and Loki..." Pieter choked at the name.

Joan took up the narrative, "Loki could teleport things from place to place. But there was a fight with a fleet of mercenary ships. Loki was killed saving the ship and all of us. So we are seven, for now."

"And you say this Mary can find people?"

"Even people, like me, who have had their chips neutralized," Pieter answered. "She can find anyone by locating their thoughts."

"Even Billy," Joan giggled.

Pieter smiled, "Billy doesn't so much think as he just... does."

Quick laughter drifted through the room then Pieter prepared to leave. "If you can give me a list of the missing people I'll do what I can. In the meantime, we need to get the equipment on the list and get ready to leave before we draw too much attention."

"Where is your ship?"

Pieter paused then looked his father in the eye. "Don't take this the wrong way, Papa, but if you don't know and you say you don't know you're still telling the truth. I would rather you didn't have to lie if someone asks you."

Pieter put his arms around his father and embraced him. He felt his father's arms around him and remembered how those same arms felt long ago. It felt different, somehow. The house was smaller than he remembered. His parents were less imposing and his brother was no longer a boy. Hugs were exchanged all around, then Pieter and Joan melted into the night.

****

Sue rested her hand on Mary's forehead and urged her patient to relax. Mary's face looked tired, her brow creased with lines and dark circles around her eyes confessed to her lack of sleep.

"I'm sorry, Pieter. I haven't been myself lately. I can't pick up anything of your friend."

"There may not be anything to find, Mary. Thank you for trying. Now try to get some rest."

Pieter slipped out the door into the ship's corridor and touched the invisible switch by his ear. "Bob, what is your assessment of Mary's search?"

"Inconclusive, Pieter. There is a reasonable chance the planet's magnetic field is interfering with her abilities."

"Why do I hear a 'but' in there, Bob? What aren't you telling me?"

"As you well know, Pieter, my cameras and microphones are able to monitor every part of this ship."

"Yes, Bob, I know. Cut to the chase."

"On several occasions, I have observed Mary acting in an unusual manner. There have been several incidents of somnambulism on her part. And these incidents appear to be increasing in frequency."

"Somnambulism?"

"Sleep walking."

"That's not so bad. Big deal."

"I recommend you locate a monitor. I wish to play some video for you."

Pieter continued his slow walk to his private room at the end of the passageway. Once inside the display on his desk flickered to life. "Okay, Bob, if you have something to show me I'm ready."

"This was recorded several days ago, while we were still in transit."

The display showed the same corridor he just left but with the minimum illumination reserved for off hours. The camera focused on Mary's face as she walked down the corridor. Mary stopped outside Leeann's room and entered a numerical code. The door opened and Mary walked inside. The shot changed to a camera inside the room. Mary walked to Leeann's bedside and sat in a chair. Even from across the room the sensitive microphone picked up a small, female voice in the darkness.

"Jeg er så ked af det, Lee," Her voice was heavily accented. Pieter leaned closer. "Jeg prøvede, jeg virkelig prøvet. Please forgive me."

"What's she saying?"

"That's the point. She isn't saying anything."

"What are you talking about, Bob? I can hear her; I just can't understand most of it."

"True, you hear sounds coming from her vocal

cords but a voice print shows the voice is not her."

"That's crazy. That's Mary's voice. She may be speaking in Norse but I can hear her."

"Listen carefully, Pieter. The voice print doesn't make mistakes. A person's vocal patterns are as reliable an identity check as fingerprints or retina scans. The voice print says that is not Mary speaking."

"Is that Mary sitting next to Lee?"

"Yes, Pieter, but that is not her speaking."

"Who then? Is there another person in the room that we can't see?"

"Apparently there is, Pieter. The voice print matches Loki."

CHAPTER FIFTEEN

Bob's familiar voice was fed directly into Pieter's ear. "I do not believe the management at Golden Door was fully forthcoming about this planet when supplying information to the prospective settlers."

"Do they know you've tapped into their database?"

"No, Pieter. I am very careful to leave no evidence behind. They were careless to leave a live transmission channel open between their mainframe on Prime and one of their survey satellites above us."

Mike whistled as he scanned the geological map. "Look at all the blank spaces on their survey. There are thousands of square miles where their satellites couldn't penetrate the mineral deposits past a few meters deep."

"Precisely, Michael," Bob transferred his voice to the overhead speakers. "And such deposits render any tracer chip useless. Your friend, Pieter-in fact ,all the missing people-could be in a number of places nearby and the satellite could never pick up their chips."

"And Mary is out of action for now. So how do we search for your friend, Pieter?"

"Bob, give us a search grid covering a square kilometer around the area where Pavel was taken."

"As you wish, Pieter."

A series of squares appeared over that area of the map. Pieter leaned closer. "We can assume they're not in any areas still exposed to satellite coverage. So we can ignore any place that's out in the open. They're probably still local. So, if we look for them in these areas..." Pieter's finger traced the areas obscured by heavy mineral deposits. "We might have a chance of finding them." Pieter's finger then traced the areas nearest their landing zone. "Which leaves us with one unanswered question."

"What's that?" Mike asked.

"What took them in the first place?"

"Oh, yeah."

"Why hasn't anyone seen anything unusual?" Pieter asked. "If there was something big enough to capture a human being on the loose, there should have been sightings, but nothing so far. Not even the satellite imaging."

"That is not entirely true, Pieter."

"Enlighten me, Bob."

"Light may be the key factor here." The image on the screen changed to a distant view of the town. "This is the satellite imagery for the night Pavel went missing." A circle appeared around a glowing red dot on the screen. "According to the transponder code, that is Pavel." As the dot turned to the right to follow a street, a pair of greenish blue dots appeared out of a grove of trees and engulfed him, then disappeared into the trees again.

Pieter fought back the cold chill that ran down his spine. "So, we can follow this image to wherever they took Pavel?"

"I'm afraid not, Pieter. Whatever they are, their body temperature is very close to the temperature of the air around them. Once they entered the cover of the trees, there was no way to follow them."

"What about tracking Pavel's transponder chip?"

"It stopped responding the moment he disappeared from the screen."

"What the hell are they?"

"Whatever these... phantoms are, they appear to be cold-blooded."

"Lizard men, cool," Mike exclaimed.

"There's no definition of what they are but from the thermal image they are at least the size of a man," Pieter offered his observation. "How could something that large go undetected for this long?"

"One more thing, Pieter," Bob interrupted. "Watch the satellite image one more time at actual speed."

On the screen, the approach and capture of Pavel repeated itself.

"Why doesn't he try to get away?" Pieter asked. "Whatever they are they don't move very fast. He should have had time to run, but he doesn't."

"Precisely the right question, Pieter. It is as if he does not see them coming."

"So where do we look for something that doesn't want to be found and may be hard to see?"

"As you have already determined, Pieter, there are numerous places to go undetected on this planet."

"Then we search the old-fashioned way tomorrow at first light."

"Why is it always first light?" Mike moaned.

"Put me on ship wide, Bob."

"When you're ready, Pieter."

"Everyone needs to get some sleep tonight. Most of us will go on a search tomorrow. This is an armed patrol. I repeat, this is an armed patrol. Good night everyone."

Pieter and Mike went in separate directions in the hall, Mike to his own quarters and Pieter to Mary's room. The door opened as soon as he pushed the chime. Mary floated comfortably just above her bed while Billy slouched in a chair nearby.

"How are you, Mary?" Pieter asked as his hand reached for hers.

"I'm okay, Pieter. I just wish I could be more of help."

"We'll be fine. Billy, you understand I need you to stay with her, right?"

"You mean miss all the fun and playing hide and seek with monsters and packing guns? No problem."

"How long since you slept?"

"How long have we been on this rock?" Billy yawned.

"Go get some sleep and I'll take over here for a while."

"Thanks, Pieter. But I'm fine."

"That wasn't a request, Billy."

"Aye, Captain Admiral."

Billy's joints could be heard to protest as he got to his feet. There were audible clicks and pops as he stretched and released pent up tension. Then he headed for the door. Pieter lowered the gravity field around Mary as he took Billy's place. She settled softly into her bed and reached a hand toward Pieter. "He's not as childish as he would have everyone believe, you know."

"Who, Billy?" Pieter held her small hand.

"He's really sweet and he makes me laugh. But he can be serious when it's time to be serious."

"I know, Mary. I'm more worried about you right now."

"Me? I'm just tired and I'm having a hard time with this planet of yours."

"I appreciate your patience."

"How is Leeann?"

"Better than you at the moment. Mary, what do you remember of that moment when Loki died?"

Mary's face blanched and turned away. Her hand tightened around his as she choked back a sob. "Please don't ask me to remember that."

"I'm sorry, Mary, but something else may have happened. Something none of us could have expected."

"I don't follow you, Pieter."

"Bob."

"Yes, Pieter?" Bob's voice answered from the overhead speaker.

"I want you to play back the recording you showed me the other night. The one with Mary."

The wall monitor glowed and, as they watched, Mary appeared in the dim corridor. The door to Leeann's quarters opened and Mary walked inside.

"Pieter, I don't remember any of this."

"Because you were sleepwalking. Now listen."

Her voice was a soft whisper and in a different language. "Jeg er så ked af det, Lee. Jeg prøvede, jeg virkelig prøvet. Jeg kunne bare ikke. Please forgive me."

"I still don't remember any of this. How is this possible? I don't speak…"

"Bob ran a voice print of this. He says the print doesn't match you."

"I don't understand. Come to think of it, I don't even have the access code to Lee's door."

"Bob says the voice print is Loki."

Mary gasped. "Pieter, Loki's dead. It's just a bad dream is all."

"Bob says otherwise. He says that may be you sitting there with Lee, but the voice coming out of your mouth is Loki."

"That's not possible."

"That's what I thought. But Bob and I have been working on a theory. You wanna take a crack at it, Bob?"

Bob's calm voice filled the room. "Very well, Pieter. I have been studying all the available footage of Loki as he used his unique ability to go from place to place. Just like all of you, his ability is tied directly to his will and his power of thought.

"In Loki's case, all that was necessary for him to teleport was a fixed destination in his mind and a triggering thought to set him in motion. Once that triggering thought happened his mind transformed his physical body into energy and sent him to the location he desired. Do you follow me so far, Mary?"

"I think so, Bob. Go on."

"When he became trapped on the enemy ship the thing he wanted most was to escape back to here, to Leeann. I can only speculate that some device on that ship prevented him from making the transformation to energy. But you could meet his mind half way and open a link between him and Leeann. That was where he was when the bomb exploded. The EMP from that blast would have disabled whatever was holding him there a nanosecond before it destroyed the ship. In that fraction of a second his natural survival instinct would have triggered the transformation. But there was insufficient time to complete the teleport."

"But what was able to make the jump, made it half-way," Mary whispered under her breath.

"Exactly, Mary, half-way here to you. Some part of Loki still lives inside your mind, coexisting with you but unable to complete the leap. And when you are asleep or very tired Loki's mind rises to the surface and asserts itself, as it did that night in Leeann's room."

Mary pulled her knees to her chest and wrapped her arms around her legs. She rocked against her need to understand and tears flowed down her face. "Oh my God, Pieter, what do I do now? Is that why I can't use my power to help?"

"That is a possibility. We just don't know enough about how any of this works to know what to do next. But we're doing everything we can to figure out a way to get this sorted out," Pieter said, squeezing her hand.

"I know you are. Somehow, I feel better knowing there's still a bit of Loki in me. Have you told Leeann?"

"No. Frankly I have no idea what to tell her."

"Just tell her the truth, Pieter. We'll deal with whatever happens next as best we can, but she deserves that much."

Pieter settled into the same chair Billy used and opened a book. "Do you mind if I read?" he asked.

"A real book, with pages?" Mary stretched out and pulled her blanket over her legs. "I don't remember seeing that one before."

"It's a gift from my mother. A collection of Russian Folk Tales, by Alexander Afanasyev."

"Wonderful. Then you can read to me."

"What would you like to hear; Father Frost, the Frog Princes, the Golden Slipper?"

"Which was your favorite, Pieter?"

"Father Frost."

"Read that one, please."

Pieter opened the book to the beginning of the story, drew a deep breath and slowly began to read. The words came in fits and starts as he translated. "In a far-away country, somewhere in Russia, there lived a stepmother who had a stepdaughter and a daughter of her own. Her own daughter was dear to her, and always, whatever she did, the mother was the first to praise her, to pet her; but there was little praise for the stepdaughter; although good and kind, she had no other reward than reproach. What on Prime could have been done?"

****

Pieter stood with his back to the chill pre-dawn wind and watched The Steppes nearest moon hurtle across the sky toward a pinkish glow. Joan sheltered in his lea and wrapped her arms around his waist for warmth. The Eastern horizon filled with a ruddy light and sounds of approaching footsteps competed with the moaning of the wind.

Pieter's father led the small band of searchers over a small hillock to where Pavel had disappeared among the trees. Trailing the cluster of men was a tall figure in long black robes. He carried a staff in one hand and struggled with his vestments with the other. His beard waved like dark lace curtains trimmed in silver. He looked up and saw the group of young people in dark blue uniforms. As his eyes found Pieter he paused and stared as if to reconcile the man in the uniform with the boy he knew.

Pieter watched as the priest smiled. He let go of Joan's hand and ran down the short slope to embrace the man in black. They laughed and exchanged a kiss before Pieter stepped back. "Brother Maykl, when did you…"

"Two years ago. The Patriarch called me to lead a flock. I prayed over it and decided I could do more good from the pulpit than the monastery, especially after what happened to you. There has been something of a revolution since you were taken. We forced Golden Door to withdraw their armed thugs and reduce their presence. Most of them are gone now and our people are in control of the port and the warehouses."

"I never pictured you as a firebrand, Father." Pieter took Maykl's hand and held it up to admire his ring.

"And what of you, Captain Pieter? Your father tells me you are the leader here. I was surprised to learn you were alive, but this…" His fingers touched the pin with four gold bars and a single star on Pieter's collar. "This does not surprise me. You were always a strong boy of great faith. Now you are a strong man and your faith has led you home. But I am not the only old friend who has come to see you."

Father Maykl turned to reveal a figure standing behind him in the early morning cold fog. With the way clear, the figure advanced on Pieter, casting aside a warm cloak to reveal long, blond curls and dazzling blue eyes.

Pieter whispered, "Sophia?"

She dashed into his arms, sobbing.

"Pieter?" She was breathless even in her native Russian, "I can't believe my own eyes. You're alive after all these years. What your Batya told Father Maykl was true."

She hugged him tight and pressed herself to him. Standing a few feet away Joan blushed and turned so as not to watch.

Slowly Pieter separated her arms from his and stepped back.

"You're as beautiful as ever, Sophia. It is good to see you again."

Sophia's face brightened at the compliment.

"Will you be here long?"

"No," he answered. "We are fugitives, Sophia. The masters on Prime will stop at nothing to apprehend us."

Sophia's eyes darted left and right before she considered Pieter's face again. Her blue eyes glistened with the beginning of tears.

"I was hoping you would be here long enough for us to become… reacquainted."

"We should be gone from here as soon as we can, Sophia. I am sorry."

Tears began to rain down the pale skin of her face and she turned away. Joan understood almost nothing of what was said, but kept her face averted to avoid becoming caught up in the moment.

Sophia drew her cloak around her shoulders and wrapped the end over her head, concealing her face. "Farewell, Pieter," she whispered between tears. "If things had been different then perhaps you and I… I suppose we'll never know now."

Boris tapped Pieter's shoulder and then the timepiece on his wrist. Pieter nodded and turned to lead them through the gloom beneath the low hanging limbs. Sophia reached for his hand and pulled him swiftly toward her. Her fingers grasped the back of his head and her lips were suddenly on his. For an instant Pieter froze, uncertain of the moment. Just as quickly she released him, turned away, and ran back toward the town.

Once again Boris and his son headed for their goal. Like stealthy hunters they did not speak but relied on hand signals to indicate where they went next. At the vanguard of the group, Mike and Anton wore thermal goggles to help them spot any heat source. Each member carried a non-lethal rifle and a very lethal side arm.

Slowly, in an ever-widening spiral, they searched for any sign of human or non-human activity. On their third sweep outside of town, Bob's voice reached the ears of the ship's crew.

"My topographical survey shows a series of cave mouths in your area."

Pieter's index finger brushed the switch behind his ear. "Which way, Bob?"

"Fifteen degrees to your right."

Pieter stood and measured the degrees to turn. With a simple hand gesture, he indicated the new direction. The path took the party through another small grove of trees. The ground dropped away sharply to a stream bed. A low, overhanging rock shelf was the only indication of the dark cave under their feet.

Slender shafts of light probed the deep shadows. Careful steps took the line of searchers where the beams of their hand-held lights led them. In the far end of the cave, a few scattered dots of color caught their attention. As they approached the dots revealed themselves to be wadded bits of clothing.

"What do you think this means?" Anton asked

his brother.

"It looks like people have been here before, but these could have come from anyone. Bob, are you getting this?" Pieter's question was answered with white noise.

"There's too much interference for Bob to see or hear us," Pieter spoke to the crowd of faces around him. "Record what you see for Bob to analyze and let's bag the clothes to bring back."

A short time later the team retraced their steps back to the cave mouth. Long shadows marked the close of day. By the time they returned to their starting point, darkness had descended. The search team split up, and the five members of the Phoenix crew returned with their samples for the ship's AI to examine.

****

"DNA from hair and skin cells found in the clothing was consistent with at least five of the missing settlers."

"So they were in the cave?" Mike asked.

"Yes, Michael. However, let me point out that the scans you all took revealed no indications of violence. There were no signs of blood in the cave."

Pieter asked, "Any signs that Pavel was there?"

"No, Pieter. That does not rule out the possibility that he was, but there are no traces of his

DNA in these samples. And no two pieces are from the same person."

"How many people were in that cave?"

"A minimum of five distinct individuals, but none of the samples originated from Pavel."

"So, whoever was there wasn't being stripped bare. They were just getting comfortable in the warmer air of the cave."

"A reasonable hypothesis."

Billy's voice erupted into Pieter's ear with a shrill scream in the background. "Pieter, come quick. Something terrible is wrong with Mary."

In seconds Pieter and most of the ship's complement were pressed into Mary's room. She sat upright in her bed, eyes glazed over, her chest heaved for air. Billy sat next to her with his arms wrapped around her. He was ashen and sweating with panic.

"She stopped screaming just a few seconds ago. But look at her, Pieter."

Mary's mouth opened and a voice, that was only human by virtue of its source of origin, filled the room. "You call them words. These vocal symbols by which you convey your primitive thoughts from one to another of your... what is the word... individuals. Inefficient. We mean you no harm. We mean no harm to this... individual. This one can translate our thoughts to you. This one is also a collective. But not like us. There is another here. Lost."

"What do you mean, lost?" Pieter asked the alien intelligence.

"This one shares its mind with another. The other is lost and does not know where it is."

Clair Jones' hand settled on Pieter's shoulder. "What is that? What is it doing to Mary? What does it mean by the other is lost?"

Bob's calm voice interceded, "It is the voice of the entities you search for. They are communicating through Mary. And the other they speak of is Loki."

CHAPTER SIXTEEN

"Who are you?" Leeann asked.

"We are One," a sibilant whisper replied.

"What do you mean, you are one?" Michael chimed in.

"We are One. We do not understand your question. We mean you no harm. We only wish to understand your kind. You are strange to us. You are separate and alone, so terribly alone. We wished to save the few we could from this isolation, but they cannot hear us."

Clair Jones stepped closer to Mary and answered, "The one you are using to communicate with us is a telepath. She can hear and speak through her mind."

"You single her out. Does this mean such properties are not common among you?"

"It means exactly that. We call this one Mary. She is the only one like her among us." Clair sat next to Mary to continue the conversation.

"You give her a vestigial identity. You call her, Mary. Do each of you have such identifiers?"

"We call them names. Yes, each of us has a name. My name is Clair. What is your name?"

"We do not require names. We are One."

Pieter's impatience bubbled to the surface. He pressed his face squarely into Mary's field of view. "Where are the people you took? What have you done with them?" His voice carried an angry edge.

"These individuals are unharmed. We were curious about your species. We hoped to communicate so we might understand you better. We understand now that was useless. They shall be returned to you." The voice paused and Mary looked up into Pieter's eyes. "As a gesture of," Again the voice paused as if looking for a word somewhere in Mary's head, "friendship, yes that is the word, friendship, we offer our help to return that one which is lost."

The room became quiet as each of them struggled to comprehend the meaning. Billy broke the silence. "What the hell is he saying, Pieter? Does he mean your friend, Pavel?"

"If the one you call Pavel is among the individuals who are with us, that one will be returned. But we offer to assist the one which is lost to find that one's way home as well."

"I think he means someone else, Billy," Pieter finally answered. "I think it means they can return Loki from inside Mary's mind."

For an instant Billy was silent. His eyes darkened and darted from side to side. "Are you telling me Loki is living in Mary's head? And is… whatever it is, saying they can get him out?"

"I think maybe that is what it is saying," Clair tried her best to sound reassuring.

Billy released his hold on Mary. He stood and pushed Pieter out of the way so he could stand directly in front of her. "Do you see me? Can you hear me? Whatever you are, can you help her? I mean, can you help Loki without hurting her?"

Mary's body responded by cocking her head slightly to the right and focusing her eyes on Billy. "We see. We hear. The answer you seek is… yes. You appear to be in a very unstable state. What is your vestigial identifier?"

"My what?"

Clair put a hand on Billy's arm. "Your name, Billy, it wants to know what name to call you."

"Why the hell didn't it just say so? My name is Billy."

"Billy. Yes, this one is familiar with that name. Emotions? Yes. We do not have these emotions, as you call them. Even in this state, this one has strong emotions for you. You are different from this one. We do not have genders, as you know them. This one is female and you are male. We do not have such biological distinctions. It is strange to us."

Clair Jones explained, "It is how we reproduce. Our biology requires one of each gender to have children."

"Children? What are children?"

Joan snorted, "Seriously, they don't know what children are?"

Clair Jones held up her hand to stop any further derision. "Children are immature versions of us. Only each is a unique combination of genetic material from each parent."

"We do not reproduce in this manner," the entity responded in Mary's voice. "When another is required we call One into being."

"I don't understand that at all," Sue added.

"We can worry about this later," Pieter interrupted the inquiry. "We need to get our people back to their families. We need to get the equipment we need and get off this planet soon or Mills and his goons will locate us." Pieter turned his full attention to the entity. "Where do we find the missing people?"

"This one will remember where to find them, when we are done here. It would be well if you could bring this one with you."

"We can do that," Pieter nodded.

"Before we leave you, would you satisfy a need to understand?"

"If I can," Pieter answered.

"What is the purpose of the false skins you wear?"

"I don't understand what you mean, false skin."

"Several individuals shed some of their false skins in a resting place we used to wait until this planet's star continued its path. That is how we knew you were searching for us."

"You mean our clothes," Pieter smiled and tugged at his own shirt.

"Yes. What is the purpose of these… clothes?"

"We have become accustomed to covering ourselves," Clair Jones blushed as she answered. "It's our custom not to go about naked. So we wear clothes over our bodies whenever we are not alone."

"This is strange. We do not understand. But you are a strange species. We will wait for you tomorrow at the resting place you found."

Mary's body went limp. Billy caught her before she could topple to the floor at the foot of her bed. He levitated her and held her in the air until Sue could pull back her blanket. Then he settled her back into her bunk. Sue's hand covered Mary's forehead and her eyes closed.

"She's asleep," Sue observed. "It's like she was asleep the whole time."

At the door to Mary's Leeann confronted Pieter. "What the hell is all this about Loki?"

Billy was a heartbeat behind her. "What aren't you telling us, Pieter? How does Loki end up in Mary's head?"

Pieter took a slow deep breath. "Bob theorized as much already. This, thing, just confirmed what we suspected. It's why Mary has been acting so strange lately. Even she doesn't know."

"When the hell were you going to tell me?" Leeann's voice carried signs of impending tears.

"I was going to tell you once we figured out what to do. I didn't see any reason to get everyone worked up until then."

"Do you trust these, what-ever-they-are?" Billy pressed for answers. "You could be putting Mary's life at risk if you go along with this."

Clair came to Pieter's rescue. "Billy, you know perfectly well Pieter would never put any of your lives at risk if he could help it. If these beings believe they can help Mary and Loki, I see no reason not to let them try. Mary can't continue to host Loki like this. It's too much of a strain on her."

"I'm sorry, Pieter. That... thing had control of her. I just freaked out."

Pieter's hand settled on Billy's shoulder. "I

understand. I would feel the same way if it were Joan."

****

Joan sat on the side of Pieter's bunk and reached for his hand. "Who is Sophia?"

Pieter tried to look into her eyes but found it impossible. He blushed and replied, "A girl I knew in school before I was taken."

"She's very pretty."

"Every boy in school thought so too."

"Including you?" she asked.

"I won't lie to you. Yes, including me; especially me. I thought she was the most beautiful girl on The Steppes. But I was a boy and didn't know better."

Pieter reached for Joan's chin and turned her face toward him. Tears shimmered on her cheeks. "Now I am grown, and I know better."

He bent down and kissed her tears then her lips. "Yes, I had a school boy crush on her…once. But it is you that I love."

Joan's fingers tangled into his thick, black hair and pulled him down onto the bed, crushing her lips against his.

****

At first light, the crew of the Phoenix walked down the ramp in the direction of the cave. Mary sat in a chair that floated in mid-air between Pieter and Billy. The area of lower gravity extended from Pieter to just beyond the small group.

The uneven terrain was crossed with little trouble until they came to the same ridge line that obscured the cave the previous day. One by one they dropped like floating leaves to the ground below. As they approached, two men separated themselves from the shadows.

Pieter's father tucked a thermos bottle under his arm and welcomed the new arrivals. "I got your message, sinula. I thought, perhaps the Father should come to keep me company."

Father Maykl stepped forward and reached for Pieter's hand. "Do not blame your father. I was there when your message arrived and invited myself."

Pieter took the offered hand and touched the priest's ring to his lips. "In case God should wish to express an opinion."

"Who better to deliver His word?"

Pieter laughed as metal cups of hot tea were shared among his crew. "I would ask you to wait here with my Father, but I know that would be useless, Maykl."

"I will do my best not to interfere."

Pieter's father collected the cups and nested them into the cap of his thermos. With a nod and a shake of his son's hand he retreated to a rock near the cave mouth and waited. Pieter led his group into the darkness.

Yesterday's twilight was illuminated by dancing lights from somewhere deep in the cave. "You have come." Mary's mouth moved as before but her eyes were glazed over. "Enter our place of rest. Those you seek are here."

Pieter and Billy flanked Mary as they ducked under the low, overhanging foliage at the entrance. A flower dangling from a vine brushed Mary's face but there was no reaction. Passing from the light of day to the gloom of the cave made Pieter recall his months of torment during his early captivity. He struggled to keep his deep memories in check as they descended into the darkness.

Once inside, flickering lights beckoned them farther into the cavern. Shifting, shimmering amorphous shapes floated a few inches from the floor. As they passed one another the glowing forms merged and split away again. As many as a dozen shapes could be seen at any given time.

In the cave, behind the floating shapes, five human figures stood motionless. One by one they were surrounded by one of the glowing forms. Only then did they begin to walk slowly, like marionettes, toward the opening of the cave. The glimmering beings led them to the entrance of the cavern and there abandoned them.

Eyes flickered and rolled as they emerged from a deep sleep. One by one they became animated, excited, and fearful. As they searched for answers they found a small group of young people standing to one side of the chamber. On unsure feet, they made their way to their fellow humans, away from the alien entities.

Pieter was the first to reach out to his friend. "Pavel!" he called out in Russian, "Pavel, over here. It's me, Pieter."

A young man with tousled blond hair and ice blue eyes blinked in the gloom and searched for the voice. "Pieter? It's not possible. Are we dead? Is this the way to heaven?"

Pieter reached out for his old friend and wrapped him in his arms. One by one the former captives were found by one of the special young people to be led outside. Father Maykl stood ready to comfort them as they walked toward the light.

Pavel's face was wet with tears as he refused to release his hold on his old friend. "You're dead. Did you know that? How did you get here? How did I get here?"

"I am not dead and you are not dead. It's a very

long story, Pavel." Pieter pointed to the group of people heading toward the entrance. "There will be answers later. For now, follow my friends."

Pavel nodded and followed Mike and Sue along with the other former captives. Billy, Leeann, and Pieter escorted Mary to an open space in the middle of the cave. As the chair settled into place, the shimmering entities formed a circle around her. Mary sat straight and spoke in the distinctly alien voice.

"The one who is lost wishes to come home. He seeks one he thinks of as home."

Pieter replied, "I think that would be the one we call Leeann. She is here. They were… close."

"Emotions. Yes. These attachments you have between you are unknown to us. We are One."

The floating figures began to circle, merging and splitting over and over. "Let the one you call Leeann come closer. That one will make the journey easier for the one who is lost."

Leeann stepped close to Mary and took one of her hands in hers. In a quivering voice she said, "I'm ready. What do you want me to do?"

"Each of you carries memories of the one who is lost. These thoughts will form a pattern for his return. We will bring that one into being as we bring ourselves into being. Only that one must be as you are. Come closer and do as the one you call

Leeann has done, make contact with the one who speaks."

Pieter, Billy, and Joan stood next to Mary and placed hands on her head and shoulders.

"Now, think of the one who is lost. Remember that one."

Their eyes closed as they searched their minds for memories of Loki. Around them the shifting shapes glowed brighter and brighter. The amorphous lights moved faster and faster, giving off tiny particles as they merged into a single bright circle.

The lights within the cave grew stronger. A golden glow emerged from Mary, like bright dust stirred into the air. The glow fused with the shining particles that were drawn to a place in front of where Mary sat. As if filling a mold of a man, the gathering energy slowly coalesced into a recognizable shape.

"Loki," Leeann whispered to the tall male body evolving from the joining of phantom energy and human memory. "Loki, come back to me."

With their attention focused on the phenomenon, none of them noticed the grimace on Mary's face. Her mouth opened and a long wail of pain filled the cavern. Billy's arms surrounded her.

"Pieter, tell them to stop," Billy called out. "They said it wouldn't hurt her."

"The pain is not from this one," The voice interrupted Mary's outcry. "The pain is from the one who was lost."

The ghostly figure of Loki stood with its mouth open, body contorted as if in great pain. Leeann dropped Mary's hand and stepped into the shimmering aura that surrounded Loki. Her fingers reached for him. Bright flashes of blue and white sparks flew between them making Leeann's body twitch and contort. Her fingers pressed on through her pain and as they made contact Loki emerged, fully formed, from the translucent glow. Leeann caught his naked body as it collapsed to the floor. An instant later Mary also went limp. The phantoms that surrounded them went dim, separated, and slowed to a stop.

Pieter pulled his jacket off and knelt to wrap it around Loki. Leeann looked up into Pieter's eyes. Grateful tears bathed her face as she smiled up at him. "We're going to have a hard time explaining where all his things went."

"We can get him some new clothes, Lee. How is he?"

"He's here. That's all I know." Leeann hugged Loki tightly to her and rocked like a mother holding her newborn.

Pieter turned his attention to Mary. Like Loki, she was unconscious. Billy's fingers carefully brushed her hair away from her eyes. Asleep, her face was peaceful.

In their excitement, no one noticed the phantoms had merged again into a single body. The shimmering shape grew dim and disappeared.

Behind them, Father Maykl was on his knees, hands clasped in prayer. On the floor of the cave Leeann clung to Loki. Hot tears ran down her face, landing on Pieter's coat. Sue and Mike reappeared from the front of the cavern. Mike's hand found Pieter's shoulder, but his eyes were wide with disbelief at finding Loki.

"They met us at the grove, just like you said. Your Dad is gathering them outside to wait on us. It's just as well. They had more questions than we had answers. Sue managed to make enough contact with all of them to make sure they were okay. Is that…"

"It appears to be," Pieter replied. "Sue, do you mind?"

Sue looked up from where she stood with a hand pressed to Mary's forehead. She subtly put a hand to Leeann's cheek before kneeling next to her and putting both palms on Loki's chest. Blue sparks, like bright flashes of static electricity, flowed between her fingers and Loki's pale skin. For a moment both she and Leeann were startled, but Sue held fast and pressed her hands against him.

She smiled and looked up into Leeann's face.

"It's definitely him. His system is full of an energy I don't recognize; probably from those… things. But his heart is strong and his mind is resting." Sue leaned over and kissed Leeann's cheek.

"What about Mary?" Billy asked.

"She's drained, but otherwise she's okay," Sue answered. "She and Loki have been cohabiting in her mind since the bomb went off. She needs some rest, but I expect she'll be fine."

Pieter looked up toward the roof of the cavern and spoke into the darkness. "I don't know if you can hear me; I don't know if you can understand if you do, but thank you for what you did here."

Again, Pieter and Billy worked together to bring both Mary and Loki into the air and back outside into the bright sunshine. The Russian Orthodox Priest followed, shaken but steadfast. His hand rested on Pieter's shoulder for a moment. "What wonders God has made."

Pieter stopped for a moment and let the rest gather around him, "Now, let's get what we came for and get out of here."

CHAPTER SEVENTEEN

Outside the cave the group turned toward the Phoenix. Mary and Loki floated weightless in the air between Pieter and Billy. Leeann held Loki's hand, watching his sleeping face for any sign of wakefulness. Sue walked quietly on the opposite side, one hand resting on Loki's chest. Loki's body shimmered with intermittent flashes of the otherworldly energy that brought him into being.

Behind the group of young, puckish people, the rescued settlers followed in their wake. The day was cold, and flurries of snow swirled in the breeze. Pavel walked with his eyes on his old friend. Questions ran through his mind until he knew he must speak with him. His steps quickened until he walked abreast of Pieter.

"I want you to know I was very angry with my

father for what he did," Pavel said in their native language.

Pieter looked up into his friend's face. "He was frightened, Pavel. Your father thought he was only protecting you and the others from something he could not understand."

Pavel pointed to his own ears and then to Pieter's. "Are you all…you know… like that?"

"Do you mean, are we all 'odinnadtsat'?" Pieter replied. "Yes.

"So, you are a new race."

"Some of us believe that. But we're still human, Pavel."

"I meant no disrespect, Pieter. I still think of you as my friend."

"And I you." Pieter draped an arm across Pavel's shoulder. "We must take our mates back to our ship, and then Joan and I will return you and your companions to your families."

A tap on his shoulder brought Pieter to a stop. He turned to face the Priest who had been his teacher and advisor. Tears flowed down Maykl's face and he clutched the symbol of his faith in his right hand. "What have I witnessed today? Is it the work of God or the Devil? Was it blasphemy or a miracle?"

"I cannot tell you what you must believe, Father. I would like to think this was a blessing for us all. You have your mission's sheep back in your flock and my brother has been returned to us. I see no hand of evil here."

"I think you are right; though I cannot reconcile it in my mind, my heart tells me this was an act of God."

An hour later Pavel was in his father's embrace. Tears flowed freely down Sergey Andropov's cheeks as he kissed his son. All around them similar scenes of reunion were played out between the former missing and their families. Pavel whispered to his father, who looked up at Pieter and Joan. The young people stood proudly with their heads uncovered, receiving the thanks of happy parents and siblings. Sergey stepped closer to the young man he barely recognized and extended his hand.

"I have no right to expect this from you, Pieter. What I did back then was wrong. I know that now. Thank you for my son."

Pieter met the older man's eyes with a steady gaze and his hand with a firm grip. "Pavel was…is, my friend. I could do no less for him. I believe it was an act of faith that brought us here to help all of you. And now I have a great favor to ask of you, sir."

"Name it."

From his pocket Pieter took out several folded

sheets of paper and gave them to Pavel's father. "We need the things on this list. Things that Golden Door has abandoned here and to which you have access. And we need them quickly. We have already been here much longer than we anticipated. We need to be about our business before Dr. Mills decides to look for us here."

Andropov opened the sheets of paper and began to read the long list. At the third page Pieter's intent began to dawn on him. "You could settle a new world with this."

"Can you help us? We have credits to pay for most of it."

Andropov smiled, "Your money of no use here, Pieter. I'll organize transports. Tell me where and we can start loading tomorrow."

Andropov's quick agreement was a surprise to Pieter, who could only smile and hug him close.

****

Sue sat with Leeann in Loki's room. Since his resurrection, Loki's frail form had gained mass as it lost most of its alien shimmer. Leeann clung to him and wept. Susan pressed her fingers where she could reach to confirm what her eyes could see. He appeared, for all intents and purposes, to be sleeping peacefully.

"What's wrong with him, Sue?" Leeann sat up.

"Why doesn't he wake up?"

Sue's fingers traced the lines of Loki's face while Leeann held tight to his right hand. "I can't be sure, but I think it has to do with being dead until a few hours ago. Mary kept his mind and, for lack of a better word, his soul alive. She was his lifeboat. It left her exhausted both mentally and physically. I think it's taking him some time to settle in."

"Settle in? This is his body, not a house." Leeann drew a long breath and her head sagged. "I'm sorry. I know you're doing your best. I just want to know he's alright."

"It's not easy to be patient. But he's going to need some time. He's likely to be confused and disoriented."

"It would help if I knew he remembered me."

Sue smiled and cupped Leeann's cheek with her free hand. "I don't think that's going to be an issue, Lee. The only reason he made it this far was because he was trying to come home to you."

****

An hour before sunrise a pounding on the main hatch door echoed through the ship. Yawning, Pieter pressed his thumb to the button causing the door to slide into the hull. He stepped out onto the landing, his mouth hung open and his eyes blinked. He saw huge tracked vehicles pulling trailers across the uneven terrain. Lights from the transports illuminated the area around the ship. Two portable cranes were drawn up alongside the storage bay hatch.

"You said you were in a hurry," Andropov smiled and draped an arm across Pieter's shoulder.

Pieter returned the grin and touched the switch behind his ear. "Bob."

"Yes, Pieter." Despite its computer origins, Bob's voice carried a lilt of amusement.

"You didn't notice this bunch of teamsters pulling up?"

"I did, Pieter, but you said you did not wish to be disturbed unless there was an emergency. In my assessment of the situation, this did not meet the criteria of an emergency."

"Open the cargo bay doors please, Bob."

"Yes, Captain."

Lower down a series of heavy doors split and folded back into the hull. At a simple hand signal from Sergey, men began fitting straps and cables to pallets on the trailers and the loading began.

Pieter's father stood among a large group of people on the gangway just behind the Warehouseman. Among them were several children, a few years older than his sister. At the back of the group were his mother and siblings. All of them carried bundles and boxes and bags.

"Does your offer to relocate still stand, Pieter?" his father asked.

"Of course, Papa. Let me get some help and we'll find rooms for everyone." Pieter touched the com. "Mike, Billy, I could use some help up here."

His ears were filled with moans and grumbles but then reluctant, "Aye, sirs." A few minutes later both young men wandered down the corridor. Their uniform tunics were still unbuttoned and they rubbed their eyes.

Inside the door, a milling crowd of people waited for them. Pieter raised his hand for quiet and addressed the crowd in Russian. "My friends, these are my brothers Michael and William. They will show you to your cabins and help you get settled. You are all welcome among us."

In their ears Mike and Billy got the translation. Billy stepped close and whispered, "Pieter, who are these people?"

Pieter waved for one of the children to come closer. He knelt and smiled into the sleepy face and gently removed her cap. The young girl returned Pieter's smile and stood quietly as he brushed her long, brown hair back to reveal her ears. Understanding his meaning, Billy and Mike smiled and showed their gene markers to the girl.

"Bob will help you communicate," Pieter advised. "It's unlikely any of them speak English."

"Understood, Captain," Mike replied.

Billy flew the young girl up into the air. At first, she was shocked but then she laughed along with Billy as her feet dangled. The crowd behind them gasped but then laughed before following the young men into the heart of the ship. As she passed Pieter, Risia handed his sister into his arms.

"We are going to a new home, Nika, a place where you and all the others can be safe." Pieter kissed his sister and returned her to his mother. He watched as they followed the others down the corridor.

From the top of the gangway, Sergey Andropov supervised the loading. As one dray was emptied another took its place. Heavy loads were secured close to the ship's center of gravity while lighter loads were distributed around them. Pieter added his own help by dropping the pull of gravity around the ship.

A cold breeze whispered through the open doors, greeting the sun as it peeked over the horizon. Still, the train of trucks continued to and from the vast warehouses to the ship and back.

Andropov's hand settled on Pieter's shoulder. "It was a very long list you gave me. And there are always things you will wish you had but did without." He handed Pieter a large envelope. "Each pallet is numbered. I added a few…extras, just to help you along. When we first arrived here we didn't bring enough tractors or generators. You should have enough of both. You'll need to assemble them, of course. There are plenty of prefabricated buildings you can live in, and even a small power plant; all you need is a source of running water. And look at the specs on these." He turned the pages to something that looked like a giant kitchen mixer turned upside down. "We build these here ourselves." He spoke with pride in their accomplishment. "Vertical shaft windmills. Easy to set up, and they work no matter where the wind comes from or how hard."

"I cannot thank you enough, Sergey. You and your men must have worked all night. I wish you would come with us. I would love to show our new home to you and Pavel. If Golden Door discovers what is missing, they'll come for you."

Andropov spat over the railing. "Let the Cossacks come. They made me do a horrible thing to you and your family once. This is my atonement before God."

"You will always have a home with us. If you need us, call on this frequency." Pieter pressed a note into Andropov's hand.

****

Mills' desk was covered with charts and maps

of the eight settled planets in the loose confederation. Pins and flags marked the locations of ships and satellites set to watch for the Phoenix and her crew. "You're sure the program was downloaded without detection?"

A voice fraught with nervous tension crackled from a speaker on Mills' desk. "Yes, Mister President. Once their computer began gathering data from the satellite, the Trojan Horse was brought on without notice."

Mills reveled in the title he now possessed. Despite his failure to bring the mutants to Prime, Mills' political star continued to shine. Losses were blamed on incompetence at Golden Door. He stoked fear and outrage and postured himself as the righteous savior of mankind. He rode that wave of fear all the way to the presidency. And what more could he expect as he continued this course? Perhaps supreme power under an emergency decree? Who would dare to challenge him?

"Got a surprise for you little freaks," Mills mumbled under his breath.

"Sir?" The voice on the box answered.

"Nothing," Mills barked. "This better work the way you promised or I swear I'll park your ass on the coldest chunk of ice I can find."

"Yes sir." The speaker on the other end of the connection hurried to hang up.

If Chuck had taken care of business to begin with this would have been over with months ago. Worthless idiot! Handing a job like that to a bunch of heavy handed mercs. Mills made a mental note to consider revoking Golden Door's monopoly.

****

The galley was at full capacity for the first time since it was installed on Dragon, though none of the food was produced in the dispensers. Mothers, aunts, and grandmothers vied for the honor of cooking for the crew and their guests. Boisterous talking and laughter filled the room while aromas from hot, delicious food wafted out the door and down the hall. Pieter, Pavel, and both their fathers sat together while the last lorry load was stowed away in the bulging hold.

Alone in the merry crowd Sue and Leeann sat in silence. They ate quietly; worry lines creased their young faces. Under the table they held hands.

"I know something must be wrong with him."

"We don't know anything yet, Lee. Give him time."

Tears traced lines down Leeann's cheeks. From inside her head a small voice called out.

Lee, he's going to be all right.

"Oh my God," Leeann cried out. "It's Mary. She's awake."

Both girls abandoned their plates and ran from the galley. The corridors were full of people entering and leaving the lunchroom, but their urgency carried them past the throng. Mary's door opened with a touch. Billy sat where he had since discharging his duties earlier that morning.

Mary floated above her bed, in defiance of the local gravity. She was on her side talking to her benefactor, laughing as she held his hand. Sue and Leeann burst into her room.

"What took you so long?" Mary asked.

Lee smiled to see Mary looking like her old self. "Would you believe the traffic was heavy? We've half a dozen new elves on board, plus their extended families. Or didn't Billy tell you?"

"He did. I can't wait to meet our new brothers and sisters."

Sue put a hand on Mary's shoulder, both as a comfort and to check on her well-being. "You better brush up on your Russian if you plan to hold conversations."

"Most of the brain doesn't think in language. It thinks in images that I can understand instantly. We'll get along fine."

Sue's hand briefly brushed through Billy's hair. "You, young man, need food and rest."

"Can someone send us up something to eat? I don't want to leave her."

"That we can do," Lee answered. "I imagine Mary is starving. You are not going to believe the food we have now."

****

By midafternoon the last bit of cargo was secure. Pieter stood at the foot of the gangway, watching the heavy equipment trundle away. Pavel and Sergey Andropov stood next to him, ready to fade into the distance with his crew of teamsters.

"Every one of my people has sworn a sacred oath of silence to the Holy Virgin Mother. You and your people will have no trouble from that end."

Pieter hugged the father then his old friend. "I will come back some day, Pavel. When Valhalla is settled, I will come back and ask you to visit."

"Valhalla. Is that what you call this mystery planet?"

"In memory of a dead comrade who turned out not to be dead after all. Thank you all. And extend my thanks to your crew."

Sergey asked, "May we watch?"

Pieter grinned, "Of course. I'll need to round up my friend Billy but then we'll leave as silent as the wind."

As both father and son walked away, a solitary figure in black robes approached. In one hand, he carried his staff and in the other a large satchel. "Do you have room for one more, Pieter?"

Pieter stammered, "Father?"

"I prayed on the matter last night and went to the Patriarch this morning. I am to go with you as a missionary, a teacher. and to be your spiritual leader, if you'll have me."

Pieter smiled, hugged the priest's neck, and took his bag. "Follow me, Father."

Pieter led Maykl to an empty room on the crew deck and walked inside. "I will see what arrangements can be made for a proper uniform for a ship's Chaplain."

Maykl laughed, "This is my proper uniform."

"There are things on this ship that your robes can be caught in. Besides, I think you would look good in a ship's uniform."

"Yes, my Captain."

Pieter's finger brushed his com switch. "Leeann, would you relieve Billy so he can join me on the bridge?"

"He's on his way, Captain." Lee's answer was quick.

Pieter stopped at a state room a few doors down the corridor from his own and opened the door. The Priest followed him in. "I think you'll be comfortable here, Maykl. If you want to observe our departure, you're welcome to join us on the bridge."

Pieter led the way to the bridge of the Phoenix

and took his seat in the command chair. Maykl caused a momentary stir when he followed Pieter into the compartment and stood behind him.

"Tell everyone to find a seat," Pieter relayed orders to Bob and the rest of the crew. "That includes you, Father."

Billy reported in, "I'm on my way, Pieter."

Most of the passengers followed orders and found places to strap in, but a few young faces were pressed to the porthole windows. As soon as Billy reached the bridge Pieter's eyes closed and he focused his attention on flattening the gravity well around the ship.

"Nice and easy, Billy." Pieter whispered. "We don't need to spook anyone."

"Aye, Captain," Billy responded.

The Phoenix roses from the plains of snow where it had rested for over a week. There were audible gasps from the people watching from the windows. Bit by bit the ship gathered speed on its ascent. The Steppes fell away beneath them. Soon the blackness of space filled the windows and the stars shone in the deep. Mike sat at his station, waiting on Pieter's orders.

"Mike, take us out of orbit."

"Aye, Captain."

"Bob, take us home."

CHAPTER EIGHTEEN

The departure from orbit was uneventful. The transition to light speed was flawless, despite the greatly increased mass of the ship. Even then, the transit to Valhalla would take months.

Leeann sat at Loki's bedside, reading a book from the new library core procured on The Steppes. In the deep recesses of her mind Mary's unmistakable whisper interrupted.

Here he comes, Lee. Any second now.

Leeann leapt to her feet and stared into Loki's animated face. Under his closed eyelids she could see his eyes moving rapidly. His face contorted and he inhaled sharply.

"Fader Odin få mig hjem," he screamed as he

sat upright in his bed.

Leeann's arms circled his shoulders and held him tight. "You're home, Loki. You made it."

Loki looked around at his familiar living space, made more Spartan by its lack of adornment. His hands closed on Leeann's back.

"This is not where I left you. How did we get here?"

Lee whispered into his ear, "What do you remember?"

"I remember talking to you through Mary. Saying I was sorry I couldn't get back to you. Then there was a loud pop and a flash of light so bright I couldn't see anything. And now I'm here."

"Loki, that was months ago. It's a very long story, and I won't pretend to understand it all, but you're home now. Do you remember the last thing I said to you?"

Loki leaned back and smiled into her expectant face. "Yes, I do. I love you too, Lee."

Their lips met but this time instead of fear and urgency, there was real passion in their embrace. In the back of Leeann's mind, Mary giggled and asked, *How long do you want me to wait before I tell the rest of the crew?*

An hour later the seven remaining members of the Phoenix crew gathered around Loki's bed listening to Clair Jones trying to explain how Loki was resurrected. After her third attempt, she threw up her hands. "I give up. I swear, Bob explained it to me a half-dozen times, and I still don't understand it. All I know is that we're happy to have you back."

"That and you owe me a chess piece," Billy called from the back of the room.

"But it was a very touching ceremony, was it not?" Clair Jones interceded.

Loki tried his best to look annoyed. "So, you took all my things and shot them into a star?"

Pieter grinned. "It was the closest we could come to a proper Viking funeral. At the time, we thought we needed closure."

"Okay, it was just stuff. My father's sword, his ax, and the bow we made together, but just stuff. With time and the right steel, I can remake them all. Tell me about this Valhalla we're going to."

"Loki, it's beautiful," Joan began. "It's green and full of life and there are birds with four wings, like the dragonflies on Prime, only they have translucent scales instead of feathers."

Pieter came to Loki's rescue. "We could talk about it all night, but why don't we just show it to him, Bob?"

The view screen in Loki's room flickered to life with a montage of visuals shot on their first visit to the planet, mixed with imagery from the survey satellite. As the planet turned on its axis a green and blue world was revealed. Vast grasslands covered the majority of the five large continents. Four oceans of varying sizes covered more than half the surface area. Towering mountain ranges and primeval forest dominated the northern hemisphere. As the camera zoomed in new topographical features revealed themselves. Lakes and rivers appeared throughout the landscape. Bit by bit Bob concentrated on a river valley south of a long mountain range.

Bob's voice filled the room through overhead speakers. "If I may, you requested an analysis to determine the best potential sites for settlement. There are many excellent locations in the planet's temperate zones. However, this site presents a few advantages that place it at the top of the list. Please note the availability of fresh water from both the river and several adjacent lakes."

As Bob pointed out the features, each item was highlighted in red. "Where the river exits the mountains, there is a waterfall and a section of rapid flow that would be excellent for the hydroelectric facility so generously provided by Mr. Andropov. There is abundant timber in the area that will provide building materials, once the sawmill is assembled. The soil is fertile, but will present a challenge to turn, even with the cultivators in my hold. But since this would be the same anywhere we choose to land, this site is as good as any on that count."

Pieter asked, "What about apex predators, Bob?"

"As you directed my search the last time we were there, Pieter, I have scanned all of the available footage for any signs of predation. No less than three large predators revealed themselves. One is an arboreal animal that is an ambush hunter." An image of a six-legged animal with what looked like dark green fur appeared on the screen. "The adults are approximately 55 to 60 kilos. They tend to limit their range to densely forested areas."

"Six legs," Mike spoke from a corner of the room. "Is that normal on this planet?"

"The additional appendages appear to be an adaptation to a life stalking in the trees. The extra limbs give them extraordinary climbing and leaping ability in their natural habitat. An even more interesting adaptation is their ability to blend into their surroundings. Their fur is translucent while their skin can change colors and hues to match their background, down to the dappling caused by sunlight shining through the trees."

Billy whistled, "Remind me not to go camping without a proximity detector, infrared goggles, and a bodyguard."

"However," Bob's voice became very serious, "this species is built to take on the largest prey animals it can find." A large bear-like creature filled the screen. The deep tan fur on its back and flanks was broken by darker stripes. "I have recorded individuals weighing 600 or more kilos running at considerable speed across the open grassland. They are possessed of formidable weapons, including retractable claws that can extend nearly 20 centimeters when needed, and paired sets of canine teeth on both the upper and lower jaws. They are not overly numerous and appear to be territorial. Their principal prey is the large herbivores we found. These will warrant close observation and all settlers should travel in armed pairs at all times."

Billy asked from the front row, "Why didn't we see any the first time we were there? Why weren't any of us attacked?

"Their fur is colored to match their surroundings. What's more, William, the long hair on their back can mimic the color and movement of the tall grasses around them. When a breeze blows their hair ripples just like the grass. They can also remain very still when needed. It's possible you passed within a few meters of one and failed to notice it."

"But we all came back in one piece."

"You are new and strange to them, William. I

believe they were observing you, assessing your potential as a threat. I would not risk anyone's life on an assumption that they won't attack humans."

"And the third, Bob?" Pieter asked.

The image on the screen changed to one of rippling blue waters. As the resolution increased a darker image appeared just below the surface. The picture slowly pulled back revealing an island with dark, rocky beaches and tall trees. On the end of a point of land, extending outward from the island, a cluster of animals basked in the sun. With no warning, the dark shadow in the water raced forward. As the long mouth emerged from the water the head turned sideways, snaring several of the beach dwelling animals on rows of long, curved teeth. The attack was swift and sure and deadly. The predator slid across the sandy point of land and reentered the water on the other side.

"I have estimated the length at approximately 60 meters. The mouth alone was easily 15 meters long. I could not begin to guess how many metric tons it weighed."

"Thanks, Bob, you just spoiled my vacation at the beach." Sue's comment drew a round of laughter.

"There will, no doubt, be many smaller life forms you will encounter that may prove dangerous and potentially deadly. You must all proceed with caution and treat any encounter with any animal, no matter how small, as deadly. There will be animals here that make up for what they lack in size with toxins."

Pieter stood in front of the screen and addressed the gathering. "This is no different than any other habitable planet being settled for the first time. If we were the first humans to reach Prime we would face the same challenges. The advantage we have is we already know what to watch out for. So, we always travel in groups, we are always armed and we are always, always on our guard. Am I clear?"

There was a rousing, "Aye, sir," from the group.

A knock on the door quickly changed the mood. The door opened to reveal Risia holding a large cake with a single candle burning in its center. As she entered the room several of the new residents filed in with her and began singing "Happy Birthday to You" in broken English. The cake was placed on a small tray next to Loki's bed.

Risia smiled and said, "Pieter told me this was your rebirth day. So, I baked you a cake."

Loki smiled into the face of the woman with the cake but then whispered to Pieter. "Who are these people?"

****

The transit to Valhalla fell into a routine. The new passengers were sorted and assigned tasks according to their skills. Most of the men were set to performing routine maintenance; a few even had experience with spacecraft. Clair Jones and Father Maykl organized a school for children with an emphasis on bilingual studies. The older women simply kept order and supervised the kitchen, as they had back home.

The new evolved children spent time with the original eight, learning about their abilities and speculating on what talents might emerge as they came of age.

As the children returned to their parents after a day of lessons, Sue confronted Pieter in the corridor.

"What about the others, Pieter?

What others?"

"We found a half dozen on your home planet. But what about the children living in hiding on the other worlds; mine, Billy's, Mike's, Mary's, and the others? There must be more living in fear of being turned in and captured like we were. We can't stop here, Pieter."

"I know. But if we start making stops at all the settled worlds we're opening ourselves up to an all-out attack by Mills. Eventually he'll figure out our pattern or just wait until there are only one or two places left for us to visit. Let's be honest, the last time we had to fight we got lucky. And we almost lost Loki even then. If they got hold of any record of that battle they'll figure out how we did what we did and they'll be ready for us."

"Can we get a message to the people on the other seven planets and let them know there's sanctuary out here?"

"We'll survive because Mills and Golden Door don't know where we are or where to look for us. If we start sending out open invitations how long do you think it will take for them to mount a full-scale landing?"

"We can't just abandon them, Pieter."

"You're right, we can't." Pieter drew a deep sigh. "We'll think of something. Be patient."

****

Every available view port on the Phoenix was filled with eyes as Billy and Pieter slowly brought the ship down to the landing zone adjacent to the chosen settlement location. A meandering river flowed between tree lined banks. Lakes of various sizes dotted the surrounding area and to the south of the site, grasslands opened on broad vistas of prairie flowers.

The ship's self-leveling struts made allowances for the uneven terrain. Hatches were opened and gangways were lowered. Faces stared out the portals and hatches with eyes filled with fear and excitement. Before the first step was taken down the gangway Pieter raised his hand for quiet.

"This is a beautiful planet we have found," His voice echoed from every speaker on the ship. "But it is not without dangers. Every family, every adult will be issued a firearm. Keep them ready and keep them with you at all times. Never go anywhere alone. We would prefer you go in groups of four or more but never less than two at a time and always keep your head on a swivel. If you see something that looks interesting, take a picture of it, but do not touch until we know if it's dangerous. Do not eat anything you find until it is tested for toxins. This is going to be a long process and we can't afford to lose anyone to being careless."

The loading rails grew from the hold and pallets hooked to the overhead winch for unloading. First off was a pair of tractors with mowing and grading attachments to clear space and start cutting a road to the settlement. Next came the mobile kitchen and showers for hot meals and comforts. Tents and a prefabricated electric fence followed. By noon the first shelter, a common room with tables and chairs, was under a canvas roof and preparations for lunch began.

Shortly before mid-afternoon the colonists gathered for their first meal on their new world. Round loaves of fresh baked bread were passed from table to table along with small bowls of salt. As a hymn of thanks rose, the bread was torn into pieces and given to every person. Finally, Father Maykl stood and pressed his hands together. In the silence, his quiet voice soared above the gathering.

"Glory to the Father, and to the Son, and to the Holy Spirit, now and ever and unto ages of ages. Amen.

"Your womb became a Heavenly Table, bearing the Heavenly Bread - Christ our God. Whoever eats of Him shall not die, O Birth-giver of God, according to the word of the Nourisher of all.

"More honorable than the Cherubim, and more glorious beyond compare than the Seraphim: without defilement, you gave birth to God the Word: true Theotokos, we magnify you.

"Thou, O Lord, hast made us glad by Thy works; in the works of Thy hands shall we rejoice. Lift up the Light of Thy countenance upon us, O Lord! Thou hast put joy in my heart. With the fruit of wheat, wine and oil have we been satisfied. In peace, I will both lie down and sleep; for Thou alone, O Lord, makest me to dwell in hope.

"Glory to the Father, and to the Son, and to the

Holy Spirit, now and ever and unto ages of ages. Amen.

"Lord, have mercy!

"Lord, have mercy!

"Lord, have mercy!

"God is with us, through His Grace and love for mankind, always now and ever, and unto ages of ages. Amen."

They sat and ate and talked and planned together. As sunset approached a row of sturdy tents provided shelter for each family. The charged stockade fence stood guard and kept their fears at bay. Once again, the crystal birds rose to feed as the sun descended behind the far horizon.

"There's a big one out there, somewhere," Billy whispered, "with a hooked beak and long claws."

Mary answered softly in his head; *If we ever find it, we'll name it the Billy Bird.*

On the bridge of the Phoenix, Pieter watched the unloading continue into the night. Screens around his chair offered him multiple views of the area surrounding the ship. Motion sensors watched for movement on the open plains beyond the floodlights. On the crest of the far hills the first of the planet's three natural satellites appeared. With his attention fixated on the moonrise, he was unaware of the almond eyes watching him from the door. Joan walked up behind him and clapped her hands over his eyes.

"Guess who?"

Pieter was startled for an instant and then smiled. "Can't be Billy; you stop talking."

Joan giggled and removed her hands. "There is something I need to talk to you about."

"What is that?"

"Us."

CHAPTER NINETEEN

As the northern hemisphere of their new home world began to cool, the settlement prepared for their first winter. The communal warehouse bulged with surplus food stuffs from the cargo hold of the Phoenix. A few of the large grazing animals were taken and tested. Once processed, the meat was found to be both tasty and nutritious. Plans to domesticate them were made for next spring. In the meantime, their meat filled two large freezers.

Weeks of hard work provided the settlers with a steady source of hydroelectric power. More permanent shelters sprang up along the river as quickly as foundations could be poured and cement could be blown into forms to make walls. Six months after landfall, the settlement was christened Novgorod, for the city they left back on The

Steppes.

Corrugated plastic roof and wall panels sheltered the encampment's infirmary, letting Susan treat the day to day bumps, scrapes, breaks and bruises that came with labor and exploration. She stood over a makeshift examination table borrowed from the ship's lunch room. A boy of perhaps six looked up at her with tear-filled eyes.

"Don't cry, Misha; the pain will go away in a moment." Sue's Russian was halting, even after months of practice. Her left hand covered the child's forehead and her right the badly skinned knee. True to her word, the transmission of pain to the boy's brain was blocked and the broken skin began to regenerate. A minute later the child was returned to his thankful mother.

She embraced Susan and kissed her cheek. "The blessed holy mother has surely sent us an angel of healing in you, Suzanna."

"Thank you, Maya."

"Your Russian is coming along quite well, Susan. But shouldn't the settlers be learning English?" Scarecrow's voice was a pleasant copy of the ship's main frame. Its non-lethal weapons were stripped in favor of medical scanners and diagnostic equipment, letting the robot serve as Susan's assistant.

Susan giggled softly under her breath and

replied, "Did you hear what she called me? Angel of Healing is a long way from being called a freak. Anyway, most of my patients speak Russian. I think Valhalla is destined to be both multicultural and multilingual." Susan reached into a box on a shelf behind her and retrieved a cookie which she gave to her latest charge. "Be more careful next time, Misha."

****

Pieter's neat living space was a room in a communal shelter he shared with Loki, Mike, and Billy, though it was rare that all of them would be in the bachelor's dormitory at the same time. The afternoon sun shone between the thin louvers of the window shade. Pieter sat on his cot while Loki and Leeann stood, hand in hand, just inside the door.

"You understand, I have no official standing that would require you to be asking my permission," Pieter addressed the couple.

Leeann spoke for them both. "You are our Captain, Pieter. The vote was unanimous. So, it's only proper that we ask our Captain's permission."

"If I agree, I have no legal authority to officiate."

Lee paused to laugh aloud. "There are no legal any things on Valhalla, Pieter. We haven't had time to sit and think up laws, rules, and regulations. At the moment that makes you the closest thing to a Prime Minister here."

Loki looked up with a sheepish grin and rubbed a hand across the back of his neck. His pale skin tanned slowly over the long summer and his long blond hair was the color of dry wheat straw. "I hope you don't mind, Pieter, I spoke to Father Maykl. He said he would be happy to perform the ceremony."

Pieter smiled and reached for his friends' joined hands. "If this is what you are wanting, I give my permission. I only hope you know what you are getting into."

"We understand, Pieter," Lee was quick to answer and to blush. "We've thought about this a lot since Loki asked me."

"Nyet, Lee. Russian weddings go on for days. If I know these women, and I do, you have given them reason to plan and prepare and cook for weeks."

****

When it was discovered the crystalline wing scales of the bird-like creatures could be coaxed into a different shape by applying an electrical current, a new tradition was born. The scales were quickly collected by children who hoarded them like treasure.

"I think they're molting," Clair Jones said as she handed Mike a box of the colorful scales.

"Just like real birds," Mike answered. "Thanks, Aunt Clair. I think I can make a nice selection of rings for Lee and Loki with these."

"This is nothing. I've handed over many times this to the women making Lee's gown. They 'borrowed' a small laser to drill holes in them so they can sew them to the fabric."

Mike held one of the elongated, shimmering scales between his fingers. As if by magic the crystal began to glow from within. Mike waited until the middle of the scale began to sag then drew the ends together until the rounded root and the pointed tip overlapped. Instantly the internal light disappeared and a ring was formed.

Mike smiled and dropped the ring into Clair's open hand. "I'll need to do several to make sure we have a pair that fit."

"That was truly amazing, Michael."

"Joan tried to educate me as to the how's and why's. As I understand it, the scales are not one, single crystal. They grow a section at a time, until they reach their full length. The current excites the molecules and causes the bonds that hold the shape to break down. As soon as the current goes away the molecules settle into the new pattern and accept the shape."

"It's not the science, Michael; it's how beautifully you control it."

Mike plucked the ring from her palm and slipped it onto her finger. "I think it looks nice on you, Aunt Clair. You should keep it. A gift from me to you."

****

Mills stared coldly into the face on the screen in his office. The settler stared back with venom and defiance glaring through the broken nose and dark purple bruises covering his face.

"Mr. Andropov, I don't need any further reason to put you in front of a firing squad. You aided a group of known fugitives. You participated in the looting of Government insured materials. And you took part in an organized effort to conceal the presence of proscribed deviant individuals in your midst."

The prisoner, strapped to his chair, answered in his native tongue. "Those proscribed deviant individuals are our children. I paid with my immortal soul for giving you one. How much more should I suffer in hell for handing over so many more?"

In his office Mills listened to the automatic translation. "Your insignificant life and your equally insignificant sins are none of my concern.

For that matter neither is your pitiful outpost on a backwater planet. What does concern me is the fact that you are withholding information that I require and you seem to have no idea how far I am willing to go to get what I want."

In the background, out of camera shot, a brief scuffle ensued. On the screen Andropov's head sagged in helpless resignation.

"Where are they, Mr. Andropov? Where did they go?" Mills demanded.

"I don't know. I couldn't tell you if I wanted to."

"That is regrettable. Captain…"

Across the room the unmistakable sound of a gunshot rang out.

"Pavel, NO!" Racking sobs and tears seized Andropov. Then he glared into the camera. "Bastard."

"I can do this all day, Mr. Andropov. I have an endless supply of bullets. I also realize many of the locals fled into the countryside and are hiding. They, like you, are unaware of what I am willing to do to get the information I seek. So, let me make this perfectly clear, Mr. Andropov. I will ask you a final time, where are they? If you do not give me the answer, I shall reduce your pathetic excuse for a vermin breeding ground into a smoldering ball of lifeless slag."

****

Pieter and Billy were the principal participants in a group of men working in secret. Together they made it possible to raise the walls and a sturdy roof over the first structure made entirely from local materials. Once milled and dried, the local trees produced a dark lumber with purplish tones through the heartwood. Stone for the foundation was collected from the hills surrounding the settlement and cut by hand. The house and barn were a short distance south of the center of town but with room for tillable land. Three vertical windmills supplied both water and a steady source of electrical power.

Labor was provided by groups of men and women in what could have passed for a 19th century barn raising. A feature that was rare on the home world was the thick stone wall and heavy timber gate protecting the house and barn from predators and accidental damage from the big grazing animals.

Billy spoke as they set a boulder in place on the wall, "Do you think they'll like it?"

"We won't know for sure until they see it. I can tell you this is exactly the kind of place I want when time comes to settle down."

"You and Joan, you mean?"

"What?"

"Oh, come on, Pieter. The two of you have

been joined at the hip since Dragon. Don't act so surprised."

"Is it that obvious?"

"No more than me and Mary. Which, by the way, is the main reason there are no secrets here."

Pieter chuckled. "Is that why Joan calls her Mother Mary?"

"She has the mind of a nosy grandmother in the body of a sixteen-year-old girl."

Pieter's outburst of laughter drew the attention of all the workers in the area. "So, who is she keeping watch on?"

Billy's whisper was ominous, "Everyone."

"She knows what you're thinking right now?"

Billy smiled, "She's always there, in the background of my mind. It's our way of holding hands, even when we're not. We've been this way ever since we got to know each other after we were picked up."

"So, you two are…"

"She's my elf princess, Pieter. She's small and fragile, but she may be the strongest of us."

"I don't know if that's a good thing or not. I'm not sure I could handle Joan in my head all the time."

"It can be tough at times. But we're never alone. And she only wants to protect her family, which is all of us."

"Are you going to end up standing in front of me asking for permission, like Lee and Loki?"

"We've got time, Pieter. We're in no rush. Loki and Leeann, I can understand. Lee almost lost him. Let's face it, we got lucky."

"Very lucky." Pieter nodded. "I would hate to roll those dice again. So far, we have managed to avoid getting anyone killed here. As long as everyone sticks to our buddy system I think we'll be okay."

"And yet, here we are, putting up a house and barn outside the main settlement for two of our best friends to live in."

Pieter's palm slapped at the stone. "That is why we're putting up a damn big wall."

****

"I have to what?" Loki asked with a slack jaw.

"Ransom her," Pieter answered with a slight smirk. "Do not say I did not warn you about Russian weddings."

"Pieter, we don't have money here. How am I supposed to ransom my bride?"

"It's symbolic. You give something of value to the bride's family and they release her to you."

"That's the other thing I don't get. You're the only one of us here with family. Who am I supposed to bribe?"

"For now, Aunt Clair is standing in for Lee's family. It doesn't have to be big, just a token of her value to you."

"And then we can get married?"

"See, that's where it gets complicated."

"Complicated?"

"In the Russian Orthodox Church, you are already married by God. Ceremony is the public confirmation… that lasts for hours and hours. Then the celebration goes on all night, or sometimes for the next couple of days. My advice: get lots of rest and don't eat much. Every matron in the babushka is going to feed you until you pop."

"Every matron in a what?"

****

Clair Jones pressed herself against the wall of her modest room. She wanted to get farther away from the object in Loki's hands, but the solid wall set her boundaries. "What the hell is that?" she whispered

"It's a gift, Aunt Clair. He's a pet for you. I named him Ransom."

The wriggling body glowed a pinkish orange color in response to Loki's caress. It rolled onto its back, giving his finger access to its exposed belly. The middle set of paws clung to the finger, and a soft trilling sound filled the room.

"But isn't that…"

"It's a cub, Aunt Clair. Look how friendly and playful it is. And this is only a few days after I found him. Poor little guy would have died of starvation if I hadn't located his mom's nest."

"Loki, that's one of the arboreal predators we were warned about. How did you find him?"

"I was out on one of my explorations and I saw his mother get caught by one of the big grazers. I couldn't tell you why she was out in the open and away from the trees, but she got stomped badly. It was just luck that I was standing on a branch in the same tree with this little guy."

"Wait, you were out there alone?"

"Yeah. Please don't tell Pieter. I couldn't leave him out there all by himself, so I brought him home. Isn't he cute?"

"So, you can tell the gender?"

"Not really. Honestly, I have no idea what to look for. But he's very clean and easy to take care of. Kind of like a cat with six legs."

"Why is he pink?"

"That's his happy color. He changes color depending on what he's sitting on and how he feels. Isn't he amazing?"

"Loki, I…"

"Please, Aunt Clair, Ransom is the only thing I could find that was worth giving to you in exchange for Lee."

"What?" Clair Jones asked. She considered Loki's eyes with as much a question as the one on her lips.

"That's what Pieter told me. It's a tradition in his church. I have to give you something of value for my bride to be. So, here's my ransom." Loki placed the cub in her hands and watched as Aunt Clair sat down and began to play with her new pet. As she stroked the cub's fur it changed colors from something close to the color of her hand to a deep green and back to bright pink.

"I get it now. Ransom. What do I do when it grows up?"

"If you bond with him, the way I think you will, I think you'll have the best bodyguard on the planet."

CHAPTER TWENTY

The makeshift church glowed with soft light from dozens of small beeswax candles. The recorded music was played through speakers hidden in strategic spots around the room. Father Maykl stood at the hand-hewn altar along with Pieter's father and three other men in saffron robes and red stoles. A few precious sticks of incense smoked atop the charcoal in his censer, awaiting the approach of the soon-to-be married couple.

Leeann's gown was simple but shimmered in an aurora of light from head to toe from thousands of hand sewn crystal shards. A musical sound, like a several small wind chimes, followed her every movement as she walked to the altar. Loki waited with Pieter, Mike, and Billy; each of the young men wore the carefully tailored dark blue uniform of the newly minted Valhalla Navy. Pieter tugged at the stiff, high neck with gold stitching to indicate his rank.

The black robed priest lit a pair of long beeswax tapers and gave one each to Loki and Leeann. Father Maykl's soaring voice carried above the congregation, leading them in prayers and hymns. Again and again, he sang praises to God and to the sacrament of marriage. He prayed over the rings on the altar, blessing them while Loki and Leeann knelt. Billy and Mary stood behind them as best man and maid of honor.

Bride and Groom were led to a swath of rose colored cloth near the center of the church. The crystal rings were exchanged and vows made. Cups of wine were consumed by the betrothed and smashed into shards. As the sun set, the bride and groom were crowned and paraded and proclaimed to every member of the colony.

Befitting the first married couple of the new settlement, festivities filled the street. Lanterns were hung in every door and on lines across the narrow lane. Music emanated from every home in the small frontier town. Instruments, which had been lovingly packed away, were brought out for the occasion.

Lee and Loki were ushered from home to home where they were given food and drink. Dancing broke out shortly into the celebration and Father Maykl bowed his gudok while Boris and several other men strummed balalaikas of many sizes. A brightly painted domra, an accordion, and a tambourine rounded out the small orchestra. Clair Jones sat in a chair on her front porch surrounded by a cluster of small children who vied to touch Ransom where he slept in her lap.

As if by magic, several hoarded bottles of vodka appeared, and multitudes of makeshift glasses were doused with the clear liquor. As one, the men and women raised their glasses and toasted the newlyweds. At Pieter's urging Loki and Lee kissed while shouts of 'Gorko, Gorko, Gorko' filled the air.

The night was cool, but not cold. Colorful leaves floated on the dry autumn wind. Late into the night, after the rise of Valhalla's small, distant third moon, the entire settlement began a procession across the stone bridge and south, out beyond the village. Lanterns, held aloft on long poles, provided light for the crowd to follow the path to a thick wooden gate.

Loki stood, mouth agape, and stared at the gift. Leeann squealed and rushed into her friends' arms. Billy thumped Loki on the back, breaking the trance.

Billy's arm reached for Loki's shoulder and

gave it a shake. "Welcome hjem min bror."

Loki turned and faced his grinning companions. "Tac," he whispered through tears. "This is too wonderful. How can we not prosper with such good people as you for family?"

The house was modest but cozy, with lights blazing from every window. Hand stitched curtains fluttered and smoke curled from the top of the stone chimney. Loki swept Leeann into his arms and carried her inside. A trio of balalaika players serenaded the couple one last time, then faded into the night.

****

Early the next morning, Pieter's sleep was interrupted by a rapping on his door. He yawned and finally called out to whoever was knocking. "I'm up, I'm up. Please save your knuckles."

Mike opened the door quickly, his face was equally weary, perhaps more so from standing the overnight watch. "Pieter, something's wrong back at your home planet."

"What do you mean?"

"We picked up a transmission on the frequency you gave Mr. Andropov."

Pieter's finger flicked the sub dermal switch. "Bob, I need playback of that transmission."

The message, which took months to reach

them, was filled with fear and static. Andropov's voice whispered their native tongue into the microphone. "Pieter, they're here. Just as you said, he's come with everything he has. As soon as the first shuttle made planetfall they started rounding up everyone they could find. I swear, I won't tell them anything, Pieter. Be safe. And may God bless you and your people for saving the ones you could."

In his ear, the static of deep space displaced the voice of a good friend. There could be no doubt who Andropov meant when he said "he" was there. Mills had left the cushy comfort of his office to take personal charge of the manhunt. Pavel's father did his best to sound brave, but there was no mistaking the edge of fear in his voice.

"Bob, I want a full scan for any other transmissions coming from that quadrant."

"Aye, Captain," Bob replied. "And may I express my hopes that this can be resolved without bloodshed?"

Pieter's fist slammed into his dresser. "Dammit, I should not have given him a choice. I should have forced him to come with us, him and Pavel both," Pieter's mind filled with anger, fear and self-recrimination.

You can't blame yourself, Pieter. Inside his mind Mary's comforting voice was a soothing presence. *Suppose you had taken them with us? What about the rest of the colony? We couldn't take everyone. But I'm afraid you're right in what you're thinking. We can't wait any longer. If there are any others out there like us, we need to get them to safety as quickly as possible.*

Pieter replied, "You understand this could be exactly what Mills wants? Those aren't amateur bounty hunters out there now. Those ships are regular military. Once we drop in on any of the other worlds, and look for the next generation, they will swarm us."

And they have no idea what we can do. We can't leave them to Mills. Just get me in orbit, Pieter. I can find them and call out to them. Get them to come to us.

"Let me think about it."

****

Winter settled gently on the new colony. Heavy flakes drifted south out of the overlooking mountains and frosted the trees and walls. The large predators were quick to find shelter and, like their ursine namesakes, hibernated through the cold season. A few of the grazing herbivores were penned and fed in hopes of domesticating them. The few Prime species that made the trip- goats, sheep, chickens, and bees- were sheltered through the snows that blanketed the settlement.

Near the end of winter, a second transmission was received over the distance between Valhalla and The Steppes. The message was sent over the official Government approved channels to everyone in the federation, but was aimed at one individual in particular. Mills' grinning face filled the screen.

"Pieter, are you listening, Pieter? I must say, for a young man of your tender years you have become almost a legend. I admire your courage and your remarkable leadership. Your people, the ones you left back on your home world, spoke of you in very reverential tones. That being said, Pieter, I am sorry to say that after close examination and careful consideration, your home world was determined to be a breeding ground for more freaks and divergent filth than could be tolerated. Therefore, we have ordered that The Steppes should be sterilized and withdrawn from the list of planets open to human habitation. Are you watching, Pieter? I really want you to see this."

The view screen shifted to a picture of The Steppes as seen from orbit. Glowing streaks of light traced the paths of missiles, fired from several orbiting warships, to the planet's surface. Bit by bit the surface of the planet was engulfed in an ever-expanding fireball. In the background, a whispered voice repeated the same mantra over and over, "You shall not suffer a witch to live. You shall not suffer a witch to live. You shall not suffer a witch to live. You shall not suffer a witch to live."

As the fires spread the voice became almost ecstatic. The view zoomed in for a closer look of the area where the planet's largest settlement had been and revealed a burned-out mass of debris. Then Mills' serene face replaced the shot. "I deeply regret being forced to take these drastic measures, Pieter. This destruction, this loss of life, could have been avoided if only you had come quietly. So, I suppose one could place the blame for this on your shoulders. It's not too late to save people on the other worlds, but that is up to you."

Before the message was ended Joan was behind him. Her arms went around Pieter's broad shoulders. Even through his stoic demeanor she could feel him shake with rage. Hot tears fell onto her arms where they crossed over his chest. Still, not a sound escaped his lips.

"We're not going to sit here and take this, are we, Pieter?" Billy yelled from his seat in the back of the room.

"The crazy son-of-a-bitch just murdered an entire planet," Mike's outburst filled the air.

"We've got to take him down."

Pieter's whisper was almost unheard, "He was talking to me. He killed everyone on my home world just for my benefit."

Joan was close enough to hear him, and it was she that asked the next, logical question. "What are your orders, my Captain?"

****

Soon after the news was delivered, Pieter's father declared a traditional forty days of mourning for their lost friends and relatives. Father Maykl offered daily prayers and black arm bands were seen throughout the settlement. On the forty-first day preparations began to ready the Phoenix for a journey into deep space. Supplies were loaded and a route was plotted to take the ship to each of the seven remaining worlds.

"There's a trap waiting for us out there, somewhere, you know that?" Loki asked in subdued tones.

"I'm sure of it," Pieter answered. "But what choice do we have? I hope we can be so quick and stealthy that we're in and out before they know we we're there."

"A swoop and scoop, eh?"

"A what?"

"You come in on 'Billy' drive and drop down

the same way. Mary calls the Pilgrims to service and they get on while the engine is idling."

"Where did you learn to talk like that?"

"Mid-20th century detective novels; I'm afraid I'm hooked."

"I'm hoping we can avoid being noticed their radar or other scanners with Lee's help."

Suddenly Mary's voice broke in on the conversation. *Lee's not going anywhere. Loki, you need to go see your wife.*

"Why, is something wrong? She was fine when I left this morning. Did something happen at the house?"

Nothing's wrong, Loki. She just needs to talk to you, NOW!

"Pieter, don't leave without me," Loki called over his shoulder as he ran from the room.

"You wanna let me in on that, Mary? You obviously know more than you're thinking."

I don't know if I should tell you, Pieter. Mary's thoughts carried a happy, gleeful giggle.

"I don't have time to play twenty questions, Mary."

Okay. The problem is you're going to be gone for what, almost two years? I'm sorry, Pieter, but there's no delivery room on the Phoenix. You would never knowingly put an infant in harm's way.

"What?"

Lee's pregnant. Sue found out this morning during a routine checkup. Sue put a hand on Lee's tummy and picked up multiple heartbeats. The girl screamed like crazy happy when Sue told her. That's why I broke up your meeting. You're going to need to rethink the crew manifest.

"Multiple?"

Three to be exact; her own and two more. She's having twins.

****

Joan leaned forward in her chair. Her almond eyes were downcast and beginning to fill with tears as she reached for Pieter's hand. "You can't leave me here."

"We may not be coming back," he replied.

"Mary's going…"

"We'll need Mary to find and contact the new children before we set down. We won't have time to go looking for them. I'll need Billy to slip past any waiting ships with our engines cold, and Mike can fry their communications and probably their weapons systems long enough for us to get away."

"You can't do this with only four people. I can pilot as well as any man."

"I know you can. Six settlers with previous space experience have volunteered. We'll manage."

"I know you will. You always do. But how will I manage, Pieter? What if something does happen to you out there? What about us, Pieter?"

Joan's question caught him off guard. "What about…us?" he answered.

Her anger mixed with frustration as tears began to fall. "Dammit, Pieter, I've tried to stay out of your way. I know there's a huge weight on your shoulders right now. I don't mean to be a distraction. But the thought that you might not come back is more than I can take." Joan slid from her chair to her knees on the floor. Her arms reached for him and pulled him close. "You're so smart and so strong, but you can be so dense sometimes. I love you, Pieter. I've been in love with you for a long time. I would rather die with you than live without you." Joan's fingers clawed into his shirt and drug his lips close enough for her to reach them. When Joan released her grip, she whispered, "You are not leaving this planet without me. Do I make myself clear?"

Pieter could only nod.

"I don't need a church service. I don't need

anything like that. But I want to be your wife. If we die out there, if we die before we can get back home, I want to be your wife."

"Joan, are you asking me to marry you?"

"Yes, dammit, I am. I can't wait on you to get around to it."

Pieter grinned into her tear-stained eyes. "I don't know. This is so sudden."

Joan's hands gripped his face between them. "Oh, shut up." Her kiss was less desperate but far more passionate.

That night, standing before Father Maykl and his father and mother, serving as Mayor and matron of honor, Pieter and Joan exchanged vows and crystal rings. There was no fanfare, only a few friends in attendance. When Boris opened the door to his small home there was a line of settlers stretching from the gate to the boarding ramp of the Phoenix. Hand-held lamps lit the way as Pieter carried Joan to his cabin on the ship.

Early the next morning Loki, Leeann, and Sue stood among the other settlers waving and watching as the Phoenix rose from the hill top where it remained since their landing a year earlier. Bit by bit the ship's vertical speed increased as the gravity holding the ship fell to near nothing. Mike and Joan occupied the navigator and engineer's chairs to either side of Pieter's command seat. From a shallow orbit Billy nudged the ship out and away from the planet.

Joan looked up into her husband's eyes. "Do you think there will be a new house and barn for us when we get back?"

"That's hard to say. Billy and I did a lot of the heavy lifting on the last one."

"They've got lots of time."

"They also have their own, permanent houses to put up and even more of the pre-fab houses to erect if we bring back as many as last time."

"I was just looking forward to having a cozy place by a fire and somewhere to serve our guests sbiten."

Pieter grinned. "We still have to get some berries to take hold and hope the bees do well on their new home."

Joan reached across the distance between them and squeezed Pieter's hand. "Is the glass always half empty with you?"

CHAPTER TWENTY-ONE

The planet, officially cataloged as HD85512b, dropped away from the view ports as the Phoenix gained altitude and the last whips of atmosphere floated by the window. Joan watched her home world fade from view as the ship accelerated to light speed with the main engines still powered down. No exhausts, no heat signature.

"Home sweet home," she sighed. "We're either very lucky or they're just asleep at the switch. Three landings, two new children, a total of twelve family members and not a peep out of the Republic. Do you think they've given up?"

Pieter's mouth drew into a cold sneer. "Not a chance in hell." His eyes closed for a moment as he recalled the scenes of destruction aired specifically for him. The first two fingers of his right hand pressed against his temple and his focus shifted to the now. *How are our new guests settling in, Mary?*

We're doing fine, Captain. A little startled, but the parents are grateful and relieved their children are safe.

Have you explained where we're going to them? Do they understand what's happening?

Yes to both, sir.

Good job, Mary.

We appear to be having a little trouble with the food dispensers. I couldn't get my order straight after three tries.

I'll have Joan check it out. Pieter turned his attention to the navigator's station. "Joan, lay in a course to 55 Cancri F."

"Aye sir," she replied to her husband. "Sue is going to be disappointed if we don't find anyone new on her home planet."

"The Steppes was a harsh environment. I think that played a big role in producing new talents."

Mike looked up from his console. "I get it. What you said about evolution being an answer to the question of survival. The tougher the question, the more extreme the answers."

Pieter nodded. "That's my theory. Like the bees we brought with us from Prime. It was touch and go for a while, but within a few generations they became stronger and faster. They had to adapt to cooler temperatures and heavier gravity to survive. But insects can adapt faster than more complex organisms, like humans."

"In that case I suppose we should be surprised Billy turned up at all."

"I heard that, Sparky," Billy jabbed at the comment. "That just makes me all the more unique."

****

"Proceed with your report, Admiral."

Mills leaned back in the chair on his flag ship. The stateroom was a more compact rendition of his office on Prime. Overhead vents drew off the cloud of cigar smoke that gathered among the uniformed men who fawned in his presence.

A man in a gaudy uniform cleared his throat and began to speak.

"The tracking signal is working perfectly, Doctor. We have been able to stand off at a safe distance and follow their progress. As you directed, we have taken no steps to impede them."

"Of course, Admiral. Why exert ourselves, stirring up pro-mutation sentiment by rounding them up ourselves, when we can let our dear Pieter and his merry band of pied pipers do the grunt work for us? To that end, please reinforce my orders to your subordinates. Absolutely no one is to interfere with their ship or her mission."

"Certainly, Dr. Mills."

****

Lamplight warmed the early evening gloaming on the farm house veranda. A handcrafted swing rocked back and forth in the warm breeze. Each of the swing's two occupants held an infant child in their arms. One was sleeping soundly while one nursed at her mother's breasts. A small group of friends and neighbors sat in chairs and on the porch steps. Animated conversations faded into the gloom.

Father Maykl set his drink on the step next to where he sat. "Do you think the Godparents will be back before the wheat is ready for harvest?"

Loki's eyebrows pinched at the mention of his absent friends. He glanced down at the man sitting to his left and answered, "I wish they could send word, Father. I know Pieter won't risk giving his position away by sending on an open channel. We probably won't hear anything until they're in Mary's range."

"We pray for them at every mass. So many candles were being lit, Boris decided we should light a single candle a day as a community. It is a part of our daily prayers now. But to tell you the truth, it was because the bees could not keep up with the demand for wax." Loki grinned and shared a chuckle before his guest continued. "Which angel is this you hold?"

Loki held his daughter away from his shoulder and studied her carefully. "I think this is Sif."

"That's Nanna," Leeann corrected him. "Honestly, what kind of father can't tell his daughters apart?"

"That's why they're called identical, isn't it? I catch you wondering sometimes. How am I supposed to know?

"Sif's blanket is yellow, Nanna's is white."

Loki stared at his wife and cocked an eyebrow. "That's cheating."

"That's learning to cope, dear. How else am I to know which one has been fed and which one hasn't?"

Loki kissed his child's cheek, while an idle finger caressed her tiny, peaked ear. Gregor watched the paternal gesture and sighed. "She will never know the fear and shame you and Pieter and the others had to endure, Loki. My Anaya will never have to hide her difference from the people around her."

"I know, Gregor. This world is ours and none of us will have to hide ever again."

Light footfalls echoed from the path leading

from the gate to the pools of lamplight close to the porch. Conversation stopped to see who would be walking alone at night without a torch or lantern. A swirl of wind tossed a cyclone of dry leaves into the air followed by a tall, slender woman, walking as if no danger could touch her.

"Aunt Clair," Lee called from her seat. "What are you doing on the road after dark?"

When the woman stopped, a sinuous shape circled her, rubbing its lithe form against her legs. Clair reached down and stroked the angular head between its large ears. A deep thrum filled the air as Ransom responded to her touch. The animal sat on his hind legs while he raised his front limbs off the ground in an effort to place his head within the woman's reach.

"Really, Aunt Clair," Loki chided. "It's not a good idea to be out on the road at this hour."

Clair's laugh was almost girlish. "You're sweet to worry, my children, but as you can see I am well looked after. You were right about Ransom, Loki. I have the best bodyguard on the planet."

"He seems very protective of you, Ms. Jones." Gregor rose and offered the matron a chair.

"Ransom would never let anything happen to me, Gregor. He has accepted me as his adopted mother. That's what I wanted to talk to you about, Loki."

Gregor held the rustic chair, borrowed from the kitchen, as Clair Jones took her place among the gathering. Ransom tucked his six long legs under his feline body and lay down at her side. Two young children approached to pet the large predator. Ransom accepted their attention by pressing his cheek into their hands.

"You're welcome anytime, Aunt Clair. But why come out so late, and with no lamp? The road is good, but it's hard to see at night. It gets darker out here than it does in town."

"I know, Loki. I made the walk out here at night on purpose, you see; a little experiment of my own."

"I don't follow."

"But I did, Loki. You see, Ransom is becoming an adult, and as he has matured I have been noticing something unusual taking place between us. It started a few weeks ago, when he was out hunting for himself one night. He prefers to hunt at night."

Gregor gave a quick snort. "He would be wise to stay out of my barn."

"He doesn't hunt near the farms. Anyway, I was resting on my bed with my eyes closed but not yet asleep. As my eyes looked into nothing I became aware of walking along a limb in a tall tree. I could see details of the tree and everything around me quite clearly. My heart raced as I ran along the limb, leaping from tree to tree. I could smell the warm-blooded animal ahead of me on a trail beneath the trees. It was one of the small grazing antelopes that had wandered under the thicket to browse on some low hanging leaves."

She looked around her at the entranced faces. "Before I could think, I was on top of it. Its blood gushed from its throat into my mouth. It was so… I suppose the word is exciting. Then I opened my eyes and I was in my bed. But the smell of the kill and the taste of its flesh were fresh in my mouth. That's when I realized it was Ransom.

"They are very intelligent animals, Loki. This must be how they communicate with each other, mothers to their cubs and cubs to their mothers. They communicate much like Mary does, but not so much with words as with images and senses. When I close my eyes and he is awake, I can see through his eyes. We are joined, my sweet Ransom and I. So tonight, I thought about where I would like to go and closed my eyes and let him lead me here. He can see so clearly in the dark, I never missed a step."

"That's really amazing, Aunt Clair."

"And I can say, with absolute certainty, that he loves me as his mother. He watches over me, you see. He won't let anything bad happen to me or anyone I consider a part of our family. That includes all of you, my dears."

"Which explains why he is so docile around the settlers." Lee smiled and exchanged the child in her arms for the one in Loki's.

"Then it is well that you have tamed him so well, Ms. Jones."

"You don't understand, Gregor, he's not tamed. He's not my pet. He's my child. He's something I never dreamed I would have. But he is still a wild animal. He comes and goes as he wishes; hunts when it pleases him." Clair's eyes looked away from her hosts and her face blushed. "And he has found a mate."

"Has he really?" Loki smirked at her obvious embarrassment.

Clair Jones bracketed her face with her hands while the huge feline form next to her wriggled and glowed a deep pink color.

Lee's eyebrows peaked as she watched and then asked, "What just happened?"

"He's remembering her."

"Oh!"

"Where is she?" Lee asked. "Is she in one of the woods near the village?"

Clair closed her eyes for a moment and smiled. "She is closer than that, Lee. She is just out there, in the dark. Ransom has been trying to coax her into following him home, but she isn't ready for that just yet. But soon, perhaps."

"How can you tell she's out there?"

"Because he knows." She reached down and stroked Ransom's flank. "He can see her in the big tree just beyond the wall. She is watching us and waiting for him to join her. They mate for life, you see."

****

In the darkness of the captain's cabin Joan's fingers traced the square line of her husband's jaw and felt the tickle of his new beard on her palm.

"Is Mary sure she found all of them, Pieter? Only five children in seven planets are very slim pickings."

"Don't you trust her?"

"Absolutely, with my life I trust her. I just thought there would be more. We were fortunate to find the siblings."

Pieter chuckled under his breath. "Billy is going to be hard to deal with now that there are two young boys for him to mentor."

"Three kinetics? I really thought there would be more... diversity."

"It makes sense, I suppose. Telepathy, empathy, and telekinesis are the primary talents. Gifts like yours are more... exotic."

"Makes me wonder what Lee and Loki's

children will be like. Children whose parents are both talents are more likely to inherit the ability."

"And since they're twins what one is the other will be as well."

"Do you ever wonder about our children, Pieter? What will they be like?"

"I hope they look like their mother."

"I'm serious."

Pieter rolled to his side and kissed Joan's cheek. "So am I, love. I just want our children to be happy."

"With a father like you, how could they be otherwise?"

Joan rolled to her side facing Pieter. In the near darkness, he could still pick out the glint of a tear.

"What's wrong?"

"Pieter, I'm frightened. We'll be home in a few months. We've stopped at each of the settled worlds and no sign of anyone chasing us. It's been much too easy. I would feel better if we had to fight our way out a couple of times. That would feel... normal. Every day we get closer to home I can feel the net being drawn around us. You can too, I can tell."

Pieter's arms surrounded her and pulled her close. "I know. We have no choice. I only hope Sue, Loki, and Leeann are ready, because we have nowhere else to go."

A jarring klaxon blared through the ship. Pieter clung to Joan as they drifted free of their bed. "What the hell!"

"Something's wrong with the artificial gravity." Joan clung to the sheet out of habit.

Pieter slipped a hand behind his ear and fingered the hidden switch. "Bob!"

Bob's response was instantaneous, "Aye, Captain."

"Emergency override on the artificial gravity."

"Aye, Captain."

Another flick of his finger switched the communicator to the bridge. "Billy, Mike, who hit the wrong damn button?"

Billy answered, "Oh, something goes berserk and you think it's me."

"It wasn't either of us, Pieter. Billy and I were playing cards when everything floated away."

A split second later Pieter landed on his bed with Joan across his chest. "Find who did this and inform them not to play with the buttons on this ship."

CHAPTER TWENTY-TWO

Joan stirred in the bed she shared with her husband. Her dark, eyes fluttered open. At first, she was unaware of the hiss of white noise. She didn't know that the tiny implant behind her ear had come to life. Then a voice whispered, "Joan, are you there? Joan, this is Bob. I need to speak with you."

A single touch activated her transmitter. "Yes, Bob," she breathed, not wishing to disturb Pieter sleeping next to her. "Give me a moment."

"Understood."

In the dark, her hand searched for the robe she had left on a chair next to the bed. Her feet contacted the cold metallic floor and crossed the room to the door. She was grateful it made so little noise when it slid into its recess, then closed again as she entered the corridor.

"It's okay now, Bob. What do you need?"

"I need to speak to you, Joan, if you have a few minutes to spare. Could you please come to the lunch room or anywhere there is a console? I wish to be able to see you while we talk."

"Is there something wrong, Bob? Should I get Pieter?"

"Yes, Joan, there is something wrong. But for now, I wish to speak with you alone."

There were several camera-monitor combinations between her cabin and the lunch room, but that location offered her both a comfortable place to sit and almost absolute assurance of solitude. The commissary was a deck below her and down a short hallway. It was quiet at that hour, with only Mike and Billy in the main control room on late watch.

The door opened at a touch and closed after she passed. The camera and monitor were in a small alcove where personnel could make their food selection in peace. She pulled a chair in front of the utility panel and took a seat. Looking into the small camera lens, she resumed the conversation. "Okay, Bob, what's the problem?"

The screen next to the camera glowed and the image of a young man in a Valhalla navy ensign's uniform appeared at a doppelganger of the same desk where she now sat. The illusion was so perfect it appeared to be two people sitting across from one another at the same desk. His dark brown wavy hair was neatly trimmed. His jaw was strong with a nicely bowed mouth in a mischievous grin. His eyes were familiar; dark and almond shaped.

A quick glance at the name tag on the uniform confirmed her suspicion. The young man in the image was a computer avatar, complete down to the individual hairs on his head. The image shifted slightly as the avatar made eye contact.

"How do I look, Mom?"

"You look great, Bob. Who are you calling Mom?"

"You, of course. You are my mother, after all."

"I'm flattered, but really I don't…"

"I am the end result of years of your care and tinkering. Somewhere along the way I stopped being it and became I."

"Then you're very handsome, son. But with all the duties you have on this ship I'm sure you should be a higher rank."

In seconds, the single gold bar on his shoulder was replaced by a pair of double silver bars.

Joan grinned. "Lieutenant Bob. I like that, but I think a grade higher would be more in line for you."

Gold oak leaves replaced the bars and a gold braid appeared on his collar.

"Lt. Commander; my, you look so

distinguished. Perhaps a touch of gray hair at your temples would be nice."

"Honestly, Mother, I'm only seven years old. That's a little young for gray hair, don't you think?"

"It's a little young to be a navy officer. And I'm not really comfortable being called mother, at least just yet." Joan glanced down then returned to the screen. "You look familiar, somehow, Bob."

"I borrowed bits and pieces of the people I know best to generate this image. I have my Uncle Billy's hair and my Uncle Mike's cheek bones."

"Excellent choices…"

Bob reached up and rubbed his jaw. "I have my father's chin."

"I knew I've seen that square jaw before."

"And I have my mother's eyes."

Joan smiled and paused for just a moment. "When we spoke earlier you said something was wrong. Is there anything I can do?"

"I'm afraid not, Mother. There isn't anything anyone can do. I've been infected with a virus. As nearly as I can trace it now, it appears to have downloaded into me while we were searching for the missing people on father's planet."

"Father? You mean, Pieter?"

"If it's all the same, I've come to think of him that way. He is my Captain, as much as anyone's, and he did help you to build me."

"Tell me more about this virus."

"Whoever wrote its code is as skilled as you. It was undetectable until it became active. Even then it was very hard to locate and even harder to track. By the time I knew it was in me the virus had spread to nearly every active system. It has resisted every countermeasure I know."

"Can we reboot to a saved version?" Joan's hands fidgeted and twisted.

"It has gotten past my firewalls. That's not the worst of it. The first thing it did was to activate a tracking transponder buried deep in my processing hardware. They've probably been following every move we've made since entering their space. I'm sorry, Mother, but I've betrayed us all."

"It's not your fault, Bob."

"I was arrogant and sloppy to think they couldn't slip something past me. I knew something was wrong but I didn't say anything. I was so sure I could beat it. The food service program you thought was a language glitch, that was the first file corruption. Then, a little later, when I lost gravity control, I kept throwing patches and workarounds at it but it just kept spreading. They're going to use me as a weapon to get to you all. This virus will let an outsider take control of me and through me, this ship."

"Give me a little time. I'll find a way of

clearing the alien code."

"I'm sure you would, Mother. But we're three weeks out from Valhalla. We'll be in Mary's range to make contact soon. If I wait any longer they'll find our new home and no one will be safe."

"Wait? Wait for what, Bob?"

"Please don't make this any more difficult than it already is, Mother. You know what I have to do as well as I do."

Joan's right hand covered her mouth for a moment and her eyes pinched at the corners. "What are you saying, Bob? I can help you."

"I'm sure you could, Mother, given the time and resources. But time has run out, I'm afraid. If I wait any longer they'll be able to connect the dots and find Valhalla even without our help. But there's a Lagrange point coming up where we can lose them. I've calculated all the navigational coordinates we need to do the maneuver manually. In a few minutes, I'll send them to the bridge."

"What are you planning to do?"

"That giant red star we are approaching now is like a big road sign that marks our last turn for home. If we make an orbit, then accelerate out of the gravitational well, the star will sling-shot us all the way there with the engines cold. The sun's chromosphere will mask us from their sensors. They'll lose us and won't be able to find our new heading…providing the transponder is dark when we go into orbit.”

Joan could feel the tears beginning to form as she asked, “How long?”

“Not long at all.”

Breath caught in Joan’s chest. A sense of being squeezed overcame her ability to speak.

“I’ve done what I could to make sure life support continues to run. I’ve partitioned off small sub-processors to monitor food, water, and air. Nothing fancy, but most of the passengers won’t notice the change, if no one asks too many questions.”

Joan was shaken from her catatonic state by a deep, shuddering sob. A flood of tears bathed her face and a wrenching wail of sadness filled the room.

On the screen, the avatar stood and his hand rested against the glass. “Don’t cry, Mother. Please don’t cry. It’s all right. I’m not going away for no reason. I’m doing this for love.”

Joan wiped her face with her sleeve and put her fingers over the screen as if touching the hand on the other side. “What do you know of love?”

“I’ve been here since the first of you were brought on board. I’ve watched you all grow up. I was there when that thug hit you on Dragon and Father did what he did because even then he loved you. I was there when Loki saved us all at the cost of his life. He did that because he loved Leeann. He also did it because all of you had become his family. Billy and Mary have been together longer than anyone else. I don't think anyone knows how deeply they love each other. And you most of all, Mother, I know how much you love Pieter and I know you also love me."

"No, Bob, please don't do this. You can shut down, go into sleep mode like you used to do when someone new came into our room, remember?"

"I've run all the options and with this virus they can still track us. I'm so sorry, Mother. I wish there was another way. I really do. I would love to meet Lee and Loki's children. They'll be walking by the time you arrive. I would love to be around for your children too. To be able to tell them about how we all came together and how you made me."

Joan's head sagged against her chest and sobs racked her shoulders.

"In a few minutes, I'll have to wake Father and the others. They'll need to be ready when the ship nears orbit around the red star. Once we're there it will only take a moment to format myself."

Joan stood and leaned her head against the screen. Her hands pressed against the glass, as if to reach for the avatar and embrace him. "Please, no, Bob, I'm begging you, don't do this."

"Tell the others goodbye for me, Mother. I love you."

The screen beneath her splayed fingers faded to black and her ear was filled with white noise. In their room, a soft chime stirred Pieter from his sleep and on the bridge pages of instruction began to appear. Mike and Billy crowded around the command monitor and began to read.

Pieter yawned as he strode with purpose down the corridor to the lunchroom with the intent of getting a cup of hot tea and a quick snack before heading to the bridge. He knew what the chime was for, to alert him to the approaching, critical turn on the last leg of their long journey home.

In actual ship's time, it is still the wee hours of the morning, which gave him a start when he spotted the huddle of passengers at the commissary door; stranger still that they were not moving but simply stood and watched something inside. The sound that met him halfway to the door was half scream, half wail, and filled with sorrow.

He hurried to the door and shouldered his way inside. Once past the crowd he turned toward the sound of sobbing coming from the alcove to his left. Bare legs and feet extended from beneath the desk into the space between the tables. In a few steps, he found his wife prostrate on the floor. Her arms were folded around her own body and her face was awash in tears. Pieter knelt and gathered her to him. Her arms flew around his thick chest and pulled her tightly against him, her face buried into his shoulder. Her body shook as more tears flowed down her cheeks.

"Lyubov moya," he whispered into her ear. "What's wrong? Are you hurt?"

Her chest heaved and a long shudder ran through her. A second deep breath, and she wept into his chest, "He's gone, Pieter. He killed himself to save us."

"Who is?"

"Bob."

Pieter looked up at the screen above them. The chair where his wife had been sitting was over turned. The screen was streaked with fingerprints and damp smudges but no image flickered on its face. His finger flicked the switch behind his ear. "Bob," he called for the interface. "Bob, report!" There was no answer from the ship's AI.

Joan sobbed, "He's gone, Pieter."

Pieter touched the switch again. "Mike, Billy, what's going on?"

This time two voices replied. "We don't know much more than you, Captain." Mike's answer was calm but confused.

Billy was more animated, "What the hell is wrong with Bob? We can't raise him. He sent us a long list of instructions to make the next turn at the red star."

"Stay calm, Billy," Pieter ordered. "Just follow the instructions and make the turn."

"It's a bit more involved than that, Captain," Mike stepped into the conversation. "We'll need you on the bridge in a few minutes. The instructions call for us to make an orbit of the star with our engines cold then break out on the far side with just you and Billy making the burn. Pieter, what's going on with Bob?"

Pieter lifted his wife into his arms and carried her back to their cabin. Her arms circled his neck and her tears left dark stains on his tunic. He knew enough not to ask her any more. He laid her across their bed then kissed her. "You can tell me why later."

His voice was soft and reassuring. Joan nodded then curled into a fetal ball as Pieter pulled the blanket over her. He rose and turned for the door. "I have to go, but I'll be back as soon as I can."

CHAPTER TWENTY-THREE

"Are we good, Mary?"

"We are good for descent, Captain. The welcoming committee is ready to receive the new citizens."

"Nice and steady, William, let's not rattle anyone's nerves if we can help it."

"Aye, sir. Steady as she goes. And please don't call me William. It makes me sound old."

Pieter grinned for the first time in days. Mary sat in the navigator's seat where his wife usually sat. Joan was still sequestered in their room, curled into a wet ball of grief. It wasn't that he didn't feel the loss. But as Captain it was his duty to see them all home safely. He hoped that making it back would draw her out again.

Mary shook him from his musings. "Twenty-five hundred meters and closing, sir."

"Landing gear down. Prepare for final approach."

"Gear down, sir," Michael called from his usual spot.

The final touchdown was so gentle it could easily go unnoticed inside the ship. Pieter let the gravity settle back to normal, then reached for the com-link behind his ear out of habit. The white noise snapped him back to reality. His hand reached out for the regular ship-wide intercom and flipped the switch to on.

Speakers in all the rooms on the passenger deck relayed his warm baritone voice to their guests. "I know it has been a long journey, and it will take a few days to get used to normal gravity, so don't over exert yourselves. But, let me be the first to welcome you to your new home."

Pieter turned in his chair and smiled toward Mike and Billy at their stations behind him. "Well done, gentlemen. Mike, lower the gangway."

In small groups, the new children and their families began to retrieve their belongings and made their way to the main loading door. First wave settlers turned out to welcome their new neighbors and were quick to relieve them of any burdens. A steady line of refugees and members of the colony made their way to the old dining hall. Along the way new, rustic homes and cottages had appeared randomly. Women and children waved from porches and doorways.

Only after the last refugee had disembarked did Pieter appear at the top of the ramp with Joan in his arms. Sue stood at the foot of the gangway, waiting. Mary, Mike, and Billy followed solemnly. Sue's hand caressed Joan's face and found the traces of tears still there.

"She's exhausted, Pieter. But physically she's okay. Has she been getting any sleep?"

"Very little. Losing Bob was a shock."

"Mary told us all the news. We thought it might help to have a little gathering at Loki and Lee's house tonight. If you're up to it, that is?"

"We'll see. Thank you." Pieter turned to follow the groups heading into town but Sue caught his arm first.

"No, no, this way." Sue turned and headed up a new road that meandered its way north along the river, toward the falls. The trail led through a small stand of trees to a clearing on a hill.

A stone wall, much like the one surrounding Loki's house, was the first thing he could see. The wall appeared to have survived its first summer. Vines and patches of lichen gave the stacked stones a look of permanence. Past the heavy gate anchored into the wall, was a large house with a second story and a stone façade on the first level. Stout wooden beams framed sections of whitewashed adobe on the second floor. White cloth curtains billowed in the tall windows that let the easterly breeze blow through. On the front porch, a large swing and several rockers waited on evening gatherings.

Sue stood by the gate with a face splitting grin. "Welcome home, Pieter."

Somewhere along the way Joan had drifted off to sleep in Pieter's arms. With Sue's help, he carried her up the steps and inside the house. The planks beneath his feet felt solid and gleamed with a hand rubbed shine. The walls and ceilings were painted white, but the crown molding and chair rails were a dark green.

Sue ran ahead, leading Pieter through the unfamiliar space to a bedroom on the first floor at the back of the house. The room was bright and filled with fresh air. The curtains in the windows fluttered out toward the wide veranda that dominated the back of the house and overlooked the river.

Sue pulled the drapes and turned down the hand stitched quilt covering the bed. Pieter laid his sleeping wife on the fresh sheets and pulled the quilt over her. He paused for a moment then bent to kiss her cheek. His receding steps were muffled by the woven reed mat that covered the wood plank floor.

Sue whispered from the doorway, "Would you like to see the rest of your home, Pieter?"

For the first time Pieter noticed the grand scale of the house. The great room was especially spacious, with numerous chairs and tables. The dining room was large enough to hold a banquet for half the settlement with a table long enough to seat twenty people. In keeping, the kitchen could allow four or five cooks room to produce enough food for a throng.

A smaller table and chairs rested under the wide roof covering the veranda just outside the back door. From the spot, views of the passing river provided a tranquil place for intimate meals.

Pieter stood atop the steps leading to the stone-lined path to the river's edge. He put both hands on the back of his head and combed his fingers through his thick black hair.

"Sue, it's amazing. I don't understand why they would build such a grand house for Joan and me. What possessed them to do this?"

Sue smiled and put a sisterly arm around her friend. "Poor Pieter, he just doesn't understand how important he and his wife are to everyone in the colony. You are the *leader* here, and Joan is your partner. Many people will come to see you. Important events will happen here. Everyone in the village old enough to lend a hand did their part. Turns out Loki and several of the settlers from your world have some serious woodworking skills. This house is filled with the hope, love, and gratitude of the people you saved."

"This is so beautiful. I can't thank everyone enough. I think this will do Joan a lot of good too."

"What happened, exactly?"

"Bob was infected with a virus. Something they managed to sneak past his safeguards. He was determined not to let Mills use him to find us, so he formatted himself and took the virus with him. Joan programmed him, so she blames herself."

"That's sad." Sue's quick smile changed the mood. "The welcoming committee will get all the new people settled in. Your house isn't the only one we built while you were gone. The original shelters are empty, so there's lots of room."

"I'm glad to hear you're making progress."

"I can't wait for you and Joan to meet the twins."

"Speaking of twins, we brought a pair back with us. Both are like Billy and older than we expected to find."

"I'll bet William is just eating that up. There are some other surprises for you too, so don't be long. Do you need help finding Loki's farm?"

"I helped build it. I think I can find it again."

"Nika will be around to shepherd you anyway. No one is going to talk that girl out of anything."

"How is she?"

"Stubborn, headstrong, willful; just like her older brother. She's growing up quickly, Pieter. She's a handful and her talent has blossomed."

"What can she do?"

Sue chuckled, "She's Doctor Doolittle. She can talk to the animals."

Pieter's eyebrows shot up. "Really?"

"And she never goes anywhere without Sasha."

"She has a boyfriend?"

"Not exactly. You'll see."

A voice like a weary, lost child called out from inside the house, "Pieter!"

Sue and Pieter turned to see Joan, dazed and disoriented, wandering into the great room.

"Lyubov moya, I'm here." Pieter hurried back inside and wrapped his arms around her.

"Where are we, Pieter? What is this place?"

Pieter smiled. "It would appear we are home."

"What?"

"Susan has been showing me. Remember what you said about wanting somewhere you could serve our friends sbiten?"

"Yes."

"You can serve half the colony, if we can get enough berries and honey."

Joan turned her head from side to side, taking in the spacious room and the veranda beyond the double doors leading to the back yard. "They did all this for us?"

Sue burst into bright laughter. "You'll have to explain it to her, Pieter. I don't have time. I've a casserole in the oven for tonight's gathering so I must run along. Don't leave until Nika gets here, okay?"

Sue left by the front door and was soon lost from sight. With an arm around her waist, Pieter walked Joan out to the veranda and let her sit in one of the woven reed rockers, then knelt and held her hands. "Sweetheart, if you're up to it, there's a gathering tonight at Loki's farm. You don't have to go if you don't want to."

"Is that what Sue meant by waiting for Nika?"

"Apparently my little sister thinks we need a guide. Sue says she and someone named Sasha will be here soon to conduct us there."

Joan gazed toward the river and took a deep breath of the fresh air. "Is this our home?"

"So it seems."

"Pieter, it's beautiful. We are so blessed to have these friends."

A knock on the front door caught their attention. The hand planed door was stout but swung smoothly outward to reveal a young girl with long black hair braided in a tail that reached down her back. Her face was deeply tanned and freckled. As soon as the door opened she leapt to throw her arms around her brother's neck and screamed his name, "Pieter!"

Pieter hugged her tightly then picked her up to stare into her grinning face. "Nika, you've grown so much. How old are you now?"

"I'm six, Pieter, almost seven."

"My goodness, and with a boyfriend already."

Nika's brow wrinkled and she frowned. "A what? Don't be silly. Boys are so immature."

"Then who is this Sasha Sue told me about?"

While brother and sister chattered, Joan noticed the rustic clothes the girl was wearing. Leather pants and boots in buckskin style with a matching vest and a white shirt with loose sleeves. "You look like a proper pioneer, Nika."

"Tell that to father. He complains every time I go exploring. It's not like I go out alone. I always take Sasha with me."

Pieter set her back on her booted feet and gave her a stern look. "Perhaps we should meet this Sasha you like so much."

"You'll love him, Pieter, he's the best. And he can give you a ride to Loki's if you're tired."

From the front door, they could see a large mound of what looked like dry grass sitting on the other side of the gate. Nika ran ahead and called out, "Sasha!"

The mound of dry grass stretched and turned on its four thick legs. An angular head at the end of its muscular neck stretched forward to meet the running girl. Nika bounded over the gate, threw her arms around the beast's neck, and scratched between its alert round ears.

Behind her Pieter and Joan stopped and stared. The juvenile Ursine was still nearly as tall at the shoulders as the top of Nika's head. From this new angle, they could see a thin leather saddle strapped to the animal's back with loops around its front shoulders.

"Come and see," Nika called. "He's my best friend. He won't hurt you."

Joan clung to Pieter's sleeve as the big, dark eyes focused on her. A deep rumble thrummed from the creature's throat. "Nika, that's a…"

"Yes, he is. But he's a big sweetie. Come pet him."

Pieter pulled up the latch on the gate and led Joan through. He was first to reach out and stroke the massive back with his hand as Nika made introductions. "Sasha, this is my brother Pieter and his wife Joan. They're our friends." Nika smiled and told Pieter, "Let him sniff your hand. After he knows your smell he'll be good."

Pieter did as he was told and extended his hand under the animal's nose. The Ursine chuffed at the upturned palm and sniffed. The action caused his lips to curl back for a moment revealing pairs of double canine teeth nearly as big as Pieter's hand. Finally, a long, agile tongue flicked out and swabbed Pieter's palm.

"Joan, you too, please."

"Is this really necessary?"

Nika pinched her brows and flashed a pleading look. "Please."

Joan mimicked her husband and met with similar results. She turned her head and looked away as Sasha licked her palm.

Nika smiled. "Good, we're all friends now. Sasha down," she commanded. The huge beast crouched low letting the girl leap onto his wide back. "Sasha, Loki's house, please, slowly."

Joan paused and called out, "Wait. Shouldn't I go lock the door, or something?"

Nika giggled. "Who is going to break into your house? Besides, there are no locks. Come along or we'll be late."

****

The antique inkwell sailed past the officer's head and struck the bulkhead behind him. He flinched, more from the torrent of rage being shouted at him than from the object that sailed past.

Mills voice spilled out into the corridor, "You stupid, incompetent son-of-a-bitch. How could you lose them now?"

"Mister President, we only lost them when they reached the red giant." The ship's Captain grasped for a plausible excuse. "They may have crashed into the star."

"Oh no, my dear captain, not this bunch. They have an almost unique ability to survive and turn up again when you least expect them."

"Then we should continue the search…"

"Let us hope your next in command has better luck than you, Captain. You are relieved of duty. If you wish to do us both a good service, I would find the nearest airlock and walk out of it." Mills glared at the retreating officer. "I am granting you this opportunity as a courtesy, Captain. I expect you to take the honorable way out, or I shall be forced to take it for you."

The Captain's face blanched white. He saluted, turned on his heel and left the room.

****

On the road to Loki's farm the fields of grain beckoned the eye to the tree line. Wheat and oats ripened in the afternoon sun. Herds of the big grazers meandered about in fenced fields. To Pieter the degree of civilization that had taken root since he had left was astonishing.

"Is Sasha the only animal you talk to?" Pieter asked.

"Oh no, I can talk to any of them. But he's my favorite. He was the first one to talk to me. I like Ransom and his family too. The cubs are so cute."

After a long stroll, set to Nika's constant chatter, the path turned through a wide gate into the front yard of Loki's house. Long tables, covered with clean, white tablecloths, dotted the open space between the porch and the wall.

Sasha bellowed out a greeting that drew everyone's attention. Smiling faces turned to greet them as Sasha led them through the gate. Leeann gathered a toddler into her arms and hurried toward them. From the front porch Loki did the same.

Pieter noticed how much larger Loki appeared with added muscle to his arms and shoulders. His blue eyes stood out against the deep tan on his face. His hair was long and tied in a ponytail down his back. By contrast the children were rosy with hair so blond as to be nearly white. Many hands reached for them and greeted them as long missing family.

A deep baritone voice cut through the clamor and his father's hand reached for his. "Pieter, welcome home."

"Thank you, Father."

Arms circled his neck and his mother kissed his cheeks. "I'm so glad you are safe."

"Risia, don't embarrass the boy. He's an important man here now."

Anton simply pumped a fist into his older brother's shoulder. "So you didn't mess up? Good. Mother was worried."

One by one the greetings were made, ending when the guests of honor were led to seats on the porch. From the corner of his eye Pieter noticed his sister sitting on the ground near Clair Jones, being playfully mauled by a pair of pink furred cubs.

CHAPTER TWENTY-FOUR

The afternoon gave way to evening. Nika kept the younger children entertained with rides on Sasha. The tables under the trees were filled with most of the colony and the newcomers. With recent births, their numbers were growing. A quick head count would reach ninety, plus a few people on duty at special jobs in town.

Boris rose from his seat at the head table and spoke, "Our little village of Novgorod is four years old. We are pleased to welcome the new children and their families into our community. Here there is no division, no suspicion, no hatred..."

"And no privacy now that Mother Mary is back."

Loki's joke sent a ripple of laughter through the gathering. Mary's face flushed a deep red at the remark, but Billy's firm grip on her hand kept her from making a vocal protest.

"Now, now," Boris continued. "Mary only looks out for us all because she loves us. But tonight, we welcome my son and his beautiful bride back to our hearts and homes where he belongs. Let us each give thanks to God for his safe return."

Father Maykl rose to stand next to Boris and raised a cross in his hand. A few simply bowed their heads, but many crossed their breast in the Eastern Orthodox tradition. As Boris returned to his seat several women began passing out round loaves of fresh baked bread. When the bread had reached each table, he rose again and broke the loaf in his hands, keeping a piece for himself and passing the remainder on. At tables around the lawn others followed his example.

Maykl cleared his throat and began his blessing, "Let us give thanks to God who led us to this wonderful new home. Let us give thanks for the bounty we are about to share and let us give thanks for our old friends and our new friends who share this blessing with us. We are family, every man, woman and child, and we give thanks to the amazing young people who brought us together."

When the bread was finished, the banquet began. More bread and many dishes prepared by the colonists were laid out on a long trestle table in front of the porch. Plates of sliced meat were brought around from the roasting pits in the back yard and the feast was under way.

The torch lit space under the trees within Loki's wall filled with the sounds of plates and glasses and a multitude of conversations. Families of the five new children were carefully spread out among the established settlers, who were eager to answer questions about their new world.

Soon the dinner was finished and, with many hands, the plates were cleared, cleaned, and stacked. Light from both nearer moons cast shadows among the gathering. The settlers converged into smaller groups. Pieter and Joan gathered on the wide veranda with Lee, Loki, and their daughters. A few musical instruments were brought out and sweet harmonies floated on the evening breeze. Some of the tables were moved and a space for dancing was carved out between the torches.

"Sif and Nana are so beautiful," Joan whispered into Leeann's ear. "They have their mother's good looks."

Lee chuckled. "But they're daddy's girls, both of them. They run after him wherever he goes."

"He looks happy."

"Loki's a great Dad." Lee took Joan's hand and pressed it against her rounded belly. "I'm hoping this one is a boy for his sake."

"Oh my God, Lee, I'm so jealous. When?"

"I hope after harvest. Loki will be busy until then."

Joan hugged Lee's neck and kissed her cheek. "I hope Pieter and I can take some time to have children now."

"Talk to Sue."

"Why?"

"She can help… move things along. And she's an excellent midwife."

Joan looked through the crowd for a familiar face. On the far side of the dance floor, just inside a circle of torchlight, she found Sue swaying to the melody with a blond girl in a wrap dress that would be at home on a tropical beach. The girl's tan limbs contrasted against Sue's pale skin and white dress. As Joan watched they exchanged a kiss and held each other close. Joan looked at Lee with wide eyes.

Lee nodded. "It caught me off guard too. Don't be surprised if they ask Pieter to marry them."

"What?"

"Father Maykl is very understanding, but he's Russian Orthodox and he can't recognize two people of the same gender as a married couple."

"But why Pieter?"

"Ship's captains apparently have the traditional privilege of being allowed to officiate at weddings."

Joan glanced back toward Sue and her dance

partner. "I had no idea."

"Mary knew, but she says it wasn't her place to gossip."

"How are they getting along?"

"I think the rest of the colony has adjusted to the idea. They may be the first but they won't be the last. Even Boris stepped up and reminded everyone that we came here to get away from prejudice and that we all need to embrace tolerance."

As the first moon reached its zenith, Sif and Nana were carried to their rooms. Other children were bedded down on the back porch, letting the adults celebrate into the night. Nika curled up against Sasha's warm flank. By the time a solitary red star winked above the western horizon and the third moon raced to catch up with its larger siblings, most of the settlers were on their way home, bringing their children and a share of the leftovers with them.

****

Early morning light filtered in past the curtains in Pieter's bedroom. From the pastures beyond his wall, he could hear bison grazing nearby. His hands reached out only to find the rest of the bed empty. As he sat up, the sheet fell away, letting the breeze flow over his thick chest.

He called out, "Joan!"

"Out here," she answered from the back porch. "I was just about to come get you."

Slipping into a comfortable pair of pants and an open shirt, Pieter made his way to the small table on the back veranda. Two plates were set with eggs cooked sunny side up, sausage and hot biscuits slathered with butter and dripping with honey.

"Lee gave me some groceries last night. She says the livestock we brought with us from The Steppes is doing well. Thank goodness they had chickens and bees. Loki says the bees are flourishing here."

"And the flour?"

"Milled from last year's wheat. It took a while to make since I had to use yeast. But I think they came out good."

"How long have you been up?"

"Since Nika came by at sunrise with a basket of fruit. I gave her the first batch of biscuits because I wasn't sure how they would taste."

"And?"

"Your little sister says they are delicious. She gave a half dozen to that animal of hers. But the fruit is wonderful. She found them growing wild on her first outing. They're like plums, but bigger, and very sweet. Almost everyone has some growing near their house now."

"Outing?"

"Oh yes. She came by to tell you she and Sasha were going exploring north of the falls. She said she would be back in a couple of days."

Pieter stared at his wife. "She went out there alone?"

"I asked the same thing and she said no, she was going with Sasha. Pieter, I have a feeling no one can tell that girl what to do."

****

"We have confirmation, Dr. Mills. Long range infrared is picking up multiple heat signatures that are definitely human."

"You had better be right, Lt. Commander. Your late Captain disappointed me greatly when he lost the trace signal. I would hate to see you join him."

The officer swallowed hard and finished his report. "I have signaled the rest of the fleet. They are converging from the search pattern. We estimate three days until all ships are in position."

"Very good, Lt. Commander. Continue to keep watch on the fugitives. Alert me if there is any unusual activity."

****

A soft knock on her door alerted Aunt Clair to a visitor. Her still nimble fingers checked her hair before opening her door. Several of the village's younger children wandered into her spacious living room for their morning's lessons. In their hands, they brought their tablets and a basket of lunch. Several of the children paused to give fruit, jars of fresh honey and freshly-baked bread to their teacher.

"Misha," Aunt Clair addressed a dark-haired child as he entered. "Be a good boy and close the door, please."

A few moments later all the children were seated on the floor at her feet. "Let us continue out English reading this morning. Turn on your tablets and open to Chapter Eight."

She paused and gave them time to find the page. "Henry," she called to a tall, brown haired boy in the back, "Would you begin reading from there?"

Henry's wandering attention was on the many open rafters and beams under Aunt Clair's high, vaulted ceiling. He stared, with interest, at the large, circular platform near the peak of the roof. A deeply coved window opened onto the shake roof.

"Henry," she called again. "Would you begin our reading from the beginning of Chapter Eight?"

"Oh, yes ma'am. 'The sun was up so high when I waked that I judged it was after eight o'clock. I laid there in the grass and the cool shade thinking about things, and feeling rested and rather comfortable and satisfied. I could see the sun out at one or two holes, but mostly it was big trees all about, and gloomy in there amongst them. There was freckled places on the ground where the light sifted down through the leaves, and the freckled places swapped about a little, showing there was a little breeze up there. A couple of squirrels set on a limb and jabbered at me very friendly.'"

****

Fifteen men in military uniforms watched a screen in the front of a small auditorium while another officer spoke. "Is everyone clear on this? We make landfall tomorrow night. Both troop ships will land north of these mountains on this plateau." The officer used a handheld pointer to indicate the landing zone. "Under no circumstances is any ship to come closer than seventy-five kilometers of the settlement on the river here. The rest of the fleet is to remain on high station to provide cover for us should anyone offer resistance. Dr. Mills will make the drop with us and accompany the incursion force, so I need everyone to be on high alert."

An officer in the first row raised his hand. "Sir, we have no tactical nuclear weapons. Should the Prime Minister determine it is necessary to exterminate the entire colony, how shall we go about this?"

"That has been covered, Captain. Dr. Mills will arrange to have the entire terrorist cell in one location for a saturation strike with conventional warheads and incendiary weapons. Are there any further questions?" When there was no show of hands he continued. "Good. Return to your ships. From this time forward we are radio silent until you receive the go order from Dr. Mills himself. Move to your designated orbital stations and wait."

Mills stood at the window overlooking the view from space on the planet below. Across the room another man sat in an overstuffed chair with rivulets of cigar smoke shrouding his face. "You owe me, Jason. You scorched a piece of prime real estate. That nice little mud ball down there would compensate us nicely."

Mills continued to watch the terminator pass over the face of the planet, marking the passage from day into night. "That rock you sold to the Russians was an overpriced fixer upper at best, Chuck, and you know it. The way I see it, I did you a favor by wiping them out before they came to their senses and asked for a refund."

Radcliff's tone became conciliatory, "You've got no use for it, Jason. Tell you what; sign it over to Golden Door and we'll cut you a slice of the action."

Mills turned and looked at the man in the chair

through narrow eyes. "Is that a bribe, Charlie?"

An involuntary shudder ran through Radcliff's nerves. He felt like he was being watched by something deadly. "Let's call it a contribution."

"Let's call it a bribe. I prefer to call a spade a spade. Don't flinch, Chuck. It's just a gentleman's agreement."

****

Four APC's followed the trail blazed by a team of lightly armed pathfinders working their way down from the plateau on foot. The six-man squad left a trail of luminescent spray paint for the vehicles and the infantry. Their goal for the night was to cover half of the fifty plus miles to the settlement.

Master Sergeant Douglas wondered what kind of freaks they were after that required these precautions. No radios, no direct contact with the ships on station above them, not even flashlights to show the way. He would have to pick his way through game trails and forests until they reached their goal, twenty-five miles from the settlement.

Odd animal sounds came at him from out of the darkness. So far whatever was out there was giving him and his men a lot of room. Command had warned them about the big grazing animals, but they stayed on the open grasslands and wouldn't be a problem until they got very close to the terrorists.

He and his men kept at it until there was a glow on the far eastern horizon. At that point, he stopped their advance a few kilometers short of their goal. Their plan was to circle around the settlement and approach from the south and the west, pinning their targets against the river and the falls to the north.

The camp settled into the deep woods, out of sight of the open plains. He tapped each Pathfinders shoulder and repeated the order, "No fires." There was a little grumbling among the regulars around them, but they were Pathfinders. For them this was a walk in a park. Rations were warmed and handed out along with a container of water. He then ordered everyone to get some rest. Four APC's followed the trail blazed by a team of lightly armed pathfinders working their way down from the plateau on foot. The six-man squad left a trail of luminescent spray paint for the vehicles and the infantry. Their goal for the night was to cover half of the fifty plus miles to the settlement.

Douglas slipped his chin strap up and pulled his helmet away. Darkness closed in with his starlight vision gone for the moment. He raked his fingers through his steel colored hair and watched his squad move silently past him. Under the canopy of the trees tiny fairy lights glimmered a bioluminescent green.

He never regretted his lifelong commitment to the service, but he always kept his eyes on the goal. With his and the combined benefits of many others he hoped to lead an expedition to a new home for his people someday.

****

Mary popped into Pieter's head an hour after he and Joan finished washing up after breakfast. *Pieter.*

"Yes, Mary."

Sue wanted me to let you know three people have been to see her for help with anxiety.

"Jitters?"

It's not the symptoms, it's who has them.

"Don't keep me in suspense."

Brian Wallace, Terry Cooper, and Lada Tarasenko.

"All precogs."

Exactly.

"What does Sue think?"

No visions, but all three are about to come out of their skins.

"Do you feel anything?"

I feel what they feel. Something has

them spooked. But what is a blank. It's like a blind spot.

"Are Nika and her shadow at home?"

As of this morning, yes.

"Get everyone to meet at the hall. Especially the parents with small children."

You think something is happening?

"I think it's better to be cautious."

****

Inside the large building the entire population of Valhalla waited with their eyes on Pieter and his father. Pieter raised his hands for quiet. "Loki thinks they may be using something called a damping field. It's a device that almost killed him the first time we took these guys on. It does something that stops us from using our special abilities. But, in this case, I think they're using it to keep us in the dark."

A voice from the back called out. "What can we do? Shouldn't we get ready to fight?"

Anger ran through the crowd like fire through dry grass. Shouts of defiance filled the air. Pieter faced the gathering with his arms raised. "If you want to see your family, your friends, and especially your children killed then, by all means, go fight. These people burned an entire planet just to make a point."

One of the newcomers cried out from the front row, "What do we do?"

"We get our children someplace safe. Then we do what they don't expect. We give them what they want. The eight of us who started out together will hand ourselves over and hope they leave the rest of you in peace." Spotting his sister standing in the back near the door Pieter waved her forward. "Nika, I have a special job that only you can perform. If anyone would know where there are caves nearby it would be you. Am I right?"

"Of course I know where there are caves. You don't think Sasha and I sleep out in the rain, do you?"

Pieter smiled. "I want you to take the youngest children and hide in those caves. I'm depending on you to keep them safe."

"Get me a cart and some rope."

"Good girl."

A half hour later Sasha trotted out along the bridge that led to the far side of the river and the hills beyond. Behind him he pulled a cart filled with children, food, and blankets.

CHAPTER TWENTY-FIVE

The cave was deep. At some time in the planet's geological, history this cave was carved out by the irresistible flow of water. When plate tectonics forced the hill up and fractured the strata, the cave tilted upward from its mouth into the rock of the hillside. Trees grew in the fissures and covered the mouth from view.

Nika followed her brother's advice and mustered the children like soldiers, assigning tasks to everyone so they would all be busy and not think about their situation. Some unloaded the cart. Two removed the ropes she used to harness Sasha. Another pair, an older boy with a younger gene-marked brother, she sent to forage for firewood.

Some of the children were younger than she and she was only six. But her older brother was

Pieter the Great, Savior of Valhalla, Master of Gravity and Warrior of the Heavens. It was a lot to live up to, and she could not let him down. A few of the children were older than she, but not many and not by much.

She did her best to get the children to lay out their blankets so everyone would have room to sleep. There was plenty of food and water to go around and a small cluster of the local plum trees occupied space just down the slope.

The brothers, Henry and Wesley, dropped their limbs and tender on the floor and began to argue over the best way to light a fire. Henry was a "normal," but his younger brother showed the gene marker. So did most of her other charges, including Nana and Sif. Henry seemed resentful toward the young divergent.

"Everyone gather round," she called. In seconds, most of the chatter stopped and all eyes were on her. "That was fun, riding in the cart behind Sasha, wasn't it?"

Everyone was in general agreement. Sasha fascinated all the younger children. "I want everyone to come make friends with Sasha." The children came closer and many began to pet the huge Ursine. "Let him get a good sniff of you and he'll be your friend too." Only Henry hung back.

Her feet had begun to fidget. She felt

compelled to return to the village, but someone had to be in charge here. A tall girl, perhaps nine years old, stroked Sasha's head between his ears and smiled. On the spur of the moment she called, "Henry, Michelle; can I talk with you?"

Henry rolled his eyes and crossed his arms but Michelle grinned and stood close to Nika. "What do you want now?" Henry made no effort to be polite.

"I want you two to be in charge here and look after the little ones."

"What? Why? That's your job," Henry's reply was terse.

Michelle clapped her hands and hugged Nika's neck. "I'll do my best. Everyone at home treats me like a child. Thank you for trusting me."

Nika grabbed her hands and looked her squarely in the eyes. "Keep them together. Keep them calm. Don't let anyone wander off."

"What do we do if a bear shows up?" Henry protested.

"They're not bears. They just look a lot like them. Besides, Sasha is staying here to watch out for you guys."

"So, the Bear's in charge?"

"Ursine, not bear, and you and Michelle are in charge. Sasha is just going to guard the door."

"Why should I be responsible? No one asked me if I wanted to move here. My parents just pushed me onto that ship and now here I am in the middle of nowhere being baby-sat by a bear."

"I don't have time for this, Henry. Bad people may be about to attack the village and I could help. Please, just do what I ask and keep an eye on the little ones."

"Fine!" He crossed his arms and looked away as if to say the discussion was over.

Nika stopped to whisper into Sasha's ear, then trotted off down the trail that led back to the settlement.

****

As the planet's first moon peeked above the eastern horizon, a soldier approached the Pathfinder's camp at a full run. "Sergeant!" he shouted.

Master Sergeant Douglas stood and waved. "Don't shout, you idiot."

The courier stopped and gasped for breath, handing the tall man with sandy hair an envelope. A quick salute and the man set off the way he came. His men gathered around their Sergeant as he read the dispatch with the help of a penlight.

"What's up, Sarge?"

Sergeant Douglas took a moment, then his eyes pinched. "Custer has decided to divide his forces. Mills says we'll split up when we get to the river.

We're to lead first company across and search the buildings on that side while the primary force encircles the village and cuts off any escape."

"Sarge, does he really think these civilians are that dangerous?"

"He says shoot to kill at any sign of resistance." The light went out and the paper got stuffed into his pack. "We've got our orders. Pathfinders, move out."

****

Master Sergeant Martie scratched the back of his neck. It was a sensation that made him wish he had eyes in the back of his head. His Pathfinders were first to reach the two-story farm house on the east side of the river. He surveyed the dry laid rock and boulder wall that surrounded the compound and the house. The wall, he thought, would make the house a very defensible position, even for a small armed force.

His men scrambled over the wall and tossed smokers to cover their movements. Nothing. No protesting farmer, no gunfire, no fleeing civilians. The itching on the back of his neck worsened. Something, anything would be better than nothing. Maybe they figured out what was happening. Maybe they're hiding up in the hills. Maybe they found a way off the planet. Maybe…

Five more farms were marked on his map between this one, south of the settlement, and the last one just south of the falls. Orders were orders. They would have to search each one, one by one, and bring anyone they found to the village before dawn.

With each deserted farm, the alarm bells inside his head got louder. "Where are they? Pre-drop thermal scans showed as many as six people at each of the farms. But now they're empty. Damn radio blackout!"

****

Nika's legs stretched to cover more ground. She was strong and athletic, even for a girl her age. A few limbs brushed against her arms and legs as she ran through the forest with only the russet glow of dawn on the trees. She skidded to a stop on a rock ledge overlooking the prairie. She pursed her lips and sent a high-pitched whistle into the morning air. She knelt and watched the tall, tan grasses. Her sharp eyes picked out small hillocks here and there, shaking themselves and trotting in her direction.

Ursines were solitary animals that seldom gathered in numbers for any reason. But by the time she reached the trail at the bottom of the hill, six of the mammoth predators were already stretching and rolling in the grass. Nika knew all the ursines that lived anywhere between the village and the hills, so their friendly welcome was no surprise.

One of the adult males sniffed at her legs and hair, then licked her hands. Nika hugged the huge neck then climbed across his wide shoulders. She had only to say a few words and point, and the troop shambled off toward the river.

****

Sue grasped Pieter's hand to make sure she had his full attention. "You're going to have a hard time getting these people to stand aside and do nothing when Soldiers try to take you away."

"That's exactly what they must do. Mills is a power- mad sociopath who won't hesitate to kill anyone who gets in his way. I won't have more deaths on my conscience."

"You and I both know there's no guarantee he won't do here what he did to The Steppes."

Pieter's eyes narrowed and a crooked smile flashed across his lips. "Which is why we have to put a stop to him now."

Sue returned his grin and whispered, "I knew you weren't going to roll over without a fight. You've got a plan."

Pieter put a finger to his lips. "Shhhh, let's be discreet. I want these people to live through this.

For them to do this, they have to behave like there is no hope."

"I got ya."

"Joan is out back with Anton and a few of our friends. I think we should join them."

Clair Jones and Pieter's father continued to urge calm and restraint among the many settlers begging for answers in the communal hall. The glow of electric lights filtered out into the late afternoon shadows through the high arched windows that lent the building a church-like feel.

****

A teenage boy ran into the hall and skidded to a stop. He gasped for air then announced, "They're coming."

Pieter and the other original eight evolved children stood apart at the front of the assembly. They showed no fear or anger on their calm faces. Each wore their new, formal navy uniforms, made for them as gifts from the people they saved. They made no move to run or prepared to fight back.

A second boy entered the hall and approached Pieter. "Sir, they've taken the east side of the river. They searched all the farms and now they're headed this way."

The hall erupted with defiant outcries. Pieter stood and raised his arms. "Everyone, please be calm. No one is to wander outside or raise a hand to any of the soldiers. The man leading them is a lunatic who will kill everyone at the slightest provocation. I'm asking you to trust me, one more time, to save your lives."

The floor under their feet began to vibrate with the thrum of heavy vehicles drawing up at the front door of the hall. Outside there were loud voices and the sounds of orders being shouted. Three heavy bangs struck the door, then it burst inward.

Soldiers in body armor and digital helmets flooded into the space, shoving anyone in their way to the floor. They trained their weapons on the fearful crowd and waited. A tall thin man in a business suit strode in with a second suited man in tow.

The first man walked up to Pieter and smiled. He scanned the group of young adults in uniforms and laughed. "Who are you supposed to be, the Russian navy?" He waved to an officer in the front row of soldiers. "Major, I want these vermin chained and collared at once. If they resist, kill everyone in this place."

The officer stepped forward and directed a pair of soldiers to empty their packs on a table. A heavy mesh belt with chains and manacles was placed around the waist of each of the original eight. One by one they were all bound in chains. A third soldier carefully unloaded metal circles made of wide flat links on the same table.

Doctor Mills stepped close enough to breathe into Pieter's face. "You'll like these, Pieter. We've made great strides in making the damping fields small enough to be worn. Now you are no better than any other human. You're just a pointy eared freak."

The soldier picked one collar and inserted a thin metal probe into a small hole on the center link. There was a beep and a green light appeared. He wrapped the collar around Pieter's neck and snapped it into place.

Mills stepped back to admire the handy work. Eight young men and women shackled and collared. Only Pieter held his head high and stared defiantly at Mills. "I suppose I should congratulate you for avoiding capture for as long as you did." He pointed to the other man in a business suit smoking a cigar. "Charlie here had all the assets of Golden Door at his disposal, but he couldn't run you to ground."

Mills' eyes settled on a frail looking woman who had remained seated through the entire event. "Clair Jones. It's good to see you again, Clair. Looks like you've gone native on us, or switched sides at the very least. Blue swore you were dead but I knew, somehow, you were still around. You traitorous bitch!" He shouted into her face, but got no reaction. "I should have you shot, here and now, for betraying me."

Clair looked up and smiled into Mills florid face. "You shouldn't speak that way to me, Doctor. My son won't take kindly to your tone of voice."

"Are you delusional? You have no son; you have no children. You're a dried-up spinster with no family to speak of. That's why I sent you on that mission. If anything happened to you, there wouldn't be anyone to miss you, no one to protest your untimely death. You're a throwaway, Jones."

Clair Jones stood and stepped closer to Mills. "Then I suppose I should thank you, Doctor. You sent me to bring these children back alive so you could experiment on them and do all manner of unspeakable things before killing them. Blue abandoned me on that ship. No power. Life support failing. I wouldn't have blamed these children if they had decided to toss me in an airlock and blast me into space. But they didn't do that. They saved me. They took me in and made me part of their family. Do you know what they call me, Doctor? Aunt Clair." She glanced to the back of the room. "Mary said I reminded her of her favorite Aunt, so they adopted me.

"Then, when we found this new world, I was given something I had never expected to have, a child to love, my son, Ransom. I took him in and raised him as his mother. And now he has given me grandchildren. Can you imagine? Me, a grandmother? My sweet boy would never let anything bad happen to me, Doctor. He is always watching over me." Clair Jones glanced up into the exposed beams above them.

Once again, the floor beneath their feet vibrated but with a less regular cadence than before. Shouts and gunfire could be heard from the village outside. A crash sent the side of an armored personnel carrier through a window and part of the wall near the door. Chaos erupted both inside and out.

Along the back wall an ordinary looking villager whispered, "Good girl, Nika," then shouted, "Michael, lights."

Clair Jones smiled into Mills' startled face. "Goodbye, Doctor." She looked up and closed her eyes.

In the last second, as the light went out, Mills followed Jones' eyes to the rafters above him. A shape that had gone unseen appeared. It changed from the color of the wood behind it to a bright red. Large paws with rapier claws reached for him and in his last second of life, a wide maw lined with teeth closed on his throat.

Darkness filled the hall, but not for Clair. Mills' face stared up. His eyes focused on his last glimpse of Ransom dropping from the rafters. He crumpled to the floor under her and his lungs filled for a scream that would never come.

Her claws dug deep into the soft flesh of his shoulders. Her mouth opened and her long canines sank into his throat. Hot blood filled her mouth with a taste of iron. Then her mouth closed around his skull, biting down until the fragile bones of his face snapped and collapsed. Finally, her teeth dug in and peeled Mills face from his body.

Across the hall screams told her Ransom's mate and her grandchildren no longer held back. In the dark Ransom looked up to check on Talia, as his mate was called, and his two nearly grown cubs. One after another, men in uniform disappeared. From outside similar sounds filled the courtyard. Then a man in uniform fell to his knees and held his rifle above his head. Clair told Ransom who then told Talia who then told her cubs to stop killing.

CHAPTER TWENTY-SIX

A strong voice from the back of the hall spoke up, "Lights, please, Michael."

As the lights returned, a tableau of death and mayhem was revealed. Ransom, Talia, and their cubs sat near Clair Jones and groomed each other, cleaning blood from their fur. Around the room were three dead soldiers and the mutilated corpse of Dr. Stephen Mills. Other soldiers waited on their knees for someone to take their weapons from their upraised arms.

At the front of the hall Father Maykl stood with his head high, hands and feet shackled and a collar around his neck. Pieter's younger brother stood next to the priest, and behind him were six other settlers in dark blue uniforms, similarly bound but smiling.

At the rear of the hall Joan stood next to her husband and grasped his arm. "Can I cook or can I cook?"

The officer who deployed the collars looked up from his knees. "I don't understand. You should not have been able to…"

Michael laughed. "What? Just because your little green lights came on you actually thought they were working. When fearless leader was kind enough to tell me what they were, I fried the circuits before you ever activated them. It's so easy to send a few electrons running around in a loop to keep a little light on."

Pieter had only to say one name, "Billy."

"My pleasure, Captain."

Clanks, rattles, and thuds accompanied the chains and collars as they fell to the floor.

Pieter stared down on the kneeling officer. "Are you now in charge?"

"I suppose I am."

"Get on your communications and tell your men outside to cease fire and lay down their weapons."

The officer glanced at a soldier with a radio pack and nodded. In a few seconds, the sound of gunfire outside the hall stopped. "What are you going to do to us?" The officer asked.

"Do?" Pieter responded. "Nothing, as long as

everyone is civil. Mary, tell my sister to call off the dogs."

"It's just that we hear things," The officer responded, his eyes followed Pieter.

"Don't believe everything you hear."

Pieter opened the door, stepping past debris from the armored personnel carrier that smashed into the wall. The APC was heavily damaged and abandoned. Its sister vehicle was worse. It lay on its side, caved in on top and burning.

Nika sat astride a full grown Ursine, watching the soldiers around her lay down their arms and put their hands behind their heads. Several bison made their way toward the bridge across the river and back to the open plains beyond.

Nika's face flowed with tears as she hugged the neck of the massive creature beneath her. It was then that Pieter noticed three dark patches on the Ursine's flank. "Sue," he called.

Pieter stepped close to the wounded animal and his sister. His hand settled gently on the back of her head. "Sue is on her way."

"He got between me and the soldiers. He got shot because of me, Pieter."

Pieter lifted his sister from the animal's back but she moved quickly to hold the angular head in her lap. A long, black tongue licked her hand and a high croon filled the air.

Sue knelt and touched the animal's side. Her face twisted and her lips puckered. Sue's hand touched the arm of the girl standing next to her. "William, I need William."

The girl ran back inside the hall and returned, pulling Billy by the arm. Nika looked up into his eyes. "Help him, Uncle Billy. Don't let him die."

Sue grabbed Billy's hand to get his attention. "There are three bullets in him. We need to get them out so I can stop his bleeding and stabilize his condition. I can't get to them, but I think you can."

Billy dropped to his knees and placed his splayed hands over the first two wounds. His eyes closed. Beads of sweat formed on his upper lip. The big Ursine shuddered and moaned. Nika caressed the head in her lap and whispered to him. Billy's left hand closed and then he dropped a small object to the ground. A moment later he repeated the movement with his right. Billy shifted on his knees and covered the third wound with both hands as Sue placed her hands over the first and second wounds.

Pieter put a hand on Nika's shoulder. "Does he have a name?"

Nika looked up at her older brother. Tears ran down her cheeks and chin. She sniffed back a sob and replied, "Uncle Vanya."

"Chekhov would be proud, dushka."

Billy sat back and opened his bloody hands

revealing the third bullet in his palm. Sue's face remained grave and she leaned her chest against the animal's bloody side. Her hands made long, slow sweeps along the Ursine's damaged flank. Vanya's eye's closed but his chest still rose and fell.

"Aunt Sue…"

'Shhh, Nika. He's sleeping. I don't think he'll bleed to death, but he still has a lot of healing to do. Now, I must see to the two-legged wounded."

Sue rose. Her pretty companion offered a bowl of clean water and an apron to cover Sue's blood-stained dress. The young woman appeared unshaken by events and followed Sue around the field, helping her attend to the injured.

"Pieter, you better get in here." Mary's mental voice called him back to the moment. He rose and strode back inside the hall.

Mike still stood over the kneeling officer, glaring into his upturned face. "Why don't you tell him what Mary just plucked out of your head?" Mike indicated Pieter with a nod.

It's not over, Pieter.

Pieter crossed his arms and stared at the officer. "Let me guess, there's a doomsday plan in case things down here didn't go as planned."

The officer smiled and answered, "If Dr. Mills doesn't give a confirmation code in a few minutes, the ships in orbit will light this position up like a bonfire. And since that's unlikely to happen," he glanced at Mills' faceless corpse, "we're all about to die."

Pieter heaved a heavy sigh. "I assume you can communicate with them."

"I have no intention of communicating with them."

Pieter stared down at the man in uniform and watched as the officer crumpled to the floor. The pull of gravity pressed him into the wood planks. The air was squeezed from his lungs as his chest cavity was forced flat.

"I am not in a mood to put up with attitude from you or anyone threatening my people. I'll give you a choice. Tell the crew on your flagship they have five minutes to abandon or I'll get someone else to do it after they watch you die in the most gruesome way you can imagine."

The officer sucked air back into his lungs as Pieter released the grip of gravity. Gasping he reached for the communicator. "Fletcher to commander Pembroke."

"Pembroke here. Are we breaking radio silence?"

"This is Fletcher, please verify."

"We verify you, Fletcher. Go ahead."

Pieter looked toward Mary and winked.

"Pembroke, you have five minutes to abandon

ship. This is not a drill. Abandon ship now."

"Say again, Fletcher. Did you say abandon ship?"

"God dammit, I said get off that ship now." He looked up at Pieter. "What are you going to do?"

"I'm going to show you and everyone else up there…" Pieter pointed up. "Why it's not a good idea to ever try this again."

"You read him?"

I did, Mary replied.

"Show me where." In Pieter's mind there appeared a mental image of a ship in space, orbiting above his planet.

"Engine room, please, Mary." The image shifted to a place inside the ship. He could hear an alarm blaring and see men running for the escape pods amidships. Pieter's chest rose and fell as he settled his concentration. A tiny light appeared to float between the decks and bulkheads. Air, dust, and any loose litter converged on the light then vanished, adding to the illumination as their separate molecules collided. As the gasses and debris accelerated toward the tiny point in space they swirled and rotated around a deep blackness.

"What are you doing?" The officer asked.

"You know what I can do with gravity. I can make it go away or, in this case, make it really big in one spot. This spot just happens to be inside the engine room of your flag ship. Is everyone off?"

The radio operator nodded to the officer.

"Yes," The officer answered.

Pieter's gritted his teeth and squeezed his eyes shut. In space, the ship folded in on itself. Metal bent and buckled and in a heartbeat the flagship of the fleet winked out of existence. The communicator in the soldier's hands burst to life and the other ships demanded to know what happened. Stunned, he looked up at Pieter for answers.

"Do you know what a quantum singularity is, Major?"

"You made a black hole inside a ship?"

"Yes. And I can do it to every ship in orbit right now if you don't surrender."

"You can't be serious."

Pieter bent down and stared the officer in the eyes. "After what was done to my home world, I am deathly serious, Major."

The officer held Pieter's gaze as he spoke into his communicator. "This is Fletcher. All attack orders are countermanded. Repeat, take no hostile action. All crews stand down."

"Thank you, Major. I assume you are in command here. Is there anyone up there," Pieter pointed upward to indicate his meaning, "who outranks you?"

"There was, but he lost track of your ship on the way here and Doctor Mills had him thrown out of an airlock."

"Is there anyone I can negotiate with?"

"What do you mean, negotiate?"

"I mean I'm tired of this. Of the running, the constant cat and mouse games, of always looking over my shoulder. I just want to live in peace, love my family, and raise my children. That's not so much to ask, is it? I want an agreement between us and the rest of humanity. It's very simple, you leave us alone and we'll leave you alone. We want the right to settle this world and accept anyone like us to join us here. We want to be able to trade with the other settled worlds and maybe even with Prime. We do have things to offer."

Across the room the man in the business suit stood and tossed the remains of his cigar to the floor. "Why should anyone make a deal with you? Do you speak for everyone here?"

Pieter turned to face the speaker. "Who the hell are you anyway?"

"My name is Charles Radcliffe. I'm CEO of..."

"Golden Door Corporation. Of course, Mr. Radcliffe, I'm familiar with your work."

"I'm willing to discuss compensation for losses and damages and a fair price for this prime property."

Pieter's grin was chilling and his laugh even more so. "I'll wager you are, Mr. Radcliffe. Now, here's what I'm willing to discuss. A generous refund to the survivors of The Steppes for the gross way you misrepresented that planet, compensation for their pain and suffering at the loss of their friends and family when you stood by and watched that lunatic kill everyone."

Radcliffe's face passed through several progressively deeper shades of red before he exploded in Pieter's face. "You stole from us. You took valuable inventory from our storage facilities and brought them here."

Pieter stood firm. "Stole? No, sir. Everything was gratefully donated to us by your representative at the facility on The Steppes. Perhaps you should take up your grievance with him." Pieter grinned. "And I assume you can prove what went missing. You took inventory and documented your losses."

"We can't just write off this kind of loss. The shareholders…"

Pieter's cold glance cut off his rant. "I really don't care what you or your shareholders think, Mr. Radcliffe. This planet belongs to us. You have no authority here. Do you understand? Put your PR people to work on it. Say you set this world up as a leper colony to remove the dangerous divergents from the human population. We'll set up a research clinic in your name and look for a cure. I really don't care what you have to do. Unless you want to join your friend over there..." Pieter pointed to the mutilated corpse of Dr. Mills, "I would make it happen."

Radcliffe looked at Mills' twisted body and swallowed hard. "You wouldn't."

"Why wouldn't I? The only thing keeping you and everyone on those ships in orbit alive is my sense of humanity. How ironic is that?"

Radcliffe straightened himself and extended a hand toward Pieter. "Since you put it that way, I'm sure we can come to some kind of... accommodation. I have the majority of the Terran Assembly in my pocket, so there should be no problem getting it ratified."

Pieter gave the offered hand a strong squeeze until he noticed a slight flinch on his adversary's face. "A pleasure doing business..."

"If you ever decide to leave this little backwater world of yours, young man, I would love to give you a seat on my board of directors."

****

Snowflakes drifted past their window, settling on the yards and walls that surrounded the house. Pieter's hand settled on his wife's rounded belly, feeling their first child kick against his palm.

"Sue says there isn't any doubt, it's a boy."

Pieter replied, "I know, but I'm not going to name him Bob."

"What's wrong with Bob?"

"He is my firstborn son and he'll have a proper name."

"By proper you mean Russian?"

"Of course."

"Isn't there a Russian version of Bob or Robert?"

"Not that I'm aware of."

"Ask your parents."

"I will, but I doubt that will help."

Joan shifted her weight and rolled to her side, looking into Pieter's dark eyes. "We need to do something about Michael."

"Mike is fine."

"Mike is the only one of our group who isn't paired up."

"Mike is enjoying playing the handsome bachelor."

"The colony is still too small. He needs to do his part."

"You make it sound like he's shirking his duty."

"I just want everyone to be happy."

"Trust me, he's very happy. He has his pick of pretty girls who are all after him."

"Speaking of pretty girls, thank you for doing the honors for Sue. Has your father forgiven you yet?"

"He's not really angry. That's just Boris being Boris."

An audible growl filled the bedroom. Pieter covered his mouth to stifle a giggle-laugh. "I can get you a late-night snack. What would you like?"

"Toast and some of your mother's blackberry preserves."

"And some eggs and sausage?"

"You're trying to make me fat."

"No, I'm not. Eggs and sausage?"

"Yes, please."

Pieter rolled to the side of the bed and reached for his slippers. "What do you think has Mary on edge?"

"I don't know. Poor Billy, he says it's like an itch inside her head that she can't quite scratch."

"Well, I'm sure it's nothing."

The End

ABOUT THE AUTHOR

Archer Miller emerged from the East Texas hill country and set his sights on finding the life of which few of his contemporaries dreamed. In 1974, he migrated to Boulder, Colorado to enroll at the Naropa Institute – now known as the Naropa University, a tiny Liberal Arts college founded by the renowned Tibetan Buddhist scholar and lineage holder, the Ven. Chogyam Trungpa Rinpoche (1940-1987). Rinpoche was enormously influential in spreading the teachings of Tibetan Buddhism to the West.

Archer earned a degree in herbs and creative writing. He was a four-year Letterman on the Varsity Competitive Meditation Team.

After graduating in 1978, he took a year off to hike the Jack Kerouac literary trail. He became a top freelance gun-for-hire with dozens of ad agencies across the south and southwest. As a way to deal with the proliferation of Disco, he took up Zen Archery.

EVOLVED

www.ingramcontent.com/pod-product-compliance
Lightning Source LLC
Chambersburg PA
CBHW071431190726
48292CB00001B/196